BROTHERHOOD OF DEATH

Augustus Swift Mysteries Book One

Stephen Taylor

SAPERE
BOOKS

Also in the Augustus Swift series:
The Cold Light of Day

BROTHERHOOD
OF DEATH

Published by Sapere Books.

24 Trafalgar Road, Ilkley, LS29 8HH

saperebooks.com

ISBN: 978-0-85495-744-6

ACKNOWLEDGEMENTS

Information, inspiration, help and suggestions came from many sources, and if anyone feels they have not been properly thanked here, please forgive the oversight. The following headings and the sources listed have been invaluable to me. If you are interested in further reading on these subjects, I can also recommend them, and I acknowledge their guidance.

For the historical period, *BHO – British History Online* and *History on the Net* were crucial in determining the chronology of the historical facts, and, specifically for studying life in Georgian London, I can recommend *Dirty Old London* by Lee Jackson and Maria Grace's blog 'To Be An Accomplished Lady'. For information on apothecaries, Lucinda Brant's blog 'The Apothecary's Apprentice in 18th Century England' was incredibly valuable. For research on the political period, Matthew White's article 'Popular Politics in the 18th Century' helped immensely, as well as William Hague's biography *William Pitt the Younger*. My thanks also go to Esther Inglis-Arkell, who pointed me in the right direction with poisons in this period, which was a fundamental plotline of this story. For research on the 'Power of Three' I consulted *Numberopedia* and *Symbol Dictionary*.

PROLOGUE

London, 1795

Brutus stirred. The two-hundred-pound mastiff had been snoring in front of the hearth, even though it was late May and the fire was unlit. The giant dog had a privileged place in the household. A faithful companion, he was always by his master's side during the day: at his desk, his dinner table, and when he walked the grounds. Admired for his powerful and muscular physique, he weighed more than any man in the house. A stranger should be wary of this guardian.

The footman responsible for locking up pulled back the heavy bolt of the front door, the clunk echoing around the hall. The dog opened one sleepy eye at the sound, let out a half-sigh, and ambled towards the door, his head lolling from side to side, spittle dripping from his fleshy jowls. He knew what his duties as a protector were. The footman stood back, allowing Brutus to stroll through the open door. Once outside, the dog let out a low bark, which was immediately answered by a cacophony of bays and howls. The dog then led the footman around the side of the house, where he unbolted the door to the kennels. The main pack, many of whom Brutus had sired, padded out to meet the alpha dog. The animals would now roam the grounds overnight.

In the distance, two men watched Newsome Hall. They were dressed in black with hooded capes, despite the warm night. But these were no chancers, scruffy rouges intent on stealing anything they could. They were educated men, and they had already been busy. They had brought several parcels covered in waxed cloth, the contents a concoction of beef, faeces, and urine. The dogs would be drawn by the smell to the irresistible, mouth-watering meal.

Ten years ago, the taller of the two men had been a young army captain, the son of a country gentleman. When his father died, he intended to resign his commission and manage the small country estate in Wiltshire. But when he returned home, he found that his father had gambled away his inheritance. The estate was mortgaged, and the debt now due. Even his commission and his monthly allowance had been paid out of the loans his father had obtained. He faced penury, knowing that his captain's salary would not enable him to pay off these debts, nor pay a dowry for his two younger sisters.

At that point, he had been recruited, his debts paid off, and in return, he was trained in many new skills. He had been a model student, and he had been paid well for his services. To the world, he was a country gentleman living off his estate, but in reality, he was something else.

The tall man looked to the night sky and saw only darkness. This was what he wanted; it was a reassurance. They listened intently, heard the footman shoot the bolts of the front door, saw the last lantern go out. Then they waited.

In the gloom, they heard the dogs getting closer — rustles in the undergrowth, the thick rumbling in the dogs' throats, the sniffing of enticing scents, and then the first sounds of the dogs gulping down the contents of the parcels. Unseen, the tall man's face creased into a grim smile. He knew that the concoction also contained something else — cyanide.

ONE

As we turned onto Greek Street, Father gave an exaggerated sigh to underline his displeasure. This was the new West End of London, and the affluence was all around us — clean streets, brightly lit shops, well-dressed people going about their privileged lives. When we walked past Josiah Wedgwood's shop, I heard Father tut his disapproval; he was never subtle. I, however, had never seen anything quite so lovely. I stared through the glass pane in wonder. Fine china tableware was displayed in cabinets, grand tables laid out for dinner parties, and fine-looking vases perched precariously atop ornamental columns.

This was my first time in the West End, and it was a view into another world for me. My father, Augustus Swift, was a physician who usually gave his time for free to the city's poor. I loved and admired him for it, but at times, I missed what others had.

'Where is this shop, Augusta?' he said. He only called me by my given name if he was irritable. I was usually called Cully, after the great apothecary, Nicholas Culpeper.

'It's just here, Father,' I replied, spotting the sign, 'two shops down.'

He stepped back and looked up at the sign — *Henry Isherwood, Haberdashers.*

Through the window, I could see fabrics hanging down in elaborate folds, so that passersby could imagine them as elegant dresses. It made me want to touch them to feel how rich the material was.

Father tutted again. 'This Isherwood fellow can obviously afford the best of physicians. Why am I here?'

'He can afford the most expensive of physicians, but not the best. You are the best, Father.'

'Ah — flattery,' he snorted.

'It's not flattery, Father, and you know it; it's only modesty that stops you saying so yourself.'

Grandpa was a Master Apothecary and had a shop in Temple Bar, where we all lived. He was a disciple of the great Nicholas Culpeper and his books, *The English Physician* and *Complete Herbal*. Father had once been apprenticed to him, and now Grandpa was instructing me in all things herbal. Grandpa was wealthy enough to send Father to Edinburgh Medical School, where he also studied Modern Medicine, Latin, Greek and Logic. Father then travelled to the Qawaloon hospital in Cairo, where he studied the Islamic approach to doctoring.

'Am I expected?' Father asked. He tugged at the clean white stock at his neck that I had insisted he wear, together with a clean frockcoat, unstained by blood or herbal concoctions. He looked handsome, I thought, tall, with a short grey beard and an arrestingly intelligent face.

'As I told you, I met his daughter Jane at my music lesson. Mr Isherwood called a physician when his wife was suffering from colic. He prescribed a physic, and as Mr Isherwood was busy with the shop, he employed a nurse to administer it. But when Mrs Isherwood didn't get any better, the nurse recommended a local healer. Jane is worried; three months have passed and her mother continues with the malady, and she is getting weaker. We're here at Jane's request.'

A bell over the door rang as we entered, and a clerk presented himself for assistance.

'The proprietor please?' Father asked. Hearing his words, Isherwood himself came forward.

Father bowed. 'Dr Augustus Swift, at your service, sir, and this is my daughter, Cully.'

'Ah yes, Jane mentioned that she had spoken to your daughter, but my wife is already being treated. I fear you have had a wasted journey, sir.'

Father tutted again, but this time at me.

'It will do no harm to have a second opinion, will it, Mr Isherwood?' I said.

Isherwood hesitated, then nodded. 'Follow me, please,' he said, leading us upstairs to the living quarters.

The curtains in the bedroom were drawn, casting the room in shadow, but I could still see a figure lying in the bed.

Sitting in a chair at the back of the room was an elderly lady whom I took to be the nurse. She was introduced as Mrs Dobbin. She was a small, sour-faced woman. I suspected that she had little in the way of nursing skills, probably taking up the duties when she was too feeble for any other sort of work. She stood as we entered the room, and I could smell gin on her breath.

'A new doctor has come to see you, my dear,' Isherwood said to his wife, keeping his voice low.

Mrs Isherwood opened her eyes slowly, gave a small nod, and then closed them again.

Father placed his medical bag on the foot of the bed. 'What do we do first, Cully?' he asked me. It was part of my mentoring.

'Ask the patient about her symptoms and then examine her, Father.'

He nodded. 'Go ahead.'

I took off my shoulder bag, placed it beside the bed, and opened the curtains. The patient reacted to the bright light with a small groan. I perched on the side of the bed and took her hand.

'Does the light hurt your eyes, Mrs Isherwood?' I asked.

'Mmm,' she replied, her voice little more than a murmur.

'Tell me about your malady, Mrs Isherwood.'

'It started with a bellyache.' She moved her hand slowly down to her abdomen. 'But now it's here.' She ran her hand up towards her chest. 'It feels as though it's burning from the inside.'

'Any diarrhoea?'

The patient tried to nod but winced at the pain.

'She is sometimes confused,' Isherwood interjected. 'And she has dizziness, headaches, and spasms.'

'I'm going to examine you now, Mrs Isherwood,' I said.

The patient didn't respond, and so I gently pulled the bedsheets down. I placed my palm lightly on her abdomen and pressed softly, watching her face closely to gauge her reaction. She grimaced when I applied a little pressure to her stomach. I also examined her hands, her eyes, and her tongue.

'Well, Cully?' said Father. 'What do you deduce?'

'I would prefer to examine a urine and stool sample, before making my diagnoses.'

'Good,' he responded. 'Never rush to judgement. But what are your first impressions? Is it biliousness?'

'No, Father, she is pallid but not yellow. It's not her liver. Certainly, there is a gastric upset, although the stomach is not distended. But the irregular pulse is puzzling.'

'What about camp fever?'

'It could be. The diarrhoea might indicate typhus. But that is often associated with overcrowding and poor hygiene, not the clean streets of the West End.'

'Scirrhus?'

'I can't feel any tumours in her abdomen or her chest.'

'So your first thoughts, Cully?'

'I am puzzled, Father; things are contradictory.'

'Sometimes they are. What does that suggest?' I knew he was testing me, and his tone was encouraging.

I hesitated. 'Maybe there is more than one malady here.'

Father smiled. 'I agree, Cully. What came first?'

'Probably a simple gut ache, maybe milk fever caused by some bad milk.'

'And what would the great Culpeper have recommended?'

I reached for my shoulder bag for Culpeper's book.

'No, don't look it up; you have studied him long enough.'

I searched my memory. 'He would recommend dandelion root, with bark from the slippery elm. I would make a hot tincture with seeds of anise, caraway, coriander, cumin and dill, and perhaps some fennel, Father.'

'And with such a preparation, what would you expect from the result?'

'A full recovery in a matter of days, a week maybe.'

'Good. So, what other malady complicates your diagnosis?'

A thought had entered my head, but I was afraid to say it aloud. It was not my place to make accusations. I glanced up at Isherwood and saw his anxiety.

'Go ahead, Cully,' Father pressed.

'I fear she may have been —' I hesitated — 'poisoned.'

'Poisoned?' Isherwood exclaimed, his eyes wide.

Father turned to the nurse. 'What have you been giving this lady, Mrs Dobbin?'

Mrs Dobbin pursed her mouth. 'I only give Mrs Isherwood the extract that Mary Gayle made up for her. Three times a day, Mary said.'

'Can I see this extract, please?'

Mrs Dobbin handed Father a small blue medicine bottle. He pulled the stopper and sniffed, then put a drop on the end of his little finger and touched it to the tip of his tongue. He passed the bottle to me.

I put it to my nose and identified dill, fennel and caraway. But, like Father, I also knew that most poisons were undetectable, tasteless and odourless.

'But who would wish to poison my wife?' asked Isherwood, clearly confused.

'Mary Gayle for one,' said Father. 'If she feeds your wife small amounts of poison but has the skill to keep her alive, then she will have a steady income from you. Who is she anyway?'

'Mrs Dobbin recommended her; she has a reputation as a powerful healer,' said Isherwood. 'She holds weekly clinics and is a stage performer. I saw her on stage and then asked her to come and see my wife.'

'And did she examine Mrs Isherwood?'

'Well, she came with her divining hen.'

'Her what?' Father did not attempt to hide his scorn.

'She brought a hen with her and put it on my wife's bed. It clucked for ten minutes or so, then settled down and laid an egg.'

'An egg?'

'You don't understand. The egg, when laid and still warm, had writing on it. It said *Scirrhus*. She has been treating her for this since then.'

'I need to speak to this woman,' said Father.

'She's been already today,' said Mrs Dobbin. 'She won't be back until tomorrow.'

'Then we shall return first thing in the morning.'

On our way home, I was anxious to speak to Father. 'I understand your assumption that Mary Gayle might benefit from poisoning Mrs Isherwood, but couldn't that also be said of her husband? Perhaps there is another woman in his life and he wants to be rid of his wife?'

'Excellent reasoning, Cully,' replied Father. 'Logic requires us to consider every possibility.' Father had a way of working things out which he called it his *philosophy of reason*. It was his own diagnostic method, part logic from his studies at Edinburgh University and part Islamic philosophy. 'But don't you think he would have poisoned her to *death* by now if that were the case? The poor woman has been kept alive for months. But you are right; we cannot rule him out. Will you talk to his daughter, Jane, and find out if there is anyone that he is particularly close to? An employee, perhaps, or maybe a family friend?'

I nodded assent, then asked, 'How will you treat Mrs Isherwood, Father? Her system needs purging of the poison, but if you prescribe tartar emetic to induce vomiting, it is likely to kill her in her weakened state.'

'Aye, Cully, it's a problem. But at least we can stop any more poison going into her system.'

I frowned. 'How, Father?'

He reached into the inside pocket of his jacket and produced the blue medicine bottle containing Mary Gayle's concoction. He gave me a mischievous wink.

TWO

Sir Thomas Maxwell-Clark, Earl Newsome, strode with his footman and his estate steward around his grounds of Newsome Hall. It was early and he was still in his nightshirt and robe.

They passed several of his dogs, some lying near the house, as if they had tried to get back to the kennels. Now he looked down at the body of his cherished mastiff, Brutus. He experienced a range of emotions: deep sorrow for his favourite animal; anger at the audacity of the attack on his property; and bewilderment at the motive behind it.

'Have you examined the bodies, Jameson?' he asked of his steward.

'Yes, my lord,' the man replied. 'There are no wounds to be found, either from a knife or gunshot.'

'So it's poison then?'

'It looks that way, my lord, and I've found the remains of it, I think. Waxed paper, licked clean by the dogs. Whatever it was they ate did for them.'

'Taking a risk, weren't they, with my hounds?'

'Yes, my lord. I'm surprised the dogs didn't have 'em.'

'But the house wasn't broken into?' the earl asked, turning to his footman.

'It doesn't appear so, my lord,' the servant replied. 'We've made a quick check, and the butler is organising a more thorough search now.'

'Local ruffians, do you think?'

The footman shrugged. 'I don't think so, my lord; locals wouldn't paint on the front of the house.'

Sir Thomas scowled. 'Show me,' he said.

The three men returned to the house and looked at the daubing beside the front door. There was a symbol, shaped a bit like a three-leaved clover with three interlocking loops connected by a circle. Below the symbol was a phrase, painted in blue: *la confrérie*.

'Is it Latin?' asked the steward.

'No, Jameson, it's French. It means fellowship, possibly brotherhood.'

'Then I don't understand, my lord.'

'It's a warning.'

'A warning? Of what, my lord?'

'Can't tell you that, Jameson, but it's a warning to me. These are troubled times,' he said contemplatively. He knew — he was the Home Secretary.

Father and I arrived at Isherwood's haberdashery at eight-thirty, just as the shop was opening. While Father went to see Mrs Isherwood, I took the opportunity to speak with Jane. I ascertained that the only woman her father was close to was her mother, as far as she knew. Jane accompanied me back to Mrs Isherwood's bedroom, and shortly afterwards Mary Gayle arrived with the day's medicine.

She was a tall woman in her early thirties, with olive skin and long black hair. She wore a black cape over an emerald-green dress. Her attire looked like it came from a high-class establishment — possibly Isherwood's itself. But it was her eyes that took my attention, large black pools framed by long, thick lashes. They fixed upon Father and then me, but her face remained a mask. Before Father could speak, Mrs Dobbin cut in.

'The doctor took away your preparation yesterday, Mary,' she said. 'Mrs Isherwood had no medicine yesterday or this morning.'

Mary Gayle took off her cape and handed it to Mrs Dobbin. The nurse held it against her chest as though it were a treasured gift.

Mary turned her dark eyes on Father. 'You are a physician, sir?'

'Augustus Swift at your service, madam.'

'Yes, I have heard of you, sir. You run a free clinic in Temple Bar, do you not?' She continued before he could answer. 'And as a physician, is it your habit to steal another physician's medicine?'

'My apologies, madam. I had not realised that you were a physician. Where did you study before joining the Royal College of Physicians?'

'I have my own qualifications as a healer,' she replied, her tone condescending. 'I have studied healing and herbal remedies extensively.'

'Oh, so you are a member of the Society of Apothecaries, then?'

Father, I realised, was stripping away Ms Gayle's credibility, piece by piece.

'I am a healer with a reputation for success,' Mary replied.

'It is always a pleasure to confer with other *physicians*. May I ask, how did you arrive at your diagnosis of Mrs Isherwood?'

'My methods are not for public scrutiny, sir. I have a living to earn — unlike you. Free clinics will only lead to penury.' Her words were hostile.

'Do you not display your methods on the stage, madam? I understand that you have a remarkable *hen* that helps you.'

'I have many aids to help with diagnoses, sir.'

'And what *is* your diagnosis of Mrs Isherwood, madam?'

She hesitated. 'My diagnosis is scirrhus.'

'I have detected no evidence of tumours,' said Father. 'Can you show them to me?'

'Sometimes the tumours cannot be detected externally; my hen found the scirrhus.'

'So it's a magical hen then, is it?'

'If that's what you want to call it, sir.'

'Can you read and write, Mary?' Father asked.

'Of course I can,' she spat. 'What kind of fool do you take me for?'

I heard father click his tongue. It was a habit he had when something coalesced in his mind.

'So, your diagnosis was made by a magic hen with the power of prophecy, and you will not tell me what medicine you have prescribed?' Father reached into his jacket and produced the blue medicine bottle. He held it out to Mary. 'Will you take your own medicine, madam?'

'I do not have the scirrhus, sir,' she said coldly.

'Is there something in the preparation that would harm you?'

'Certainly not.'

'Then come, let us both take it.'

Mary hesitated. 'Very well. But the preparation is not to be taken on an empty stomach. I have not eaten this morning.'

Father turned to Isherwood. 'Will your kitchen be able to find some food, please, sir?'

The haberdasher nodded and went away to arrange it.

'Will I be allowed some privacy to eat, sir?' Mary asked.

Father nodded and we removed to Isherwood's office, along with the haberdasher and his daughter, leaving Mary with Mrs Dobbin and Mrs Isherwood.

I asked Father if he would really swallow the preparation. 'If it *is* poisoned,' I said, 'it will be dangerous.'

'If I have to,' he replied, 'then I will. But I doubt it will come to that.'

'Why have we left them alone?' I asked.

'The woman is playing for time.' He looked at me. 'Work out the logical course of action, Cully.'

I tried to remember what Father had taught me. He wanted me to use his *philosophy of reason*, but his mind was far more analytical than mine. I hesitated before speaking.

'Mary Gayle earns her living by deception.'

'And?'

'We need to establish the *value* of her deception — the value to her.'

'And what is that value?'

'The value to her is — well, absolute, I think. Her whole life is a deception.'

'So what is our strategy?'

'I don't know, Father. The woman will defend herself — she has no alternative.'

'Exactly, Cully. But what if our strategy is to offer Mary Gayle a way out?'

Before I could reply, there was a knock on the door and one of Isherwood's kitchen staff came in. 'I've taken food to the mistress's room, sir, but there's no one there, other than Mrs Isherwood,' she said.

Father turned and winked at me, his *philosophy of reason* justified. 'I think you will find they have made a run for it,' he said.

'Devil take the woman!' cried Isherwood. 'This proves that she and Mrs Dobbin have been poisoning my wife and swindling me. I will send to Bow Street for a Runner.'

'Poison is difficult to prove, sir,' said Father. 'For most poisons, there are no tests. Leave revenge for another day. Unless…' He paused. 'Who has been running your household since your wife was taken ill?'

'Why, I have, sir — but I confess to neglecting it during business hours.'

'Then I would suggest that you take an inventory of your personal belongings, and in particular your wife's jewellery. There has been scope for petty pilfering. Call in the Runners if you find anything missing.'

'Damn them both!' Isherwood exclaimed. 'But how did Mary get the hen to lay an egg with writing on it?'

'She is a music hall entertainer, Mr Isherwood, and she can read and write. She may have written on the egg using a solution of vitriol so that it burned into the shell. Then it was probably a case of sleight of hand. It's not so difficult to create an illusion.'

We all returned to Mrs Isherwood's room and Father asked me to examine her again. She was as before, except that her pulse was more regular.

'She is a little stronger, probably because no poison was administered in the last twenty-four hours. Let's try to build up her strength over the next few days and hope that the poison leaves her system naturally. I will make up some broth, and Cully here will stay and administer it.'

'Your visitor from Bow Street is here, Sir Thomas.'

The Home Secretary looked up from his desk at his private secretary. 'Send him in will you, Bradbrook?'

Bradbrook returned a moment later with a broad-shouldered man wearing a long black greatcoat and low-crowned slouch hat. 'Constable Abel Stoll, sir,' the secretary said by way of introduction.

'Thank you, Bradbrook,' said the earl. 'Please stay, if you will?'

Stoll took off his hat and nodded uncomfortably to Sir Thomas.

'You can sit if you want, Stoll,' the Home Secretary said. Stoll did so.

'You've been recommended to me by Sampson Wright, the Chief Magistrate at Bow Street,' said Sir Thomas. 'He says you have a fine investigative mind.'

'It's good of him to say so, Sir Thomas.'

'I have a job for you, Stoll. Two nights ago, all my dogs were poisoned while patrolling my grounds, but my house was not broken into.'

Stoll took out a notebook from the breast pocket of his uniform and began making notes. 'What time would this be, my lord?' he asked.

'Sometime after midnight and before five-thirty in the morning.' He pushed a piece of paper across his desk. 'This is a copy of a symbol that was painted by my front door.'

Stoll examined the drawing. 'I don't recognise the symbol, sir, but these words are French — *la confrérie*. Brotherhood, I believe.'

The Home Secretary couldn't hide a look of surprise. 'You speak French, Constable?'

'Some, sir.'

'Well, what do you think?'

Stoll gave an uneasy cough. 'Are you sure this is a matter for Bow Street, sir? It doesn't look typically criminal to me. It could be political? Surely you have people at the Home Department who can advise you?'

Sir Thomas took out a snuffbox from his waistcoat pocket, pinched some of its contents onto the back of his hand and then snorted it up each nostril, leaving a brown stain on his nose. He took out his silk handkerchief and flourished it before his face. 'Yes, I have agents who can advise, but they don't immediately recognise the name of this brotherhood; it seems to be new. This is a warning to me. They are investigating, but the Home Department itself is new, only founded a dozen or so years ago in 1782.'

'So you want me to be the man on the ground? Look for strangers in the area, see if I can identify the culprits?'

'Exactly, Stoll. And you will report directly back to me, not Bow Street or the Chief Magistrate, do you understand?'

'Yes, sir,' the constable replied. 'But what about — resources?'

The Home Secretary looked at his private secretary for guidance.

'I think he can draw any additional resources from Bow Street, sir,' Bradbrook said. 'You will have to brief Samson Wright, though, sir.'

Sir Thomas nodded. 'If you need help, get it from Bow Street, but tell the other constables as little as possible. Discretion is the keyword here, understood?'

'Yes, sir, discretion.'

The earl stood up to signify that the meeting was over. Stoll followed his lead. 'And Stoll,' Sir Thomas added, 'urgency, if you please.'

THREE

Bob's Chop House was busy. Constable Stoll took a table by himself and ordered pea soup, cold meats and bread, with a jug of ale. When his pewter tankard arrived, he took a deep swig, then wiped his mouth with the back of his hand, exhaling appreciatively. He was thirsty, hungry, and his feet ached.

He had roamed the city all day, for word on the street. As night fell, he had turned his attention to Covent Garden, where he knew the high and the low mingled.

He had first-hand experience of the London crowd, its unpredictability, and with gin as the king, it could explode into life at any time, and that frightened the city fathers. There had always been a fear of riot. The mob was usually ready for mischief, and gin was often its fuel; he knew that all too well.

Stoll had visited all his contacts, his informers, questioned them about any new gangs in the city, but he had drawn a blank. He had worn his Bow Street uniform during the day but had been back to the station to change into plain clothes — a three-piece tweed suit. He took his pocket watch from his waistcoat. It was ten after nine. The night was the time to visit the theatres and the cockpits. He dipped crusty bread into the pea soup, breathing in the aroma of the dried peas simmered in stock with celery, onion and rich seasoning.

He looked around between mouthfuls. Bob's Chop House attracted more than the casual diner. It was also a place for hard drinking and gambling. In short, it was one of the lowest of establishments in London; its clientele, however, was of a surprisingly mixed variety. Sporting gentlemen were looking to gamble with some of the city's more successful villains.

Card games were in play, and some women supported the winning players, no doubt looking for custom. The card games themselves were part of the entertainment, and much of the noisy crowd gathered around them.

Stoll licked the last of his meal from his fingers and went to join the crowd. He joined in with the banter and skilfully directed it to the criminality that was currently on the streets. Certain lines of enquiry emerged for him to follow, but they were for another day; nothing of this new brotherhood surfaced. As he mingled, however, the hair on the back of his neck stood up. He'd been around long enough to know when he was being watched. He looked around and saw a pair of menacing blue eyes across the room. A scar ran down from the watcher's right eye to the corner of his mouth. A villain had recognised him; it was time to move on.

Cockpits were attached to many a disreputable inn, but the most infamous were on the south side of St James's Park, near Gray's Inn Gardens. Stoll started his tour of them but had had little success. It was coming up to ten-thirty when he reached the Royal Cockpit in St James's Park. His mood had soured; he didn't like these places. The smell of human sweat mixed with animal excrement did nothing to improve his temper. With the stench of piss and ale, and the roar of the crowd, it all added up to a noisome attack on the senses.

The cockpit consisted of tiers of benches surrounding a raised platform. As Stoll entered, a fight was in progress. Two cocks matched by weight and fortified with steel spurs on their feet were in the process of maiming each other. The crowd bayed its approval or disapproval, depending upon which fowl their money rode. There was a crescendo of sound that rose with every gash. Suddenly, one of the combatants collapsed, signalling that the fight was over. The wall of sound diminished only slightly as the audience turned to the business of settling wagers.

Stoll feigned enjoyment in the revelry, the stimulating bloodlust, the excitement of the wager. Alcohol was consumed without restraint, tongues loosened by the atmosphere; it could be the best source of information he would find all day.

He manoeuvred himself next to a sporting gentleman — a young buck in his early twenties, his smart frockcoat dirtied by the benches. He engaged him in conversation between fights, skilfully moving the topic to unrest on the streets. The man looked back at him with inebriated eyes. 'Sir,' he said, 'it's not the criminal on the street that I fear, it's the radicals. Sedition is all around us. That scoundrel Pitt, the Prime Minister, should do something about it before London suffers the same fate as Paris.'

The moonlight caught in the tall man's eyes in the warm evening. Otherwise, his black hooded cape rendered him almost invisible. In the shadows, he stood watching Pear Tree House, the elegant London residence of Earl Darwin, Cabinet member and Lord President of the Council. The house was in the affluent West End, with its wide streets and grand homes. Fronted by two wrought-iron gates, the magnificent residence proclaimed its splendour to the world and the status of its owner. The tall man looked past the railings to the lavish property within, assessing his task — how to gain entry to the building.

It was the third night he had been here, noting the routine of the household. These were dangerous times for the wealthy and well-to-do, and the owner knew to take precautions. At night, all the doors and windows were heavily bolted, to keep out intruders, and to protect the family and contents within.

But the tall man had discovered a garret window to the rear that was left open at night, probably by a servant unable to sleep in the warm evenings, seeking some cooler air. It was inaccessible, right at the top of the house — but it would do for his partner.

Just after two o'clock, some rolling clouds hid the silver moon to provide temporary cover. The tall man's task tonight was that of lookout. The conditions were not ideal, the moonlight was an enemy, but now there was an opportunity. He whispered to his partner; they made their decision.

Within moments, the small man was scaling the wall at the rear of the house. His skill was that of a climber. The tall man had recruited him. At the age of sixteen, he had been part of an acrobatic troupe; he was agile, small of frame, but surprisingly strong for his size. He travelled the country with the company, where he also put his skills to another use, burglary. But he was young and foolish and had flashed his money about in the taverns, bragging about the thefts. An informer took the usual forty-bob reward for his apprehension by the watchmen. Thrown into gaol — his fate after trial either hanging or deportation — it took him only two hours to escape. He broke through the timber ceiling and dropped down to the floor outside.

The tall man had found him in a tavern. He had taught him to read and write, had given him a new identity. He was now a man of property, three run as brothels near Covent Garden, their purchase financed by his new profession.

Now he was putting his expertise to use in the service of the Brotherhood. He climbed deftly, drainpipe to ledge, ledge back to drainpipe. Nearing the top, he took advantage of the gargoyles provided by the architect — lion-headed troughs cut to carry water from the roof. Strong fingers helped him traverse, taking his weight when there was no foothold beneath him.

On reaching the garret window, he eased himself through the opening and dropped silently to the floor. The room was small, with just a single bed and a nightstand beside it. The sound of snoring filled the space, and he tiptoed to the door to let himself out. Tentatively he descended a flight of stairs, stepping on the outside of the step to minimise creaking.

He followed the lingering aroma of the previous night's meal towards his destination, the kitchen. Tonight the small man would not be a thief; however, his reward would be a substantial fee, if he got away without anyone knowing he had been there. He glanced around the kitchen but failed to find the object of his search. He opened the door to the larder, but there was no window inside, and he needed light to continue his search. He took a candle from his pocket along with his tinder pistol. He cocked the flintlock mechanism and fired it. The flint struck against the steel and sparks flew onto a charcloth. He blew on it, creating a small flame, and lit the candle wick from it.

He now saw what he was searching for — the tea caddy. It was locked. He took it back into the kitchen and sat down at the servants' dining table. The key would be with the housekeeper. Placing the candle down, he took a bunch of delicate metal tools from his pocket. He inserted one of the steel implements into the lock and turned it, listening for resistance. He had it open in under thirty seconds. He sat back, pleased with himself.

The small man took out an envelope from his inside pocket. He opened it to reveal an odourless and tasteless powder, which he sprinkled onto the tea. Then he relocked the caddy and gave it a shake, dispersing the powder as evenly as possible. Before he left, he had one last task to perform. From another pocket, he took a roll enclosing a small brush and a vial. He turned the caddy on its side and painted a symbol on its underside.

We always sat down to the evening meal together. Mother, Father and I lived with Grandpa Matthew over his apothecary shop in Temple Bar. Father held his free clinics in the back room on the ground floor. We had only one servant — Betsy, our housemaid — but Mother insisted on a good table, laid with a damask tablecloth, silver cutlery, and real wax candles. We also had a bottle of burgundy and three wine glasses tonight. Betsy brought in our evening meal. Tonight we had white soup made from veal stock, cream and almonds, thickened with bread, followed by a platter of baked fish and vegetables.

Grandpa was reading the *London Penny Post*. Noticing Mother's hard stare, he folded it up and turned his attention to his soup.

'I see one of Pitt's Cabinet died yesterday, Augustus,' he said as he picked up his spoon.

Father looked up at him. 'Which one?' he asked.

'Some duke or other,' Grandpa replied.

'Well, it would be with a Tory government,' Father scoffed. He had no time for Pitt and his government.

'The paper says foul play is suspected,' Grandpa added, then blew on his spoon to cool the hot soup.

Father's interest was piqued. 'Why?' he asked. 'How did he die?'

'The paper doesn't say other than he was taken ill in Cabinet and died in the Prime Minister's office. Do you think it could be an assassination, Augustus?'

'I wouldn't rule it out, Matthew; Pitt's government breeds repression. They see any protestors as a rabble to be put down, whether it's against poverty or voting. He's a man out of his time.'

'I don't think murder is a suitable conversation for the dinner table, Matthew,' said Mother in her Scottish accent. She turned to Father. 'And you, Gus. Cully is not yet eighteen, remember?'

'As my assistant,' said Father, reaching for his wine glass, 'Cully has seen more of the world than most young women see in a lifetime. Only the other day, she correctly diagnosed the poisoning of Mrs Isherwood.'

'And you allowed that, Gus?'

'Nonsense, Iona. Cully here is probably the best-educated young woman in London. She has Latin, logic, and rhetoric, and she knows a wide knowledge of herbs and some anatomy. Her grandfather and I have made sure of that.'

This was dangerous ground, I knew. I desperately wanted to continue as Father's assistant, but Mother had hopes of my becoming a refined young lady and marrying well. The last thing I wanted was to spend my days embroidering and taking tea. I was only learning to play the piano because Mother had insisted upon it.

Mother flung down her soup spoon. 'And tell me, Gus, just how will all that learning find Augusta a suitable husband? A gentleman will not want a wife cleverer than he is.'

I bit my lip. It was never good when Mother used my given name. But she wasn't finished.

'Will she be allowed to join the College of Physicians?' she asked.

'No, Iona, you know they don't admit women,' Father replied.

'Well, maybe she can apply to the Society of Apothecaries?'

Father sighed. 'No, my dear, they won't allow her either. But she *can* help out in the apothecary shop, where her knowledge will prove invaluable.'

'And what will happen when Matthew dies?' Mother looked up at her father-in-law. 'He's hale and hearty,' she added hastily, 'but he's sixty-six, is he not?'

'Sixty-six, but aged to perfection,' Grandpa put in, unable to suppress a wheezed chuckle.

'Will she be allowed to continue his work?'

'No, my dear,' answered Father.

'God, in His wisdom, felt it right to send us a daughter and not a son, Gus. You should accept that and not try to make her into something that she is not.'

'Yes, my dear.' Father seemed resigned to having lost the argument — this was serious.

'And while we are on the subject, isn't it time you got some more private patients? Our income is currently dependent on the apothecary shop.'

'Do you want me to give up my free clinic?'

She sighed. 'No, Gus,' she said, her voice softer. 'Your clinic is important to you; I know that. But some private work will help pay the bills.'

'Yes, I know. And you're right, Cully will be eighteen in a few weeks. We must start looking for a suitable husband. Can I leave that to you, my dear?'

Mother nodded, and a knot tightened in my stomach. Why couldn't I take over the apothecary shop? I knew I was capable.

'You didn't allow *your* parents to find *you* a suitable husband, did you, Mother?' I demanded.

Mother paused. 'That was different,' she said, twisting the wedding ring on her finger.

'Why was it different?'

'Your father and I —' she hesitated — 'well, it was a love match. That's the difference.'

'You married Father and then immediately went away with him to Egypt. That's hardly traditional, is it?'

'I loved your father very much. And my father approved of him; he was his tutor at Edinburgh Medical School. He introduced us.'

'And did Grandpa approve of him taking a young lady halfway across the world?'

'Well, no, he didn't, but —'

'I bet he didn't,' I cut in. 'But that's not the point. You want me to be something that you yourself rejected when you met Father.'

'It wasn't like that. I thought that I was marrying an exceptional young doctor who would be successful. That I would own a fine house and be prosperous — until your father got it into his head to study Islamic medicine.'

'So why didn't you break off the engagement?'

'I was too much in love. I couldn't wait three years for him to come back. So I insisted on going with him. I had no comprehension of what it would be like.'

'And what was it like?' I was intent on making my point.

'Insufferable heat and endless biting insects, that's what it was like.'

'And what else?' I knew what else — she had told me many times as a child when she had put me to bed.

She breathed a long sigh of resignation. 'Camels and turbans, Pashas and Beys,' she said wistfully. 'Arabs and Ottomans, silk dresses in vibrant reds and golds with diamond insignia, magnificent Arab stallions resplendent with gem-studded bridles.' Her eyes slid away and I could tell that her mind was back in Egypt. 'A boat trip on the lazy Nile; palm trees guarding its bank; thousands of white butterflies taking to the air as we walked through the lush greenery of the floodplains.'

'Now that's hardly settling down with a *suitable* husband, is it, Mother?'

She snapped back to the present. 'But we were in danger so many times,' she added, but I hoped that I had put her off the idea of marriage for the present.

FOUR

Bradbrook ushered Constable Stoll into the Home Secretary's office, where Sir Thomas gestured for him to take a seat. Bradbrook stayed, along with a fourth man whom Stoll didn't recognise. The constable gave his report on the word on the street.

'So, no new gangs are working in London?' Sir Thomas said, leaning back in his chair.

'No, my lord, none that would know how to poison your dogs and then leave without a trace.' He felt uncomfortable before such an imposing figure, his London accent coarse compared with the Home Secretary's silky tones. He was, after all, just the son of a greengrocer.

The Home Secretary steepled his fingers before him.

'Can I speak freely, my lord?' asked Stoll. Sir Thomas waved a hand for him to continue. 'I spoke to a young sporting gentleman in a cockfighting pit. He told me that it wasn't the criminal on the street that he feared but the radicals. "Sedition is all around us," he said. He was drunk, of course, but there is unrest. I doubt the poisoning of your dogs was the work of a criminal gang. I would suggest the investigation be continued in places where radicals may meet, perhaps the coffee houses, the theatres, the gentlemen's clubs.'

'That is our conclusion also,' said Sir Thomas. He looked up towards the fourth man. 'This is one of our agents, Mr Hazeldean. I have charged him with doing just that.'

Stoll nodded a greeting. 'So Mr Hazeldean will take over the investigation?' he asked.

'Yes, but not immediately; I have another job for you first, Constable.'

'Sir?'

'You may have read this morning that Earl Darwin died yesterday. Tragic, he was a good man. Well, we have now heard that his wife and eldest son have also been found dead. It looks like they were poisoned. I don't have to tell you, Stoll, this strikes at the very heart of government; the earl was a Cabinet member.' He looked at his secretary and gestured for him to continue.

'We want you to go down to his London house and take over the investigation from the local constable,' said Bradbrook. 'Hazeldean here will go with you. He can talk to the family while you talk to the servants.'

'Right away, sir,' Stoll said as he stood. He didn't take offence at the apparent slight.

As the carriage rattled to a halt outside Pear Tree House, Stoll peered out of the window. It was early June and warm, but it had been raining since dawn. He took in the extensive property, glancing up to the substantial windows and then at the smaller ones in the garret where the servants would sleep. The cabbie came round, unfurled the steps and then opened the door. Hazeldean stepped down first and made hastily towards the front door to get out of the rain. Stoll followed him.

The footman answered the bell and led them to the drawing-room, where Hazeldean introduced them. Stoll looked at the young earl; he was no more than seventeen, he thought, clearly shaken by the death of his parents and older brother. The burden now, unexpectedly, fell on him.

Hazeldean turned to Stoll. 'You may relieve the local constable, Stoll, and then start your investigation. We'll meet again at six o'clock to compare notes.'

'I would like to sit in on your debrief, Mr Hazeldean, if that is acceptable?' said the young earl. The Home Department man looked surprised but nodded. The earl turned to the footman. 'Please ask Coleman to accompany Constable Stoll,' he went on. 'Tell him to allow the constable access to the entire house.' He turned back to Stoll. 'Coleman is my father's — my butler,' he explained. 'He has all the keys. And, Constable, I want answers.'

Stoll nodded. 'Understood, sir.'

At six o'clock, Stoll entered the library, where Hazeldean and Earl Darwin were waiting for him. The young earl gestured towards a seat, which he took. He reached for his notebook, while Hazeldean outlined what he had ascertained.

'The earl and I believe that his parents, the late Earl and Lady Darwin, and his elder brother Sebastian were poisoned at breakfast yesterday morning. They all died within two hours of being taken ill. Earl Darwin died shortly after reaching Downing Street, actually in the Prime Minister's office. Lady Darwin and her son died here, at Pear Tree House. We haven't established how they were poisoned or why the new earl and his sister Georgiana were not. They all took breakfast together.'

Stoll looked at Hazeldean in his smart grey frockcoat and sighed inwardly. *It has taken you all day to establish virtually nothing,* he thought, when it became clear that the agent had no more to say. It was time for him to report.

'I have spoken to the cook and the footmen, sirs,' he began. 'I understand that the Earl and Lady Darwin's habit was to take tea with their breakfast. The new earl's habit is to take a draught of light beer, and his sister takes drinking chocolate. It seems clear, therefore, that the poison was in the tea.'

'But how did it get there?' enquired the young earl.

'Either the cups were laced with the poison, or it was in the tea caddy, sir.'

'And have you determined which?'

'Yes, sir, it was in the caddy.'

'How can you be sure, Constable?' the young earl continued.

'Whatever was added is tasteless, colourless and odourless, but there's something in there all right.'

'How can you be sure if it's colourless and odourless?' asked Hazeldean.

'Because when I turned the caddy over, there was a symbol inscribed on the bottom.' He took a piece of paper from his pocket and handed it to the earl. 'I have made a copy of it.'

The earl frowned. 'This means nothing to me.'

'I think it will mean something to Mr Hazeldean.'

Hazeldean took the note and nodded. 'This is the same symbol painted on the wall of the Home Secretary's house.'

Stoll looked at the earl. 'I fear your father's death is a political assassination, my lord.'

The earl looked at the Home Department man, who simply nodded confirmation.

'Have you interviewed all the servants, Stoll?' asked Hazeldean. 'If there was no break-in, then it must be one of them.'

'Yes, sir. Most of the servants have been with the family for years. The only exceptions are two scullery maids, but they are only fourteen and fifteen. They are unlikely to have been politicised. I asked all of the servants if any of their colleagues attend political meetings, but it appears not.'

'Do you believe them, Constable?' asked Hazeldean.

'I do, sir. It's more likely that one of the maids has a beau. Perhaps she lets him into the house at night when everybody has gone to bed.'

'But they would be instantly dismissed if found doing such a thing,' said the young earl.

'Aye, sir. They run a significant risk, but it happens, I assure you.'

'Has one of them confessed?'

'No, sir. Though I'm confident I would have got it out of them if such a thing had happened.'

'So how did the poison get into the house, Constable?' asked the earl.

'Well, if it wasn't a servant, then it must have been a break-in, sir.'

'But we already know there was no forced entry; the servants have checked.'

'I have rechecked all the windows myself, and yes, none were forced. However, if you look out of the window from one of the servant's rooms at the top of the house, you will see traces of mud on the gargoyles and drainpipes. There is also an ear missing from one of the lion-headed gargoyles, and I found the missing piece on the ground below; the broken edge shows that it's recent. I believe the wall was expertly scaled, and the intruder got in through an open window.'

The young earl turned to Hazeldean. 'What happens now?' he asked.

'I'll need to report back to the Home Secretary,' replied the agent, as if Stoll's good work was his own. He would take the credit, Stoll knew. 'All the Cabinet members, I believe, are now at risk.'

'And my household?' asked the earl anxiously.

'The foul deeds have already happened here, my lord; I don't think you are still in danger.'

Stoll cut in. 'You must tell all your servants to close and bolt all the doors at night. No window can be left open, no matter how hot the day has been. In the meantime, we'll take the tea caddy away with us; I'm sure the Home Department will have experts that they can call on to identify the poison.'

The same evening, Sir Thomas sat discussing the case with his private secretary.

'Stoll is such a coarse fellow,' he complained. 'Do we want him interviewing aristocrats, Members of Parliament?'

'The man has a keen investigatory mind, my lord,' replied Bradbrook.

'But we have good men here, don't we? What have they found out?'

'As you know, sir, the Home Department employs a number of spies, informers and agents provocateurs. We have an insight into where the sedition is, who the perpetrators are. We have a list of names to be watched — but none of our agents has identified this particular group, or who runs it. I think we have to recognise the seriousness of the threat that faces us if we don't want a Parisian-style terror here in London.'

'Dangerous times, eh, Bradbrook?'

'They are indeed, sir. We seem to be dealing with a secret brotherhood, not some rabble shouting in the streets and throwing stones — and we don't know who is behind it. Is it the Irish? Is it religious? Whoever it is, it's sedition.'

'Aye, and the Prime Minister has personally charged me with putting an end to it. Pitt feels we cannot give way to calls for change; that's why we voted down the Reform Bills of 1792 and 1793. He fears that reform is the thin edge of the wedge. It will inevitably lead to the overthrow of our whole system of government; we don't want to go the way of the French, do we?'

'No, but when you brought the radicals to the law for treason before, the judges didn't support you, did they, sir?'

'Members of the London Corresponding Society, you mean? Hardy, Horne Tooke, and the like, damn their eyes. We were right, though — they are dangerous men, mark my words.'

'But the Prime Minister was humiliated when they were acquitted, sir. The jury took only minutes to acquit John Horne Tooke.'

'Pitt is aware of that; he won't let it happen again. He's decided we must bring in new legislation if we can't get them under the existing law. They won't escape justice next time, not when my new Treasonable and Seditious Practices Act comes to law. The Prime Minister believes we need to strike at them hard, stamp out any form of subversion. If they say or write anything to bring the king or his government into contempt, then we'll charge them with treason, and this time they won't escape justice.'

'And the other Bill, sir? The Seditious Meetings Act?'

'Excellent, is it not, Bradbrook? Any public meeting of more than fifty persons will have to be authorised by a local magistrate. That'll stop them in their tracks.'

'Yes, my lord, no doubt about it.' The secretary hesitated. 'But any such Act will itself be provocative, will it not, sir?'

'Then so be it!' The Home Secretary thumped the desk. 'These people must realise who governs this country.'

Bradbrook nodded. 'Perhaps if we attach Stoll to Hazeldean as his advisor? The coarseness will be less apparent if Hazeldean asks the questions.'

'Yes, yes — do that, will you, Bradbrook?' Suddenly, Stoll's coarseness seemed less significant.

FIVE

'Come in, Constable Stoll.' Hazeldean beckoned for him to sit. 'Welcome to the Home Department.'

Stoll looked around the office. It was spacious, and there was a smell of waxed wood and floor polish — so different from the cramped conditions at Bow Street.

'Has the magistrate explained the position to you?'

'Aye, sir. I have been seconded to the Home Department to work on the poisonings.'

'That's right, Stoll, and you will report directly to me. I will decide what to take to the Home Secretary. Do you understand?'

'Aye, sir.'

'Any questions?'

'Yes, sir. Will you be taking me into your confidence?'

Hazeldean blinked. 'About what?' he asked.

'About what the Home Department has already found out, what it suspects.'

'I don't think it will be necessary, Stoll. I will tell you what you need to know and what I want you to investigate. Why do you want to know, anyway?'

'Perspective, sir. I want to know what motivates these people, whoever they are. It'll determine what questions I ask, where I start looking.'

'And what do *you* think their motives are?'

'Well, sir, in both poisonings, there was no theft — why? Was it blackmail, then? They have demonstrated they can kill someone as elevated as a Cabinet minister, but, as yet, there has been no demand for money. So, am I correct to assume that what they want must be political?'

Hazeldean raised a surprised eyebrow. The magistrate had chosen his man well. 'Yes, I think you are right so far, Stoll. What else do you want to know?'

'They are sending a message — do we know what that message is?'

'We believe so.'

'And will you disclose that to me, sir?'

Hazeldean swallowed. 'No, Stoll, you don't need to know that.'

The constable paused. 'I take it, with all your resources, you have identified *who* they are.'

'No, actually, we haven't.'

'But you have their symbol; surely that is a clue?'

'You would expect so, wouldn't you?' Hazeldean sighed. 'We have agents everywhere, and we think that we know where the sedition is, who is behind it — but this brotherhood isn't known to any of us. It must be new.'

'And the poison? Have you identified it?'

'No, we haven't identified that either. We have consulted the king's private surgeon, and he agreed with you that it was colourless and odourless.'

'Pity.'

'Pity, as you say, but the identity of the poison is not critical, is it?'

'It could be, sir. If we can identify it, it may enable us to find the supplier, then establish a chain back to the poisoners.' Stoll glanced at his superior. 'With due respect to the honourable surgeon, he is not an expert on poisoning. But I think I may know someone who may advise us.'

'Who do you have in mind?'

'Dr Augustus Swift.' Stoll noted Hazeldean's blank expression and explained further. 'I was called into a case some weeks ago in which the physician — Dr Swift — identified that a goodwife was being slowly poisoned. The poisoners were Mary Gayle, a music hall entertainer and so-called healer, and Mrs Dobbin, a nurse. Gayle was clearly behind it, but she claimed that Dobbin was poisoning the medicine she provided. We found some stolen items belonging to the patient in the nurse's lodgings, and Gayle offered to turn king's evidence. The nurse was convicted of theft and attempted murder. She is to hang in a few days.'

'You think this Swift fellow will be useful?'

Stoll nodded.

'Then I need to talk to him.'

It was just after eight o'clock when there was an unexpected knock at the door. We had not long finished dinner, but it was still light and we had sat down to a game of whist. I was playing with Father, Mother with Grandpa. Betsy brought a card and gave it to Father.

'Who is it, dear?' asked Mother.

'It's a Mr Hazeldean from the Home Department, and a constable from Bow Street. They want to speak to me. Shall I tell them to come back in the morning?'

Mother shook her head. 'No, you should speak to them, Gus — and if they want you to do something for them, please explain that they will have to pay. The government can afford your fees,' she added.

Betsy showed the visitors into the drawing room, where Grandpa, Father and I waited expectantly. The younger man looked to be in his late twenties, with a thin, sallow face and pale blue eyes. He wore a smart grey frockcoat with a freshly laundered stock at the collar. When he spoke, he had the clipped tones of a gentleman.

He introduced himself and then gestured to the constable. 'I believe you know Constable Stoll from the Isherwood poisoning case, sir; I was told that you identified the substance.'

'Good to see you again, Constable.' Father reached out and shook both men's hands, then gestured for them to sit.

'Apologies for calling so late,' said Mr Hazeldean, 'but we have something of importance to speak to you about.' He glanced at Grandpa and me. 'Something confidential.'

'We run a family business, sir,' said Father. 'Physician and apothecary services, and my daughter Cully acts as my assistant. We all contribute, and we know how to keep a confidence, I can assure you.'

Mr Hazeldean fidgeted in his seat. I could tell that he was uncomfortable with the situation. 'Very well,' he said. 'I want to consult you as an expert on poisons.'

'I hardly claim to be that, sir,' said Father.

Hazeldean shot the constable a hard stare, as if accusing him of wasting his time.

'But I would struggle to suggest anybody better qualified,' added Grandpa.

'Have you nobody attached to the Home Department who can advise?' asked Father.

'We have sought medical advice, but we have not identified the poison in question.'

'Then we'll help if we can —' began Father.

'Will there be a fee for this consultation, sir?' I interrupted, heeding Mother's words.

Mr Hazeldean shot me a reproachful look. 'Yes, of course.' He then proceeded to tell us about the poisoning of the Home

Secretary's dogs and the deaths of Earl Darwin and his wife and son, presumably from a poisoned tea caddy. As the story unfolded, I could see Father's expression darkening.

'So you want me to help that scoundrel Pitt and his government? Look at the state of this country — only a tiny minority of people are eligible to vote. Many of the constituencies are rotten boroughs where just a handful of voters send members to Parliament — and large towns such as Manchester send none. They deny any political rights to ordinary people. Riots are frequent in our towns and cities, and it's a wonder, sir, that we have not had a radical rebellion already. There's an appetite for reform in the country, led by educated men with sympathy for the French Revolution's aims. France declared war on us in 1793, and the country lives in fear. And what is the Prime Minister's response to all this? Does he move to allow reform to avoid revolution? No. His answer is *repression*, the outlawing of any sort of protest. His government votes down any attempt to bring change to Parliament, so corruption and patronage continue. Good God, man, they tried reformers for treason last year — treason!'

I looked at Grandpa, who just shrugged his shoulders. We both knew Father was passionate about his beliefs. Hazeldean and Stoll, however, were stunned at Father's tirade.

Hazeldean coughed nervously. 'Well, you are entitled to your views, Dr Swift,' he said.

'But that's the whole point, sir,' said Father. 'I'm *not* allowed my views, not according to the Prime Minister. And you want me to help him?'

I agreed with Father, of course, but now was not the time for a political debate. Fortunately, Constable Stoll spoke up.

'Dr Swift,' he said, 'I am a simple policeman. In my mind, the fact that the victim is a member of the Cabinet is irrelevant; it is still murder, is it not?'

Father sighed heavily. He recognised the truth in the constable's words. 'Yes, you are right, Constable Stoll.' The rancour had gone from his voice. 'We have to find the poisoners and stop them. Have you brought the tea caddy with you?'

'Aye, sir,' Stoll replied and handed it over.

Father opened the caddy and sniffed. 'We have a colourless and odourless substance. We must consider the options,' he said.

'And what are the options, Dr Swift?' asked Hazeldean.

'Hemlock and aconite are deadly to humans and animals,' Father replied. 'The toxins in hemlock cause muscular paralysis, leading to respiratory failure and eventual death.' He noticed Hazeldean's look of confusion. 'The victim cannot breathe — they are basically asphyxiated whilst still awake. A nasty death. Hemlock can be identified by the blotches it leaves on the skin. The monkshood plant contains highly toxic aconite. Initial signs of poisoning include vomiting and diarrhoea. In severe cases, it may cause death from respiratory paralysis or heart failure. From what Constable Stoll says, the symptoms do not appear to match the cases in question. I'll need to talk to the doctor called to attend to Earl Darwin, but I think we can disregard these two poisons.'

'What else could it be, Dr Swift?' asked Constable Stoll.

'Belladonna and mandrake have been used in traditional medicine for hundreds of years. Both plants, however, are also highly toxic. Belladona poisoning causes nausea, hallucinations, sweating and increased heart rate. Mandrake grows in Spain and Portugal. It's the root that's poisonous. It affects the liver and kidneys, so it isn't usually as fast-acting as other poisons. Mandrake poisoning would not cause death in a few hours, like that of the Darwins. I would be surprised if either were the poison used in these deaths.'

'So what *should* we be looking for, Dr Swift?' asked Hazeldean expectantly.

Father looked thoughtful. 'The fact that we are looking for something odourless and colourless would suggest something chemical, perhaps arsenic, strychnine or cyanide.'

'I don't know these poisons,' said Stoll, frowning, 'unless you mean the arsenic young ladies put on their faces to give them a pale complexion.'

'I mean precisely that, Constable. But a few grains can kill a man. And it is tasteless and odourless.'

'And what of the other two?' asked Stoll.

'I came across strychnine in the Middle East; it arrived there from China and India, where it's been used for centuries. It is a nasty poison and an unpleasant way to die. It causes uncontrollable muscle spasms and frothing at the mouth. Death is due to spasm of the respiratory muscles, resulting in respiratory failure. A Swedish chemist discovered hydrogen cyanide a few years ago,' Father continued. 'It is sometimes called prussic acid and is now used in blue paint, but it was also found to kill people very quickly. Exposure results in seizures before the victim passes into unconsciousness. It affects the body's ability to absorb oxygen, and death follows. It's characterised by a blue discoloration of the skin — often the lips and fingertips.'

'Blue paint, sir?' interrupted Hazeldean.

'Aye, blue paint,' answered Father. 'Is that relevant?'

'It is, sir. In both cases a symbol was painted at the scene, accompanied by the words *la confrérie* — and the colour was a brilliant blue. Turn over the caddy and see for yourself.'

Father did so and saw the symbol. 'If the colour is relevant, then we may have found our poison, gentlemen,' he said. 'I would like to examine the bodies to confirm.'

'And where would one get this poison?' asked Stoll. 'Do you stock it?'

Grandpa answered. 'No, we make up our own remedies, and we have a supplier who provides the necessary components. We *could* use cyanide as a preparation to get rid of vermin, but we don't; we offer other poisons for that. Our supplier sources most of his ingredients locally, but he would have to import cyanide.'

'So the source of the paint and the poison could be the same?'

'Could be,' agreed Father.

'Something for you to follow up, Stoll,' said Hazeldean as he stood up to leave. Another thought occurred to him, and he turned to Father. 'Dr Swift, would you be interested in a consultancy with the Home Department?'

I saw Father and Grandpa share an uneasy look. I knew he would view this as working for the enemy, but I wasn't going to let him miss this opportunity. I cut in before he could respond.

'Will there be a retainer, sir?' I asked.

'Certainly. We'll pay a retainer and a further fee for each consultation.'

Father nodded a reluctant acceptance.

'Good,' said Hazeldean. 'You can start by examining the bodies. I'll get you clearance.'

SIX

The London season was in full swing, and Sir Edgar Rowland, Duke of Howdon, was entertaining at his London town house in the West End. He was a personable man, witty and well-liked in his own set — an excellent host and placed high on others' guest lists. His entertaining was a *must* in London society.

The dining and drinking started in mid-afternoon and would go on late into the evening. He was a man of rank, and there would be few restraints at his party.

Sir Edgar greeted one of his oldest friends as he arrived. Earl Alton shook his hand vigorously, while their wives leaned in and kissed each other's cheeks.

'These are rum times, Ralph,' said Sir Edgar, whose friend was a politician.

'Aye, rum indeed, Edgar,' replied Earl Alton. 'There is sedition all around us. The government is trying to keep a lid on it.'

'You should do as I do, Ralph. I ignore it and live my life as I've always done.'

'So you still have your string of horses then, your hounds, your hand-made guns? It must cost you a fortune.'

'It does, Ralph, but then I am a sporting gentleman, am I not?'

'You're an inveterate gambler, you mean!'

Both men roared with laughter, but the duchess shot them a troubled glance — she was less amused. The truth was that the duke was selling off parcels of his land and mortgaging his country seat in order to fund his gambling and socialising.

Earl Alton spoke. 'But those days are gone for me, Edgar. I have inherited my title now, I have an estate to run, and I am a Cabinet Minister. As the Lord Privy Seal, I have to set an example.'

'But that's not for the likes of me, Ralph.'

'We'll leave you to welcome your other guests,' interrupted the countess, taking her husband's arm.

'Will you take a turn at the card table later, Ralph?' asked the duke as they turned away.

'Maybe, Edgar, maybe.'

The London town house was crowded with guests, and there was an excellent show for them; the food was at its finest, and all the ladies and gentlemen were dressed in their most elegant clothes. After dining, the guests danced to the music provided. There were also other entertainments, players giving renditions of popular plays and recitations from some of the best-known literary figures. It was just after ten o'clock when the dancing was interrupted, and two small tables were erected in the drawing room, each table having four lace-edged napkins, one placed on each corner.

The game was to be whist, and some gentlemen took their places at the two tables. There was a spare seat at one of them, and Sir Edgar looked around for his friend.

'Where is Earl Alton, the scoundrel?' he called. The throng parted as the earl made his way to the front. 'Will you play some hands with me, like we used to do, Ralph?'

The earl took his pocket watch from his frockcoat and studied the dial. 'It's getting late, Edgar; I think I'll pass.'

'Nonsense, the hour is not late at all. The Earl Alton I knew would play until dawn.'

The countess put a restraining hand on her husband's arm, but it was too late. 'Just a few hands, my dear,' he said as he took a seat at the table.

He looked around the table at his three competitors. Alongside the duke was a young army captain in dress uniform and a wealthy wine merchant, well known at the gambling tables.

Card-playing at such gatherings was as much an occasion for the other guests as it was for the players themselves. It was a spectator sport, and the guests gathered around the tables to watch the tactics. There was polite applause for well-played hands. They were the centre of attention; all eyes were on them.

'Well played, sir,' said another young military man, who stepped forward and patted the captain on the shoulder after he had played a winning hand.

The wine glasses on the corner napkins of each table were filled regularly by the servants, who were alert to the merest of hand gestures.

After about an hour's play, the earl's winnings were mounting. Responding to the polite applause, he stacked his chips neatly between games, happy he was now the player to watch. However, as he picked up his next hand, his fingers went into spasm, and the cards scattered, cascading down to the polished floor. He looked up for his wife as his body started to convulse. The alarmed onlookers watched in horror as his face turned purple, a vein pulsing in his forehead, his eyes flashing in terror. Something was seriously wrong. The earl tried to speak but could only make a choking sound. He tried to stand, but when he did so, his body went rigid, and he fell to the floor, saliva trickling from the corner of his mouth.

The countess gasped and rushed to his side as the seizures continued.

'He's had a heart attack!' shouted the duke. 'Is there a physician present?'

Nobody came forward, but the young soldier knelt on one knee beside the earl, loosening the stock at his throat. 'He seems to be having trouble breathing,' he said. He turned the earl over and saw a gaping mouth, lips curled and twisted, eyes bulging. 'Can you hear me, my lord?' he asked. There was no response.

The countess put her hand to her mouth, and tears welled in her eyes.

'Boothroyd!' the duke called out for his butler. 'Send for a physician right away.'

Foreboding was writ large on the onlookers' faces. The soldier placed a cushion under the earl's head and felt for a pulse. It was there but erratic. His breathing became shallower, and he was dead within half an hour.

It was twelve-thirty when Father and I arrived at Lord Howdon's town house. We had retired for the night when we were roused by banging at the front door — a Bow Street Runner sent by Constable Stoll, summoning us.

Father identified us to the footman, who showed us through to the drawing room. As we walked, I noticed a floral scent; there were vases of flowers everywhere. I looked around at the opulence. Although it was the middle of the night, there were many candles, all mounted in sconces backed by mirrors so that the light reflected back into the room. The walls were pale green and I noticed marble fire-surrounds and shuttered windows.

Constable Stoll had taken charge. He had cleared the room except for a diminutive, slender man with a doctor's bag who I assumed to be a physician, and a portly man with a red face, introduced as the Duke of Howdon. He sat at a card table with a body at his feet, which had been covered with a drape.

'The deceased man is Earl Alton,' said Stoll. 'The local physician here pronounced him dead at about eleven forty-five. His first thoughts were that death was the result of apoplexy.'

'A brain haemorrhage. So why have you sent for me, Constable?' asked Father.

'Lord Alton is a member of Mr Pitt's Cabinet — and I also remembered what you said about cyanide.'

'Let me see,' said Father, going down on one knee. He pulled aside the drape and examined the deceased's lips and fingertips.

'Am I correct, Dr Swift?' asked Stoll.

'You are — it's cyanide all right,' said Father. 'He's been poisoned.'

Turning to the duke, Stoll said, 'Can you assemble all your guests in one room, please, and all the servants in another?'

'Boothroyd!' the duke called. The butler arrived almost immediately. 'Have all the servants assembled in the servants' hall, will you? The constable wants to talk to them.' Boothroyd gave a small bow and went about his task.

'And your guests, my lord?'

'You won't need to talk to my guests, Constable,' said the duke. 'I will vouch for them.'

'My lord,' said Father authoritatively, 'this is not a death by natural causes; it is murder, and the murder of a Minister of State no less. Constable Stoll and I have the authority of the Home Secretary to investigate this suspicious death. Shall we get Sir Thomas out of bed to settle this argument? No? Then you will have the guests assembled for questioning, if you please.'

The duke sighed heavily. 'Very well,' he said, 'but most of my guests have already left.'

'Why did you let them go?' Father snapped.

'They are my guests, sir,' the duke blustered. 'I was thinking about their sensibilities.'

'And what about catching the earl's killer?'

'None of my guests will have had anything to do with that, sir.'

'Maybe, maybe not, my lord. But they may have valuable information, may even have seen who the poisoner was. Please assemble those that are left, and then let the constable have a list of the guests who have gone.' Father turned to Stoll. 'We'll talk to the servants while the duke is doing that,' he said and strode out of the room. Constable Stoll and I followed him.

In the servants' hall, the staff were lined up like soldiers on parade. I saw Father counting them; there were sixteen in all. The men were dressed in bottle-green livery, with silver braid and epaulettes, white stockings, white gloves, and powdered white wigs. Constable Stoll took charge.

'Are they all servants of *this* household?' he asked the butler.

'No, Constable,' Boothroyd answered. 'Four are from another household and are here just for tonight to help with the party —' he pointed — 'the four on the end.' They were two footmen and two maids.

'They are wearing the duke's livery, I see,' said Stoll.

'Aye, sir; we keep spare livery jackets just for this purpose.'

'And who was serving drinks in the drawing room?' Two footmen raised their hands. 'Just the two of you?'

The two footmen looked at each other in some confusion; then one of them stuttered, 'Arthur was serving with us, sir, and then later another footman that Mr Boothroyd hired.'

'And where is Arthur?' Stoll asked.

'He's not here, Constable,' the butler responded. 'We've been unable to find him.'

Stoll turned to the two hired footmen. 'And which of these two was helping you in the drawing room?'

'It was neither of them, sir,' the man stuttered again. 'But he was wearing our livery.'

I heard Father click his tongue.

'Right,' said Stoll. 'I want a full search of the house now.'

'What are we looking for?' Boothroyd asked.

'Arthur, of course. Search every room and cupboard, even if it only contains a mop.'

The butler snapped his fingers and sent groups to various parts of the house. They scurried away.

Father conferred with Constable Stoll and Boothroyd. It was only a matter of minutes before we heard a scream — one of the maids, I assumed.

We followed the sound to a small room close to the servants' hall. The maid was now crying, her face buried in the housekeeper's bosom, who was trying to console her. The housekeeper pointed towards a door, which stood slightly ajar. Stoll opened it wide; it was a small cloakroom, with coats and spare uniforms hanging on hooks. Slumped against the back wall was the body of a servant, a livery jacket spread loosely across his chest. The constable glanced back at the housekeeper.

She responded with just one word. 'Arthur.'

Father entered the cloakroom and crouched down. He put his fingers against the servant's neck, feeling for a pulse. He looked up at Stoll and shook his head.

'Another poisoning, Dr Swift?'

It's possible, but if it is, it's not cyanide. The lips and fingertips are not discoloured.'

Father pulled away the livery jacket and sat the body up to check behind. 'Look!' he exclaimed suddenly. A slender blade had been driven into the back of the neck.

'So, he was stabbed,' said Stoll. 'Have you much experience of stab wounds, sir?'

'Oh yes, I have dealt with many over the years. They are surprisingly common, whether accidental or otherwise.' He paused, studying the wound. 'The point of entry is under the back of the head, where the spine goes into the skull. Arthur would have died instantly.'

'So he would have gone down like a sack of potatoes, making no sound to attract anybody.'

'Right, and whoever did it knew what they were doing — possibly someone with military training, not some tavern brawler handy with a knife. And I think there may have been two of them: one to hold Arthur and one to find the exact spot. It's a specialist knife as well, a thin, lightweight blade. This is an assassin's weapon, and they have left it in the wound, so there is hardly any blood. With most stabbings, the victim dies from severe blood loss — we call it exsanguination. There should be a lot of blood, but look, there isn't.'

'So the killer takes Arthur's jacket — no bloodstains on it — and takes his place?'

'That would be my speculation.'

Constable Stoll nodded and reached for the livery jacket. He put his hand in the side pocket, and then withdrew a piece of paper. Unfolding it, he revealed a symbol in bright blue.

'Seems you are right, Dr Swift. We have another assassination.'

SEVEN

The following day, Swift was summoned to the Home Department to see the Home Secretary himself. Sir Thomas Maxwell-Clark, he noticed, was in a foul mood when he arrived. The summons was on Constable Stoll's recommendation, as the Home Department agents had no idea who was behind the recent assassinations of Earl Darwin and Lord Alton. Sir Thomas was in the middle of berating Hazeldean when Swift was ushered in.

'It's got to be a new organisation, sir. Otherwise our agents would know about them.' Hazeldean's voice was shrill with exasperation.

There was a temporary lull in the dispute.

'You have little to say, Dr Swift,' Bradbrook, the secretary, said.

'Well, I would say you are both wrong,' he said. 'Your logic is flawed.'

Sir Thomas turned cool eyes on him. 'And why would that be, sir?'

'Because both assassination attempts have been successful, have they not? Whoever they are, they are good, outstandingly good. This is not an organisation operating from a standing start.'

'If that's true,' said Bradbrook, 'then we are at a dead end, because we certainly don't know who they are. So where do we start looking, sir?'

'We look to logic and reason. In conflict situations you must always try to keep your opponents in the dark, hide your objectives, because that will give you the upper hand. They have done exactly that to you.'

'They have indeed,' agreed Constable Stoll.

'Think of it as a card game, gentlemen,' Swift continued. 'It is said that if only chance is involved, no good players will emerge. But we know that isn't true. Good players do emerge because they have evolved tactics — reading their opponent's play, understanding what they are trying to achieve.'

'And?' said Bradbrook.

'And so you have to do the same. But remember — the answers you are looking for will be skilfully hidden. They will be defended. Think of it as concentric circles; you have to break through each circle, or layer, in turn.'

Bradbrook gave a small nod of understanding. 'Go on,' he said.

'Well, the first circle to break through is to establish their motive; what are they trying to achieve by assassinating Cabinet members? Until you know that, you can't advance.'

'And what do *you* think their motive is?' asked Hazeldean.

'Well, they haven't sent any demands, so we have to apply logic, as the ancient Greeks taught us. We need to extract a *valid inference*.'

'Meaning?' asked the Home Secretary.

Father turned to him. 'Meaning, sir, why aren't you dead? This organisation has poisoned two of your colleagues, so why not poison you?'

Sir Thomas looked to his secretary, but Bradbrook had nothing to offer.

'The poisoning of your dogs and the subsequent assassinations of Earl Darwin and Lord Alton are a message to you, are they not?' Swift added. 'And through you to Prime

Minister Pitt. I think that is a *valid inference*. And if I am right, it will also be a *valid inference* that you know what that message is.'

The Home Secretary stared at Swift and then sighed heavily. 'Yes, you are right, sir. I know it is a message sent to me and the Prime Minister.'

'And what is that message, Sir Thomas?'

'I am introducing new legislation later in the year to help fight sedition. We need strong leadership at this time.'

'New legislation?'

'The Treasonable and Seditious Practices Act, and the Seditious Meetings Act.'

'Which will do what?'

'If anyone says or writes anything to bring the king or his government into contempt, then we'll charge them with treason. And any public meeting of more than fifty persons will have to be authorised by a local magistrate.'

'Am I to understand that the purpose of these Acts is to gag free speech?'

'No, sir, the purpose is to stop sedition; we cannot afford to allow rabble-rousing to continue.'

'Then allow some reform; it's long overdue.'

'Pitt feels that we cannot give way to calls for reform. It will be the thin edge of the wedge. It will inevitably lead to the overthrow of our whole system of government. We'll go the same way as the French.'

'But that is illogical, sir; you are making the same mistakes as the French by denying reform.'

'You are impertinent, sir,' said the Home Secretary.

'And you deny the mood in the country, sir. These are educated men looking for reform — men rediscovering humanism from the Ancient Greeks, men who look to science, men pursuing insight and reason.'

'Educated men who live in Ivory Towers, you mean,' responded the Home Secretary. 'These people must realise who governs this country.'

'And who does govern, sir? Good God, we executed a tyrannical king for high treason because he believed in an absolute monarchy and his divine right to rule, and then we forced his son to accept a constitutional role. And now we have Hanoverian kings who are just puppets to the will of Parliament. Have you not just replaced this beheaded king with your own tyranny? Pitt's Cabinet are dukes, earls and lords, aristocratic men of property. Isn't the reality that these Bills are really to protect *yourselves*?'

'Be careful, sir,' hissed the Home Secretary. 'You were called here to advise on poisons, not to make political speeches. If you speak like that after the new legislation is enacted, then you may well find *yourself* tried for treason.'

But Swift was in no mood to be cautious. 'Mr Pitt's government is out of step with modern thinking. Being in power for generations has left you unable to contemplate change. The country is transforming, sir; wealth is no longer purely in aristocratic hands. The middling classes are now prospering. You just fear the loss of *your* divine right to govern.'

'I think you had better go, Dr Swift,' growled the Home Secretary, his eyes blazing.

Swift too was angered, but he had said his piece.

Bradbrook squirmed nervously in his seat. 'Let's not be too hasty, Home Secretary,' he said. 'Let's hear what Dr Swift has to say about his next concentric circle of reason, as he puts it.'

'Go on then, sir,' said Sir Thomas, the rancour in his voice still evident. 'If you are a logician, tell us what your reason tells you.'

Swift took a breath before he spoke. 'The symbol the organisation left behind,' he said. 'What can we infer from that?'

'Are they not just telling us who they are so that we can identify them? Eliminate the copycats?' said Constable Stoll.

'That reasoning is sound,' Swift said, 'but I think there is more to it. Symbols have great potency; that's why so many organisations use them. Even our country recognises that, with the Great Seal of the Realm used to proclaim and validate the rule of law. I believe that we can make a further *valid inference* — this symbol has a meaning; it is proclaiming something. It is telling us something about them, their history, their prowess.'

'But nobody at the Home Department recognises it,' said Bradbrook. 'If it has meaning, then we don't know what it is.'

'Consult the Cabinet Office, preferably somebody who has been there for many years. In the meantime, I'll contact some of my old colleagues from university, see if they know anything about it. Constable Stoll can interview the guests who were at Lord Howdon's house party last night.'

Glances were exchanged and heads began to nod. There was no other strategy put forward.

The Oxford Mail Coach was uncomfortable, and I ached all over. We had travelled many miles along cobbled streets and dry rutted roads. It had not proved difficult to convince Father that I should accompany him on his journey, but now I was unsure if it had been such a good idea after all. When I could stand it no longer, I pulled on the leather strap and lowered the window. I breathed in the fresh air but ealized I had exposed myself and our fellow passengers to the road's dust. I was relieved when I saw the passenger opposite also open his window. The cool air, it seemed, was worth the added dust disturbed by the iron-clad wheels as they rolled over the uneven surfaces.

'Heads back in the carriage, please!' shouted the driver as he manoeuvred the team through an archway barely wider than the carriage itself, and I ducked hastily back into my seat. The carriage came to a standstill. The long uncomfortable journey was over, and we were in Oxford.

Father had written to an old friend at Edinburgh University; they had been undergraduates together. He was now a lecturer in history, and Father had asked him if he could advise us on the meaning behind the mysterious symbol. His friend had recommended Professor Margett at Oxford. He had written to him on Father's behalf and arranged a meeting.

Professor Margett met us at his door, thrusting out a large hand to Father, which he shook. He was an upright older man, not bent by age, and was completely bald. I noticed that the top of his head was a little sunburned, suggesting that he spent time outside. He must have been a vigorous man in his youth, I thought, and he had taken that vigorousness into his old age. He seemed surprised to see me, but when Father introduced me as his assistant, he bowed politely and invited us to sit down.

His room was as I imagined of an academic, wood-panelled and lined with bookcases, although there seemed to be as many books stacked on the floor as were on the shelves. The room had a mix of smells: beeswax, floor polish, brass metalwork, and, of course, books.

'Our colleague at Edinburgh speaks very highly of you, Dr Swift,' said Professor Margett. 'He says you have as agile a mind as he has ever encountered.'

'That's very kind of him,' Father replied. 'Did he explain what I wanted to talk to you about?'

'He did, sir.'

'There is a secret organisation causing all sorts of trouble back in London. I am hoping that you may have been able to identify the maxim *la confrérie*, and the accompanying symbol.'

The academic gave a wistful sigh. 'There is little hard history I can tell you about, sir. No scholarly publications identify it as a movement that influenced the course of history.'

'So you think it is a new organisation, as the agents at the Home Department believe?'

'The Home Department, sir?'

'Yes, I act as a consultant for them on poisons.'

'Ah, poisons, that may be relevant, Dr Swift — but I'll come back to that. The fact that there is nothing published does not mean that this society does not exist. I have spent many hours searching the university's archives, and I have found something. Just notes written by one of my predecessors, but I think they are relevant.'

'Yes, Professor?' asked Father eagerly.

'I think they are, or were, an organisation called the Brotherhood of the Parole.'

'*Parole*, from the French, you mean? *Parole d'honneur* — their members are bound by their word of honour.'

'Precisely, their word; that is what defined this group. It was part of their governance never to leave any written record.'

'Like Socrates, you mean? He never wrote anything down.'

'Not quite; Socrates wanted his words to be heard. With the Brotherhood, it was part of their secrecy. Written words were something that could incriminate them.'

'And what was their objective, Professor?'

'To re-establish the Catholic Church as the state religion by way of a Catholic monarch.'

Father's forehead furrowed in thought. 'This is unlikely to be the organisation I am looking for, sir. The society presently active in London does not seem to be Jacobite.'

'Don't confuse the Catholic cause purely with the Jacobites, sir. It was much more complicated than that. Predominantly, the 1745 Rebellion was about Scottish nationalism; it just happened that Charles Stuart, the Young Pretender, was a Catholic. He belonged to the Stuart dynasty's Catholic side, as did his father James, the Old Pretender, being descendants of James II. But *English* Catholics fought with him, for example the Manchester Regiment, as did French and Irish regulars. And in the earlier rebellions, French and Spanish fleets were launched against England in support of the Jacobites because it suited those countries to do so; they were our enemies. The Jacobites were pawns in a much bigger game.'

'So you're saying that this society — the Brotherhood of the Parole — primarily supported the Catholic cause, not the Jacobite one?'

'I am, Dr Swift.'

'But what this society is doing now doesn't seem to tie it to the Catholic cause either. It would appear that they are murdering members of the government in an attempt to warn Pitt not to enact gagging legislation. On the face of it, it is about radicalism, about parliamentary reform.'

'I see your dilemma, Dr Swift. But then we know so little about this society.'

The was silence, and I took the opportunity to ask a question of my own.

'You mentioned earlier that poisons may be relevant, Professor. Why do you think that?'

'What little we know came in 1740, when one of the society's men was discovered at Markfield Hall, a Catholic aristocrat's house. He was a known Jacobite supporter who had been betrayed by a double agent. He was the target, but when the king's men arrived at the hall, they discovered the Brotherhood of the Parole man there. It soon became clear that he had sworn an oath of secrecy and wouldn't even give his name. He was handed over to officers of the Grenadier Guards, and under questioning and probably torture, he confessed to being a member of this organisation and identified its symbol. This led to just two other arrests, as the man claimed he only knew two other members. Apparently, it was part of their governance that each member knew only two others, so that the other members could not be identified. Messages were only by word of mouth to protect the leaders. They were managed by a coordinator who never revealed his identity; he always wore a hood, and no one knew his name.'

'And poisons?' I asked again.

'Well, they recruited men with various skillsets, and this particular man disclosed that one of the two men he knew was a poisoner. After naming him, that man was also tortured and confessed that the society was responsible for many poisonings. They could eliminate people without there being any suspicion of foul play.'

'Was this believed at the time?' asked Father.

'He put forward some names of victims, and he was right; their deaths had not been considered suspicious, but they also found no evidence to substantiate his claims.'

'There wouldn't have been; there are no tests to identify most poisons.'

'Their whole structure was based on elusiveness.'

'They've been hiding in the shadows all this time,' said Father.

'What was your predecessor's conclusion about this Brotherhood of the Parole?' I asked.

'That they reluctantly accepted defeat and that they were on the wrong side of history, then disbanded. Look at the events of the last hundred years: the Glorious Revolution of 1688 overthrows the Catholic James II; the 1701 Act of Settlement required the monarch to be Protestant. Queen Anne dies in 1714, succeeded by the Protestant Hanoverians, who come with ready-born heirs. A series of failed Jacobite rebellions culminating with the 1745 Rebellion, defeated at Culloden. Whoever they were, they were thought to have been dispatched to history.'

'Until now,' I interjected.

Father turned to me. 'If it is the same organisation,' he said uncertainly, rubbing his chin.

EIGHT

The following Monday, Father was again called to the Home Department. After his injudicious words last time, he was surprised, and concluded that they must be desperate for ideas. He agreed to let me observe the meeting, but the Home Secretary refused point-blank to see Father, and he made his report to his private secretary, Bradbrook, and the agent Hazeldean.

'This secret organisation,' said Bradbrook, 'the Brotherhood of the Parole. Do you think it is the one we are looking for?'

Father replied hesitantly. 'I can't say it's a *valid inference*; there are still questions that need to be answered — but on balance, I believe it is. If it *is* them, though, we are looking at an organisation that's been hiding in the shadows for half a century, if not more.'

'If you're right,' said Hazeldean, 'and they operate this *parole d'honneur*, this word of honour, then it explains why our agents don't know of them. But how on earth do we stop them? It's a sorry state of affairs, all right.'

'And the Home Secretary wants them stopped before the government enact their *new* legislation,' added Bradbrook. 'They have been hiding for fifty years or so, and now we have only weeks to find them.'

'What did you establish at the Cabinet Office, Mr Bradbrook?' asked Father.

Bradbrook looked to Hazeldean, who answered. 'Nothing so far, but they're still looking. I can go back to them again now we have a name, this *parole d'honneur*. It may help narrow things down.'

Bradbrook looked at Father. 'Dr Swift, you previously mentioned something about breaking through concentric circles, or layers, to get at the truth. Can you expand on that now?'

Father sat back in his chair. 'We broke through the first layer in order to make a *valid inference* as to their motive — that they are intent on stopping Pitt's gagging legislation. The second layer was to establish their identity, and my *valid inference* was that they had left a sign at all three locations because symbolism is potent. But what I have learned about their secrecy now makes me question that inference. Why would an organisation which has remained carefully hidden for half a century suddenly reveal its existence?'

'And do you have an answer for that?' asked Hazeldean expectantly.

'Yes, I think so. You are uneasy because you only have a few weeks to stop them. But the same timescale applies to them as well; they have no time to waste. My *valid inference* now is that they want you to understand the dangers that they pose. They haven't time for you to come to that conclusion over several months, because the legislation would be law by that time. They are deliberately showing you a part of their hand, but you failed to realise that.'

'But, thanks to you, sir, we now have,' said Bradbrook. 'We now know that we are facing a formidable foe, with an ability to hide in the shadows. So how do we flush them out?'

'One layer at a time, sir,' answered Father.

'And what is the next layer we have to penetrate?'

'Their weakness; we have to find it.'

'Have they any? They operate in small groups of three and never write anything down, so there is nothing to incriminate them.' There was exasperation in Bradbrook's tone.

'The weakness is the man at the top,' said Father. 'He sits like a spider at the centre of this web.'

'But the society is set up so that their members don't even know who he is.'

'But he knows who *they* are.'

'So cut off the head of the snake, you mean?' said Bradbrook. 'But where do we start? The man could be anywhere.'

Father took a pinch of snuff from his waistcoat pocket. 'You put forward hypotheses and test them until you can make a *valid inference,*' he said, before snorting up the powder.

'Such as, sir?'

'Well, the original organisation was set up to re-establish the Catholic Church as the state religion by way of a Catholic monarch. That doesn't seem to be their intention here, but their leader is likely to be a descendant of the founder. I think we are looking for a man from a Catholic family. And he's not an outsider. He knows his way around power. I would infer that he is a member of an aristocratic family and is close to the government.'

'I don't think that makes things any easier,' interrupted Hazeldean. 'That'll bring some extremely influential people under suspicion.'

'Yes,' said Father, 'I think you have your work cut out.'

We were just sitting down to eat our evening meal when Mother spoke. 'There's a letter for you on the mantelpiece, Gus,' she said. 'Hand-delivered this afternoon.'

Father retrieved it and broke the seal. His brow furrowed as he read the words.

'Who is it from?' Mother asked.

'It's an invitation to a dinner party this Friday at the house of a Henry Lawton in the West End. Why on earth would he want to invite us?'

'Who is Henry Lawton?' Mother asked, ladling soup from the tureen into Grandpa's bowl.

Father looked blank, but Grandpa recognised the name. 'He's a prominent banker and an outspoken Whig Member of Parliament,' he said. 'But, unlike me, he gets the *credit* he deserves.' He wheezed a chuckle.

'Oh, Grandpa!' I moaned, shaking my head at another of his terrible jokes.

'He speaks about electoral reforms regularly in the House of Commons,' Grandpa continued. 'You have to accept the invitation, Gus; it may bring you some work.'

'No, I don't think so,' Father answered. 'And anyway, Iona, you would need a new gown. There wouldn't be time for the dressmaker to make one before Friday.'

'I agree with Matthew,' Mother said. 'It'll be good for business, and you can take Cully as your partner. It's a chance for her to be seen out in society. She is an eligible young lady, after all.' She shot Father a knowing look.

I wanted to attend with Father, but I felt suddenly anxious. Images flashed through my mind of grand ladies and gentlemen in their elegant clothes, footmen leaning over to fill my wine glass, witty repartee flying back and forth across the dining table, handsome gentlemen bowing and taking my hand.

'But won't she also need a gown by Friday, Iona?' asked Father, breaking into my reverie.

'She will need a whole new wardrobe if she is to be shown off, but I'll go to the dressmaker first thing in the morning to see if I can cajole her into making one in time.'

'What about Jane Isherwood?' I suggested. 'I could borrow one of her dresses.'

Mother smiled. I had never indicated any desire to socialise before, and I could see that she was both pleased and surprised. I had surprised myself. 'Yes, that may work,' she said, 'and I will make any alterations required. But I am still going to the dressmakers to see about that wardrobe.'

Upon arrival at Mr Lawton's impressive residence, the footman took my cape, revealing my borrowed attire — a silky sky-blue gown with white lace at the collar and cuffs. I caught my reflection in a mirror as we walked along the hall. My blonde hair was tied back in a chignon that exposed my neck, and Mother had used a hot iron to create the curls that fell in front of my ears. It was all very different to my usual simple cream dress with an apron over the top, a muslin buffon around my shoulders, and my hair tucked into a cap. Now I was a fashionable young lady, and I wasn't about to let Father down.

The footman announced us as we entered the drawing room. Father shook hands with our host, Henry Lawton, who introduced us to his wife and son, Edward. Father was wearing his best black frockcoat, which looked splendid at a meeting of the Apothecary's Guild, but less impressive compared with the other guests' excellent tailoring. Father didn't seem to mind, however.

Edward offered me a glass of punch, and I glanced at Father. He nodded, but I could see the reluctance in his eyes. I was manoeuvred to a side table where the punch bowl resided, and Edward used the ladle to fill my glass with the pink liquid. I sipped it, not knowing what to expect. It was surprisingly sweet, not like the whisky that Father so favoured.

Edward was a handsome man, I thought. He had fair hair, and blue eyes with long lashes. He wore a grey frockcoat, with a satin waistcoat and delicate lace cuffs. He was easy to talk to, but I recalled Father's words: *The gentry are well educated, but know little of use.*

I knew Father would disapprove of him, but I liked him. I knew what I wanted in life — to take over the apothecary shop. I knew I was capable, and I had made it clear to Father and Mother that it was my intention, yet here I was, enjoying the attention Edward was paying me. The gong sounded for dinner, casting these thoughts from my mind as we made our way to the dining room. The protocols of society required that the guests were seated according to their status, which meant that Father and I were the last to sit. I sat facing Father, with Edward next to me on the same side as our host.

I looked around the table; there were fifteen guests in their finery. They all seemed to know one another, and conversation was between small groups. Edward made small talk with me, but Father sat silently, and I wondered at the purpose of his invitation. Mother had made him promise not to talk politics, after what he had said to the Home Secretary, but there was little else he had in common with these people. Well, at least he had an excellent meal to compensate, the aroma filling the room as an army of footmen arrived to serve us.

After the meal, we ladies repaired to the drawing room and left the gentlemen to their cigars and brandy.

Swift was enjoying an expensive cigar and a dark cognac in a balloon glass when Henry Lawton turned to him with a playful smile.

'Is it true, Dr Swift?' asked Lawton conspiratorially.

Swift frowned. 'Is what true, sir?'

'That you asked the Home Secretary why he wasn't dead?'

There was an outbreak of laughter.

'Well, yes,' he said guardedly. 'I was trying to make a point. Somebody had had the opportunity to kill him but hadn't taken it.'

There followed a spontaneous round of applause. 'Bravo, sir,' several of the guests said.

'You know you are the talk of Parliament, sir?' said Lawton. 'Old Maxwell-Clarke was seething afterwards, apparently.' There was more applause. 'And did you say that Pitt was as tyrannical as King Charles I had been?'

Swift nodded, embarrassment taking him.

'We understand, sir,' said Lawton. 'We all know about the planned gagging legislation, and all here agree that it's an attack on our freedom of speech, something every Englishman is proud of.'

Swift considered his reply carefully. 'I asked the Home Secretary if Pitt hadn't just replaced this beheaded king with his own tyranny. Are not these Bills just to protect *themselves*?'

'Well, that told the old bugger, sir,' said one of the other guests.

'Aye, maybe,' said Swift. 'But I doubt now if I will get any further work from the Home Department.'

'You are a Whig at heart, Dr Swift,' said Lawton.

Swift had promised his wife he wouldn't talk politics and put his consultancy at risk, but he was being drawn into precisely that. This dinner party was, in essence, a gathering of Whigs, he realised.

'Sirs,' he said, looking around the room, 'is not *your* party similarly founded on the rich aristocratic families? You are no different from the Tories in that respect. You also benefit from a voting system that allows a small number of men to control the votes.'

'But we are progressive Whigs, sir, as is our leader Charles Fox. We see the reform of the voting system as crucial. We stand for religious tolerance and a constitutional monarchy with the king subject to Parliament. We are not like the Tories.'

Lawton changed the subject. 'I'm told that you studied medicine at Edinburgh University, yet you run a free clinic, Dr Swift. That can't be good for business, can it?' His tone was conversational, but Swift detected a touch of disdain at such altruism.

'My apothecary shop supports my family, and I've studied Latin, Greek and Logic as well as medicine. Even if I say so myself, I believe I am the best physician in London. I offer much more than just bleeding my patients, I assure you.'

'If that is so, sir, then you could earn substantial fees for your family.'

'My wife would agree,' Swift said, to some amusement. 'It was in Egypt that I learned the most about medicine, sirs.'

'You have travelled in the Levant, sir?' one of the guests asked.

'Aye, sir,' Swift replied. 'I worked at the Qawaloon Hospital in Cairo; it's been there for hundreds of years. The hospital is maintained by the state budget and is therefore free to all. They look after the health of the citizens. Perhaps now you can understand why I run a free clinic. Being poor should not deny you an education and healthcare.'

'But we have five free hospitals in London, Dr Swift,' said Lawton, 'providing treatment for those who can't afford it, including the London Hospital.'

'Aye, sir, but they are funded privately by generous subscription. They do their best, but they are, in reality, seriously underfunded. They should be funded from the state budget.'

That view did not seem to win much support, Swift saw. They may have called themselves progressive, he thought, but they fell well short of his enlightened ideas. The conversation moved on to other subjects, and he realised why he had been invited; it was because of his notoriety. He had been the entertainment.

NINE

Sir George Cornysh pulled the door closed behind him as he left the house on Stephen Street. It was built in the classical style, with stuccoed brick to look like stone, columns, decorative plaster mouldings and paned sash windows. He had bought it for his mistress.

He took his pocket watch from his waistcoat and scanned its face — fifteen minutes after ten. Darkness had fallen on this midsummer night. He intended to walk to Tottenham Court Road and then on to Oxford Street, where it would be easier to find a hackney to take him to his club on St James's Street. He set off at a brisk pace, swinging his cane, his cape swirling. Then he halted abruptly. Two of his Cabinet colleagues were dead, murdered. He mused on that thought, turned, and strode back to the house, looking about him for a runner.

He called over a raggedly dressed man and flipped him a coin to fetch him a hackney, and the man ran off in pursuit of his task. Sir George was agitated as it would now delay him, but his humour eased when a carriage came quickly around the corner. He barked the name of his club as he took the step and climbed in. As the carriage set off, he sat back, his hands resting on the head of his cane.

The journey should only have taken a few minutes, but after ten he looked out of the window, irritated. He did not recognise where he was. The cabbie was going the wrong way. He lifted his cane and used it to bang on the roof — there was no reply.

The carriage swerved at pace around a corner, throwing Sir George to one side. He reached up and grabbed the leather loop to steady himself.

'You damned fool!' he thundered at the cabbie above him, but the pace continued. He peered out of the window into the black night, seeing little more than an empty street. A few moments later the cabbie pulled firmly on the reins and the horse pulled up rapidly, throwing Sir George forward in the cab.

He was righting himself when the door to the carriage was flung open, and a tall man dressed in black with a hooded cape and a black kerchief wrapped around his face jumped in.

'Damn you, sir, this is my carriage!' Sir George bawled. His belligerence turned to alarm as he realised, too late, that he was in jeopardy. He raised his cane to hit the fellow, but before he could, a cudgel rose and then fell on his skull. Sir George was momentarily stunned.

'Now just sit still, if you please, Sir George.' The attacker's tone suggested he was a man used to being obeyed. The driver, a smaller man also dressed in dark clothing, climbed down and opened the other door.

Seeing the second man, Sir George realised the full horror of his situation. The Home Secretary had advised caution, offered a soldier as his bodyguard, but damn it, a man didn't need such a thing when visiting his mistress. He swung the head of his cane at the smaller man, but his adversary nimbly dodged it. The tall man lunged forward, brandishing his cudgel, and brought it down once more on his head. He fell back insensible in his seat.

*

'Go!' yelled the tall man. The small man climbed back up onto the top of the hackney and took the reins. He shook them vigorously, and the horse lurched forward.

Inside, the tall man bound Sir George's hands and then gagged him, before sitting back. They made their way south of the river, down Rotherhithe Street to Mr Williamson's wharf, a dark and deserted place at that time of night — just empty warehouses and a lead pipe factory. The horse was agitated, blowing and snorting from its exertions, loud in the silence.

They carried the unconscious man to an unused warehouse. The small man went around the rear, expertly scaled a high window and dropped down to the ground within. He pulled back the bolt that locked the warehouse from the inside and opened a side door.

Father was engrossed in a medical textbook when the messenger arrived. The boy came straight through to the clinic at the back of the apothecary's shop, where I was cleaning our instruments ready for the next day, and delivered the note to me as Father's assistant. I read it aloud. A Mr Gilbert had been taken ill, and Father's immediate services were requested. The boy said he didn't know the nature of the illness. It was close to dinner time, but far from being annoyed, Mother said that she would keep his dinner warm for him. A consultation meant fees, and that was what we needed.

'Where do you think you are going, Cully?' Mother asked as I put my cape around my shoulders.

'I'm going with Father,' I said, 'as his assistant.'

'You can take that cape off. I know it is light now, but it'll be dark soon after nine.'

Father hesitated, then nodded. 'Your mother is right, Cully. The dark streets are no place for a young lady,' he said.

I wanted to argue that he was there to protect me, but thought better of it. Father gathered his bag, went down the stairs, and out into the night.

Swift made his way towards St Giles, looking for Hyde Street, the address given in the message. He crossed Drury Lane, which meant negotiating the horse dung and urine left behind by the city's thousands of working horses. The stench was acrid, mixed with the soot and smoke that filled the air. He took his kerchief from his pocket and placed it over his face, although the stench of the streets was nothing new to him. The further he walked, the more reservations he had; St Giles was an overcrowded slum, notorious for its poverty, crime and gin shops. He found the address and looked up at a dilapidated building split into multiple occupancies. He was unsure whether to go in, then sighed deeply and climbed the steps to the front door.

He knocked and waited. He heard shuffling behind the door, a voice mumbling obscenities. The door opened to reveal an old woman in a pinafore. Thick white makeup covered her face, a large black beauty spot on her cheek, but it did little to mask her dishevelled appearance. Swift noticed that there appeared to be only one tooth in her mouth.

'I'm the physician,' he said. 'I've come to see Mr Gilbert.'

The old woman stepped aside. 'Second floor,' she said. As Swift crossed the threshold, she screeched, 'He's here!'

A broad-shouldered young man appeared from the first door. He was not dressed as gentry, but his clothes were clean and appeared to be new.

'Take the doctor to Mr Gilbert's room,' said the old woman.

The young man turned to the staircase without speaking. His feet stomped heavily on each step as he climbed. Swift fell into step behind him, his tread lighter, quieter. On the second floor, he turned left across the landing and knocked on a door. It opened a crack.

'Physician,' the young man growled.

The door opened fully, and a clean-shaven man appeared, perhaps in his mid-thirties. He was dressed like the first, clean and smart, but with nothing to draw attention to himself.

'Dr Swift?' he enquired. 'Dr Augustus Swift?'

'Aye, sir,' Swift replied. The man stepped aside for him to enter.

The room was sparse, with just a bed, a chair, a side table with a basin, and a water pitcher. Sitting upon the bed was a third man. He was fully dressed, his frockcoat draped over the chair. The door closed behind Swift, but only after the young man also came in. There was no explanation for his presence.

Swift looked at the man on the bed; he looked hale and hearty, but Swift assumed him to be the patient. 'You need a physician, sir?'

'I need a *particular* physician, sir,' the man replied.

A realisation took Swift. This man was well enough to have attended his clinic; he didn't need him to call. His voice suggested an educated man at odds with the neighbourhood in which he purported to live. Too late, Swift realised it was a trap. He willed himself to make all his actions slow and deliberate, nothing that would provoke these men. He put his bag down on the side of the bed. Opening it, he took out a piece of paper. He unfolded it slowly as the three men watched on. He offered it to the man on the bed, who lowered his eyes to see that it contained a white powder. He raised his eyes again to Swift, who smiled at him — then he blew the dust into the man's face.

The second man grabbed Swift from behind, holding his arms against his body, while the younger man produced a cudgel from under his frockcoat and clubbed him. Swift slumped to his knees.

The man on the bed jumped up, coughing and rubbing his eyes to get rid of the powder. 'Get him up!' he yelled at his companions.

Swift was hauled to his feet. The man pointed a menacing finger. 'You will pay for that, physician,' he said, 'before I kill you.'

Swift's eyes darted to the man's raised arm; just visible beneath the voluminous bishop sleeve was the top of a tattoo, but he recognised it nonetheless. It was the symbol of the secret organisation.

'But killing me was always your intention, was it not, sir?' said Swift.

A thin, humourless smile appeared on the man's face. 'I was told you were a clever man, Dr Swift. Yes, that is our commission. It was just business before you blew that powder in my face, but now it is personal.'

'No doubt you are acting on behalf of the Brotherhood of the Parole?'

The man's eyes widened. 'What do you know about the Brotherhood?' he growled.

'I know you are sworn to secrecy on pain of death. I know that you three form a group, taking orders from your leader, though you don't know his identity. Likewise, you don't know the identity of any of the other members.'

'Your death is now unavoidable, Dr Swift — you *do* know too much.'

'I know you've made a mistake.'

'Oh yes, and what would that be?'

'This address — you can be traced back to here.'

'Do you take me for an amateur, sir? It will be dark in under an hour, and then a carriage will arrive. Your body will be bundled in, stripped naked, and then weighted down and thrown into the River Thames. If your decayed corpse should ever resurface, which is unlikely, there will be nothing to identify you. Bodies are fished out of the river every day; no one will be interested in another one. And we'll be long gone from here, our job done, with nothing to connect us to this house. The old lady has been paid to keep her mouth shut, but she doesn't know our identities anyway. So what mistake have I made, Dr Swift?'

'The powder, sir. It will be in your lungs by now, and is poisonous. I am an apothecary as well as a physician, sir, and that was my extract of monkshood. Has the feeling gone from your legs yet?'

The man frowned. 'Why would a physician have poison in his bag?' It was a good question, but Swift had planted a seed of doubt in his mind.

'I use it to ease swelling and calm seizures.' He paused. 'In small doses, of course. If you want to live, then you need *me* to administer the remedy.'

The man looked unsure. He had his well-worked routine carefully planned out, and now, suddenly, he didn't know which way to turn. Swift took the hesitation as an opportunity to assess the danger. His eyes darted around the room, looking for a possible escape, but he saw none. There was something else, though: ink stains on the inside of the man's hand — a clue, perhaps, to the man's occupation.

'He's bluffing, *Première*,' said the second man. 'Let's kill him as we planned.'

'It's not *your* life on the line here, is it?' barked *Première*. 'I need to think.' He turned back to Swift. 'Give me the remedy now,' he snarled.

'Now, that wouldn't be logical, would it?' Swift's voice was calm. 'If I give you the remedy, then there will be nothing to stop you from killing me.'

'Then we'll beat it out of you,' said the younger man. He seemed anxious to use his fists.

Première nodded and sank a hefty fist into Swift's midriff. The air left his lungs, winding him. His mind was now in turmoil; he was bluffing, but his deceit had only partly been successful.

'Well?' said *Première*.

'I won't be able to give you the remedy if you beat me insensible,' Swift groaned.

'I agree, sir.' He turned to the younger man. 'Not his head or his hands, *Troisième*. Stay with his guts.' Another blow sank into Swift's stomach and he dropped to the ground, struggling for breath.

Suddenly there was a loud banging at the front door. The three men froze, listening intently. 'Quiet,' hissed *Première*.

They heard the old woman shuffle to the door. She was talking to the caller, but they couldn't make out the muffled words.

'*Troisième*!' *Première* gestured with his head towards the door. The younger man nodded and left the room, leaving the door open. They listened as his footsteps thudded down the stairs. Swift held his breath as he heard *Troisième* tell the man at the door to be gone.

There was the noise of a scuffle, blows being exchanged, then the sound of footsteps on the stairs. Swift noticed the difference in the weight of the tread. They all looked towards the open door — and then the uniform of a Bow Street Runner came into view.

Relief coursed through Swift's veins like an elixir — it was Constable Stoll.

With his truncheon drawn, Stoll quickly assessed the situation. He saw Swift held by a man, slumped forward and clearly in distress. He saw another man sitting on the bed, whose eyes darted to a frockcoat draped over the chair, and concluded that he had a weapon concealed there. Stoll did not hesitate. He must not let the man arm himself. He swung his truncheon down in an arc, hitting the knee of the man on the bed. As the man bent forward, he brought the baton up with the same movement and hit him on the forehead. The man cried out in pain, clutching his knee and head.

Stoll turned towards the other man, who let his captive go. Swift stumbled to the bed to support himself, taking great gulps of air.

Stoll's opponent took a cudgel from his frockcoat, and the two men squared off against each other. The man stepped forward and raised the cudgel above his head, then brought it down in a diagonal arc towards Stoll's head. Stoll saw it coming, crouched low, and heard the weapon swish past his face. It was a close call. Stoll now swung his truncheon at the man's right knee and heard the crack as it hit bone. He aimed it at the right wrist with the backhand movement, and the weapon dropped with a cry of pain. Stoll was an expert in quickly disabling an opponent, and he had done just that. He connected again with the left knee, but he was reaching, and the blow was not as powerful as the first.

Nevertheless, the man brought his hands down to his injured knee, leaving his head unprotected. Stoll connected powerfully, and the man went down. The fight was over.

Stoll rushed towards Swift. 'Can you stand, sir? We have to get out of here before they recover. It will be three against one, and I no longer have the element of surprise in my favour.'

The physician stood unsteadily. Stoll put his arm around his shoulder, taking some of his weight, and the two struggled down the stairs. They saw the younger man's prone body in the hallway, blood seeping from a gash on his forehead. They stepped over him as he started to stir, while the old woman mumbled obscenities at them from a doorway. Once outside, their progress was slow, but they only had to reach a busy street. From Hyde Street, they staggered on until they approached High Holborn, where they felt able to slow down. Stoll waved down a hackney, and within minutes they made their escape.

TEN

A message was delivered to our house in Temple Bar at a quarter to noon. Addressed to Father, it looked important, so I took it up to his bedroom. When I entered, he was talking to Constable Stoll, who had called to see how he was doing.

Father was in bed. He looked pale and drawn after his beating, his quick eyes dulled, but as he spoke I realised that, unlike his appearance, his intelligence had not been dimmed.

'Can you get me a cudgel, Constable Stoll?' Father asked. 'If I'm attacked again, I need some way to defend myself.'

Constable Stoll stroked his chin. 'A cudgel on its own will be of little use to you, sir. You need to know how to handle it.'

'Will you teach me the technique?'

'Gladly, but it'll take time. For the present, I think it best for you to arm yourself with a pistol.'

'But that will only give me a single shot, will it not? There were three of them, remember?'

'I can get you a double-barrelled pistol. That will give you two shots before you need to reload. Villains would see it and think twice about attacking you.'

Father nodded in agreement and I took the opportunity to speak.

'A letter for you, Father.' I stepped forward and handed it to him. He looked at the envelope and saw it was Henry Lawton's stationery. He broke the seal and opened it.

'This concerns you, Cully. It's from Edward Lawton — you remember, we went to the dinner party at his father's house.' I stared at him — how could I forget? 'Upon my soul,' he went on, 'he asks permission to call on you.' He handed me the letter. I could feel my heart beginning to pound. 'Fetch your mother, will you, Cully?'

I called Mother from the landing at the top of the stairs. She had been doing the household accounts and was happy to take a break. When she entered the bedroom, I handed her the letter. As she read it, her small smile broadened into a wide grin.

'Such a fine gentleman,' she said. 'The dresses I ordered for you are ready for collection, Cully,' she added.

'Are you not concerned, Iona?' asked Father.

'Why should I be? Edward is from a good family, Gus,' she replied. 'I hope your prejudices are not going to get in the way of this opportunity?'

'I have met the sons of gentry before,' Father began. 'Aristocratic thugs and libertines, with no restraint on their actions from the law. They do what they want — drink, gamble, womanise.' I had heard him say it many times before.

'But from what Cully has told me, Edward is a well-educated young man.'

'Aye, which means he will record his occupation as "Gentleman" while pursuing a life of pleasure, without labour or study. He will not run an estate as his father does. He'll live in a little cocoon, as do most gentlemen of rank in London society, and the plight of the vast majority of his fellow countrymen will not even enter his consciousness.'

'He is a polite young man, Cully says.'

'Aye, he will be polite to those of rank, but he'll see no obligation to be courteous to the lower classes. Upper-class young men look for a wife who will be a social asset to them, and that'll mean a dowry. He won't want a clever wife; that would be intimidating.'

Mother frowned. 'I know how you regard these young men, Gus, but this is a bit strong, even for you. We will invite Edward here, and I will act as a chaperone.'

'You don't understand, Iona.'

'What don't I understand?'

'This is not a good time, that's all.'

'Father, what is it?' I asked him.

He coughed hesitantly. 'I wasn't lured to that house to be robbed. It was an attempt on my life. If it hadn't been for Constable Stoll here, they would have succeeded.'

Mother gasped. 'But why would anyone want to kill you, Gus?' she asked in disbelief.

I knew the reason. He was getting too close to exposing them. 'It's because you're working for the Home Department, isn't it?' I said. 'You think they're from that secret brotherhood.'

'Logic would suggest so, Cully.'

'And you think we're all in danger?'

Father looked directly at me and nodded.

Mother put her hand to her mouth. 'What do *you* think, Constable Stoll?' she asked.

'I must agree with Dr Swift,' he said. 'We have both seen their faces, which breaches their cloak of secrecy. I have sent my wife and daughter away to her sister in Northampton. My advice would be for you all to go away as well.'

Silence fell; we exchanged glances, but nobody seemed to know what to do.

'I must stay,' Father said eventually. 'This is my livelihood. It's my responsibility to provide for my family.'

'I will stay with you, Father,' I said boldly. 'And I'm sure Grandpa won't leave.'

'This is no time for bravery,' Father said. 'We are in danger; we have to face that.'

'And we will,' said Mother determinedly. 'If I can travel to Egypt and put up with the insufferable heat and endless biting insects, then I can put up with this threat.'

'Right,' I said, coming to a decision. 'We make this house impregnable. All the doors and windows must be bolted, day and night, never mind that it's summer. The apothecary's shop must be closed, as will your consulting room for the clinic, Father. We'll find empty premises close by and run the shop and consulting room from there. And nobody consumes any food or drink unless Mother prepares it.'

Mother nodded. 'What about Betsy?'

'She will have to live in,' I said. 'We'll put a cot up in my room. She can share with me.'

'But all the supplies and preparations for the apothecary shop are here,' said Father.

'We'll hire an errand boy. Grandpa can prescribe from the new premises and send his prescription with the boy to me. I will make it up. Can you make do without me at the clinic, Father?'

Father opened his mouth to speak, but was interrupted by a knock at the front door. We all looked at each other again, our glances laced with fear.

We heard Betsy answer the door, followed by a muffled conversation, then measured footsteps on the stairs. There was a creak on the landing as they paused outside Father's door. Then the door slowly opened, and Betsy's head appeared. We all exhaled. The threat to our safety was making us uneasy.

'A Mr Hazeldean to see the master,' Betsy said timidly, giving the calling card to Mother.

Father shifted in the bed, but Mother put a hand on his shoulder. 'He will have to meet with you up here, Gus. After all, you *were* injured on Home Department business.'

Father lay back and nodded. 'Will you show him up, please, Betsy?' he said.

Hazeldean took the chair next to Father's bed. He flicked the tails of his smart grey frockcoat as he sat down and Mother followed Betsy back downstairs.

He turned to Father. 'You are unwell, sir?'

'I was badly beaten last night,' answered Father, 'during an attempt on my life.'

Hazeldean looked surprised, and Father told him the whole story. 'You were lucky that Constable Stoll was there to help you, sir.'

'I was on my beat in St Giles when I saw Dr Swift,' the constable explained. 'I called after him, but he didn't hear me. Knowing the area to be a rough one — more so at night — I decided to follow him. I saw him go into a house, and so I waited just down the street. When he didn't come out, I went in. If I hadn't had the element of surprise, I fear we would both have been killed.'

'Are you sure it was an attempt on your life, sir?' asked Hazeldean. 'Not an attempted robbery?'

'Aye, I am sure, sir. They were members of the Brotherhood of the Parole.'

'Will the Home Department deploy constables to protect us, Mr Hazeldean?' I asked. 'After all, Father was attacked because he is advising you.'

'I'm afraid that your father is not the Home Secretary's favourite person at the moment, Miss Swift,' Hazeldean answered. 'But your family will need to be careful.'

'Careful, sir?' I repeated. 'This secret organisation has poisoned the Home Secretary's dogs, broken into a Cabinet member's house and poisoned three people, and poisoned another Cabinet member in front of a houseful of guests, and you tell us to be careful? Is that the best you can do?'

'Cully!' Father gave me a hard stare. 'That will be enough.'

I was in no mood to apologise. Father and Constable Stoll had run for their lives, and we were denied protection; I was angry.

Hazeldean had the good grace to look a little sheepish. 'And there's been another development,' he said.

Father stirred in his bed. 'Go on,' he said.

'The night before last, Sir George Cornysh, the Cabinet Minister, disappeared. He visited his mistress and then took a hackney at about fifteen minutes after ten. He hasn't been seen since.'

'Do you think he's dead?' asked Father.

'No, at least we hope not. The Home Secretary received a ransom letter this morning telling him Cornysh will die if he goes ahead with the gagging legislation.'

'And will he? Go ahead, I mean?'

'That is certainly his intention. And we are charged with finding this organisation and putting it out of action.'

'You say "we", sir. Am I still working for the Home Department, then?' There was surprise in Father's words.

'Bradbrook and I have convinced the Home Secretary that you are vital to the investigation. It wasn't easy, but he's agreed — though he will not meet you personally. You will work through Bradbrook, me, or Constable Stoll.'

'I'm not sure I want to continue, sir. It means putting my family at risk. The obvious solution is for the Home Secretary to withdraw his legislation.'

Hazeldean stared at Father. 'There is a man's life at stake, sir.'

'I fear that events may have overtaken us, Dr Swift,' put in Constable Stoll. 'We have seen the faces of three of their members. They know we can identify them, if not their leader. We are in danger whether you work for the Home Department or not.'

There was silence while we took this in. I realised the constable was right.

'We have to catch them,' Father mumbled, his gaze distant. Then I heard him click his tongue and knew he had remembered something. 'Did you notice the hands of the one they called *Première*, Constable Stoll?'

'No, sir. What did you see?'

'Ink stains on the inside of the man's palm. A clue, perhaps, to the man's occupation. A printer or an engraver?'

Stoll nodded. 'I'll start visiting these establishments to see if I recognise anybody.'

'Take somebody with you,' said Father, looking at Hazeldean. 'These men are dangerous.'

The Home Department man nodded his agreement. 'When we last spoke, Dr Swift, you advised that we need to identify the man at the top. Are we any further along in breaking through that layer?'

'No, that will be the final circle. We have others to penetrate first,' said Father. 'We broke through the first circle to establish their motive, and the second to establish what their symbol represents. Circle three shows us why they have revealed their existence after fifty years of hiding in the shadows. We now need to pierce the fourth circle to establish their weaknesses.'

'But you said their leader was their weakness, sir,' said Hazeldean.

'Yes, he is; if he falls, so does the organisation. But to get to him, we need to exploit any fault we can find in their operation.'

'Can you see any?'

'Possibly,' said Father, then, 'their communication, for instance. We know they do not leave a paper trail, as part of their code of secrecy. It has served them well, but it also imposes limitations. So the leader has to replace it with some other form of communication.'

Hazeldean's brow furrowed. 'I'm not sure I follow, Dr Swift.'

'Symbolism, sir.'

'I know symbols can be potent, but —'

'Extremely potent, sir; when Saladin besieged Jerusalem and the city fell, he had the Christian Cross taken down from the Dome of the Rock and dragged around the city streets. As a symbol, it was more powerful than a thousand proclamations. I think the tattoo on *Première*'s arm indicates that they probably use symbols as part of their initiation, their rituals; symbols are important to them.'

'Professor Margett told us that the leader never reveals his identity, Father,' I said. 'He always wore a hood.'

'Exactly, Cully, so we have to ask ourselves — how does he call them to the meetings in the first place?'

'Ah, I see, by symbols,' I replied.

'Our country has a history of espionage. In Elizabethan times, there was an obsession with codes and cyphers. Thomas Cromwell had an army of spies working for him, infiltrating possible enemy groups, especially the Catholics, and the Catholic families under suspicion reciprocated. They both developed expertise in deception. But in the end, they found that codes and cyphers can be intercepted and broken.'

'So the secret organisation has used symbols rather than codes?'

'I think so, Cully, and they have already revealed the symbol of their organisation. Now we know that, it will not only incriminate any of their members, but could also point to a trail that will take us to the leader.'

'I'll authorise more men to work under Constable Stoll,' said Hazeldean.

'Don't get carried away, sir,' said Father. 'Let's assume that you arrest the three men from last night — we will still be no nearer to identifying their leader because they can't identify him either.'

Hazeldean pursed his lips in frustration.

'I've been thinking about this at some length,' Father continued. 'The leader wears a disguise, but I think there is some clue as to his identity.'

'A clue, sir?' asked Hazeldean expectantly.

'Yes, his knowledge. How does he know about Pitt's proposed new legislation? It's a valid inference that the man is at the heart of the government.'

'Yes, and if you are right, sir, that narrows it down,' said Hazeldean.

'I think we can narrow it down further, sir. He sent the three men after me — how does he know about my involvement? Could he in fact be someone at the Home Department, or have an informer there?'

'Is that your *valid inference*?'

'It's a possibility, but no. A few days ago, I received an invite to dine at Henry Lawton's house, the Whig politician. I went with Cully, not sure what was behind the invitation. It turned out that they wanted me to tell them about my meeting with the Home Secretary and if I had indeed asked him why he wasn't dead. They seemed to think it was a great wheeze. Looking back, I think it was also an opportunity to find out what I knew and whether I was a danger to their plans. My *valid inference* is that the leader was at that dinner.'

'How many people were there, sir?' asked Hazeldean excitedly.

'Fifteen — and if you eliminate Cully and me, that means we are looking at thirteen possible suspects. Six were wives, and we must ask ourselves if it is dangerous to eliminate them; if we do, it leaves just seven.'

'Then I think it's time I put our agents to work, Dr Swift. I'll have dossiers of each attendee drawn up.'

ELEVEN

A week later, Mother was busy making preparations for Edward Lawton's visit. She had decided that keeping busy would take her mind off the danger we all now felt. Similarly, I had busied myself with reorganising our business. I found rented premises on Essex Street, just around the corner. I called in a tradesman, and all the doors and windows at Temple Bar were now heavily bolted. Grandpa had taken to keeping a pistol in the new shop. Father, too, had a double-barrelled weapon on him at all times, acquired for him by Constable Stoll.

A young lad had been employed as a messenger delivering the prescriptions to me, but that left nobody to run the free clinic, as Father was still not well enough. Grandpa and I attempted to fill in, but that left at least one part of the business unmanned at any one time.

The previous night, Father had left his bed and joined us for the evening meal. It was good to see him feeling better, but we were all concerned that he would return to work before he was ready.

'How was business today?' he asked between spoonfuls of soup.

'It's been busy all day, Father,' I replied.

'Who ran the clinic?'

'The patients are directed to the new apothecary shop, where Grandpa prescribes for them. If he is unsure, I am called over. I know the patients from assisting you.' I tried to concentrate on my soup, but I knew I was not fooling him.

'I'll start work tomorrow,' he said.

'You will not,' said Mother. 'You need another week's rest before I will allow that. Your belly is still bruised black and blue, and you can't stand for long periods. Your body needs to heal.'

Grandpa put his spoon down. 'I think I may have a solution,' he said. 'I went to the Guild meeting last night. You remember that old Will Turnbull died a couple of months back? Well, his widow has applied to the Worshipful Society of Apothecaries for permission to continue the business, and they have agreed to let the business trade in her name.'

'How's she going to do that?' asked Mother. 'Anne's not an apothecary.'

'A young apprentice called Rafe Bullimore was running the business during Will's illness and has continued since his death. I spoke to Anne last night. She wants to sell the business as a going concern and needs to continue trading until she finds a buyer.'

'Is she finding it difficult to find a buyer?' asked Mother.

'No, she has one, but the buyer doesn't want the apprentice, so she is considering turning down the offer. The lad is only twenty and has eighteen months of his apprenticeship to go. You know how it works — he was bound by apprenticeship indenture for seven years. The indenture is legally binding, and money was paid by Rafe's father to Will, in exchange for him agreeing to train the boy in the profession and provide lodging, food and clothing for the duration of the seven-year apprenticeship. Anne had thought of offering him a partnership, but the Guild won't allow an apprentice to trade as the proprietor.'

'Has Anne asked you to take over the apprenticeship?' I asked.

'Aye, she has. It will solve both her problem and ours.'

'Will our business support this young man?' asked Mother.

'Anne will pay part of the money they received from Rafe's father to us. She says he is a first-rate young man.'

Father nodded. 'Then let's talk to him tomorrow.'

A message was sent to Rafe Bullimore early the following morning, and he presented himself straight away. Father and Grandpa interviewed him in the apothecary at Temple Bar. I also attended, but my mind was elsewhere — Edward was calling that evening.

Rafe was tall, with the shadow of a beard on his chin and a long pigtail tied at the nape of his neck. Despite his coming at short notice, his stock was clean, demonstrating that he had made an effort with his appearance.

Grandpa asked him about the famous herbalist Nicholas Culpeper. Although Rafe knew of him, it seemed that Will Turnbull, his previous master, had not been such a devotee as Grandpa. This was a black mark as far as Grandpa was concerned, so he then threw questions at him, but Rafe answered them all correctly. Father then asked Rafe to make up several prescriptions, and the young man set about his task with enthusiasm. He was comfortable behind the counter, I saw.

'When you complete your apprenticeship, Bullimore, what trade will you be entering?' Father asked. I could see the mischief in his eyes.

The young man frowned. 'Sir, I will not be entering a trade. I will be entering a profession. The House of Lords ruled as far back as 1704 that apothecaries can both prescribe and dispense medicines. To the vast majority of people, the apothecary is their physician, not the barber-surgeon.'

'Well said,' said Father, a smile appearing on his face. Then he became more serious. 'Never forget that apothecaries are valid members of the medical profession. I studied anatomy at Edinburgh and know all the bones and organs, but all that counts for nought when I sit beside a patient. I rely on my apothecary training to treat what I have identified.'

Rafe nodded his agreement. 'Never, sir,' he answered.

'Good,' said Father. 'Now, let's see how you fair at diagnoses.'

By ten o'clock we were all impressed with Rafe, and Grandpa agreed to take over his apprenticeship. He was to return at twelve o'clock, we decided, but there was something we all had forgotten.

'We have nowhere for him to sleep, Father.'

'Did you have your own room at Will Turnbull's?' asked Father.

'Aye, sir. He was a good master; he took me into his home, and I ate at his table.'

'You will eat at our table too, Rafe, but sleeping accommodation is a problem.'

'I will be content to sleep at the back of the shop,' he said.

'No, no,' said Grandpa, shaking his head. 'Would you agree to share my bedroom for a short period, until we get things sorted out?'

'Aye, sir,' he said, 'that would be acceptable.'

'Good,' said Father. 'You will learn from me and Matthew, as well as Cully.' He turned to me. 'The Guild won't accept my daughter as an apprentice, but I assure you she is as good as any apothecary in London.'

That was quite a commendation, and I blushed slightly. When Rafe looked at me, he too blushed, but not, I think, from embarrassment. I believed it was because we had locked eyes.

That evening Edward called to attend on me. My family had eaten earlier so that I could dine with him, with Mother as chaperone. The chemise gown that Mother had had made for me was tasteful and elegant. She had gone to the Jewish merchants in Monmouth Street to keep the cost down but had managed to buy a lovely fabric of royal blue, decorated with small white flowers. It had a low neckline gathered with a drawstring, a high waist, and a skirt hanging in a straight line.

Mother had styled my hair as she had when we'd gone to Edward's father's house. It was shining, tied back in a chignon, with curls falling beside my ears.

When Edward arrived, he first addressed Mother. 'Mrs Swift,' he said, 'and how is it with you today?' He bowed with all the politeness required of a man of his station.

Mother bobbed a curtsy. 'Always happy to see you, Mr Lawton.'

He then turned to me and pretended not to recognise me. 'And who do we have here?'

'Mr Lawton, this is my daughter, Augusta — but you have already met, sir,' Mother answered, giggling like a young girl.

'No, it cannot be. Why, I do believe you are even more beautiful than the last time we met.' He bowed and kissed my hand.

Mother had brought me up to display good manners at all times, although Father had told me that the rich and privileged believed that they did not owe any politeness to people of the lower orders. But for today, all our manners were on display.

Over dinner, Mother was keen to tell Edward of my accomplishments. 'She has Latin and some Greek,' she boasted, 'and is a fine harpsichordist and pianist.'

I blushed at my mother's forwardness.

'You have Latin, Augusta?' There was some surprise in Edward's voice, and then he quoted some Latin. I understood it; it seemed to be poetry, but I did not recognise it. He said it was by a Roman poet called Ovid. Unfortunately, my Latin had come from medical textbooks and not books of poetry.

Fortunately, Edward did not make me feel uneasy about my lack of knowledge of poets. On the contrary, he was attentive throughout the meal. He asked about Father's work, his apothecary background, his medical training in Edinburgh, and his visit to the Levant to work in an Egyptian hospital. When I told him that Mother had accompanied him to Egypt, he was anxious for her to tell him all about it.

He then asked me to play the piano for our entertainment. I agreed to do so, and I played some Mozart. When I finished, he applauded enthusiastically, and I silently thanked Mother for sending me to music lessons after all. We then played a duet together; Edward followed my lead with great skill and even navigated the tricky bits with dexterity. We laughed together as we did so. But then our hands crossed on the keyboard, and I faltered. It was only the briefest of touches, but I felt myself blushing furiously. I shot Edward a sideways look, but saw no embarrassment on his face. He put his hands back on the keyboard and picked up the next couplet, then waited for me to follow his lead. I did so, and we finished the piece without further mishap.

'Will you also sing for us, Augusta?' he asked.

I felt my cheeks burn again. I had never sung for anyone before; this was one step too far. 'Oh, I couldn't possibly,

Edward. I am no singer.' I held my breath, hoping he would not insist.

'Shall we sing a duet, then?' he said encouragingly.

I let out a sigh of relief, my heartbeat easing; yes, that was preferable to singing alone. We looked through my pile of sheet music, choosing 'Jesus Christ the Apple Tree'. We sang together — Edward had a robust baritone voice — and Mother applauded enthusiastically when we had finished.

I had a wonderful evening. Edward was funny and cultured, and I hoped he would want to call again. Before he left, he kissed my hand again.

'Perhaps next time,' he said, 'we can visit Vauxhall Gardens together to take in the entertainment there?' He turned to Mother. 'And the invitation, of course, applies to you as well, Mrs Swift.'

'That would be splendid, sir,' Mother answered while bobbing a curtsy.

TWELVE

Sir George Cornysh began to stir as consciousness slowly returned to him. He opened his eyes but shut them immediately as his head started to pound, as though a dinner gong was repeatedly striking inside his head. He tried to move his hands, then realised they were manacled behind his back. His mouth was stuffed with a rag or kerchief and tied tightly in position He forced himself to open his eyes again, this time squinting, but saw only the dirt ground on which he was lying.

His neck was sore, but he managed to turn his head sideways. He was in a large, empty room with high, painted-out windows. Yet there were silver linings at the edges of some of them that revealed it was daylight outside.

He listened — nothing. Or were there some muffled voices in the distance? He moved his legs and realised that they were not shackled like his hands. He swung his top leg away and managed to roll over onto his back, but that now trapped his hands behind him. There was a stab of pain, and it forced him to sit up.

Almost immediately, there was some relief from the discomfort racking his body. He looked around, his eyes adjusting to the dim light. He forced himself to kneel and then gingerly got to his feet. He could see a door in the gloom. He edged forward, but when he was halfway across the room, he was pulled up short. He looked back and saw a chain attached to his manacles, the other end studded into the ground.

He staggered back and sat down inelegantly, resting his back against the wall. He was exhausted. After a while, his mind started to give way to sleep. As he drifted off, he became aware of a foul stench. He realised that he was by the Thames — it was the smell of the river that all Londoners knew well.

When Sir George woke again, those few rapier strands of daylight were gone; there was only darkness. But as his eyes adjusted to the gloom, he saw a shadow at the upper window. It dropped silently to the ground, then he heard a bolt slide open. *The room is locked from the inside*, he thought. The door creaked open, and lantern light appeared. Two men were behind it — a tall man and a smaller man. They stepped inside, closing the door behind them, and walked towards him.

The tall man held the lantern higher, and a small circle of light enveloped them all. Both men were dressed in black frockcoats, with black kerchiefs covering the lower halves of their faces.

'I see that you have been making yourself comfortable, Lord Cornysh.' The tall man spoke with the clipped tones of an educated man.

Sir George studied the figure in front of him and saw the candlelight dance in the tall man's eyes. There was something — what was it?

'Comfortable is not the word I would have chosen, sir.'

The tall man waved his hand, and the small man crouched down behind Sir George and undid the manacles. He brought his stiff arms around the front, massaging his wrists to get back the circulation, but before he could do much more, the small man relocked the manacles at the front.

'Are these necessary?' he asked, gesturing at the restraints.

'You can eat and drink like that,' the tall man said matter-of-factly. He lowered himself to the floor before Sir George and took a flask from his pocket. He unscrewed the lid and handed it across. Sir George gulped down the contents. It was light beer.

'Don't drink it all at once,' said his captor. 'That will have to last until tomorrow night.'

Sir George put the flask down. A linen parcel was then taken from the tall man's other pocket and handed over. He unfolded it to reveal bread and cheese. It was poor-quality fare, but he devoured it anyway. When he had finished, he sat back against the wall.

'Is it money you want?' he asked.

'I've already been paid, sir.'

His heart leapt. 'So you've come to release me?'

'Oh no, I said *I* had been paid.'

'So, how long do you intend to keep me here?'

'As long as I am told to.'

'By whom, sir?'

'That doesn't concern you.'

'Is this all to do with Pitt's damn gagging legislation, then?'

'Now, that doesn't concern *me*. I'm just paid to keep you hidden.'

Sir George knew the answer, of course. He could see that these were not common criminals, and in all probability, it was political.

'Is my life in danger, sir?'

'You should face that possibility. It is down to your friends to save your life.'

'The Home Secretary will have men out all over London looking for me. It's only a matter of time —'

'Only a matter of time?' the tall man interrupted. 'Well, maybe — if that helps you to deal with your predicament.'

The tall man signalled to the small man with a nod of his head. He knelt and undid the wrist shackles, pulled Sir George's arms forcefully behind his back, and relocked them.

Sir George grimaced. 'Can you not leave my arms at the front?' he grunted.

The tall man looked at him expressionlessly. 'Afraid not, sir. You will only pull your gag down and shout out.'

'What if I give you my word, sir, not to cry out?'

'Still no, I'm afraid. I don't know whether I can trust you.'

With that, he kneeled beside his captive, stuffed the kerchief back inside his mouth, and tied it in place with the gag. The two men stood, the lantern held high to check nothing had been forgotten, then they walked back to the door. The tall man left, the short man shooting the bolt behind him. He then climbed up to the upper window to escape. Sir George's world returned to darkness.

Constable Stoll had been to the Worshipful Company of Stationers. They controlled, amongst other things, the printing trade in London. He now had a list of the printers who traded in the city; his search could begin. Hazeldean had arranged with Sampson Wright, the Chief Magistrate at Bow Street, for four other Runners to assist him. His list ran to eighty-six business addresses.

It was four o'clock, and his team was weary as they approached Dunkin and Brownlow on the Strand. It was their fifteenth property of the day. They had been to thirty-two others on the previous two days. Stoll nodded to his team. He did not need to issue any further instructions; they knew the routine by now. One Runner went around to the back entrance; two remained outside the front door. Stoll and the other constable went inside.

Dunkin and Brownlow was one of the larger establishments they had visited. Constable Stoll's eyes darted around the workshop, but he recognised no one. It was a busy scene — men shouting to one other, the noise of printing machinery, the smell of ink and paper. At the sight of their uniforms, the noise lessened as the workers looked around at them. A man walked over, wiping his ink-stained hands on a rag. He did no more than raise an eyebrow inquisitively.

'Who is in charge here?' asked Constable Stoll authoritatively.

'That would be Mr Brownlow.' The man gestured towards the corner of the building. 'That's his office over there.'

They walked over. Stacks of printed paper awaiting binding were piled up outside. The door was open, and they could see there were also stacks of print inside. It was as much a storeroom as an office. A man sat at his desk with his back to the door. Stoll knocked. 'Mr Brownlow?' he enquired.

The man turned around and straight away Stoll recognised him. It was the one called '*Première*'. But the man also remembered Stoll. He looked about his desk frantically, searching for a weapon with which to defend himself. The best the man could see was a wooden mallet; he grabbed it and jumped to his feet, his chair tipping backwards and crashing to the floor. He faced Stoll and his colleague challengingly.

'If I remember rightly, Mr Brownlow, or should I call you *Première*, the last time we met, I also caught you without a weapon to defend yourself.'

'I'll take my chances,' the man spat, raising the mallet above his head.

Stoll sighed. 'Put the mallet down, if you would be so kind.'

The man merely growled and gestured for them to come and take him. Stoll drew his truncheon, and his colleague followed.

'There are two more Runners outside the front door and a man posted at the back. You are going nowhere, sir.'

Realising that he was cornered, Brownlow put the mallet down on the desk.

Stoll reached forward and grabbed it quickly, but as he did so, Brownlow let out a shout.

'*Troisième!*'

Stoll heard a scuffle in the main factory and looked behind him. There was a man fleeing for the far end. *Première* had given a warning to another of the men, he realised. Not to worry; one of the Runners would apprehend him.

Constable Stoll stepped forward and manacled his prisoner. He then called all the men in the workshop to attention. Their bewildered faces turned towards their shackled employer. 'I want you all to roll up your sleeves, please.' The men grumbled but did as they were asked. Stoll walked along the line and looked at the exposed arms, but there were no tattoos. 'Damn!' he cursed; he had wanted all three men.

'Is anyone not at work today?' he asked, but the men seemed reluctant to talk. 'Well?'

One of the men spoke up. 'The gaffer's brother-in-law, Jack Broad. He's not been at work all week.'

Stoll turned to Brownlow. 'Where is your brother-in-law?'

Brownlow cleared his throat. 'He's away on business.'

'And what sort of business would that be, Mr Brownlow?'

'Printing business.'

Just then the Runner he had positioned at the rear of the premises came through the door at the back of the workshop, a man with a bloodied head in tow. *Troisième.*

'And who do we have here?' asked Stoll.

'Mickey Broad,' said the constable. 'Ran straight into my truncheon, sir.'

Stoll grabbed the young man's arm and pulled up his sleeve. There was the tattoo. He lifted the arm into the air so that all the workers could see.

'Have any of you seen this symbol before?' he asked.

The same man spoke up. 'Jack Broad's got one like that,' he said, then, 'Jack is Mickey's father.'

Stoll smiled. He had now identified all three members of the group. But one of them was still missing. Then a thought struck him — if Jack Broad had not been seen at the workshop all week, then perhaps he was reconnoitring the whereabouts of Augustus Swift and possibly even himself. If he and Swift were dead, who could identify them in court?

Sir George Cornysh woke when his legs were kicked. He opened his eyes to see a lantern being held high above him. It was the tall man, the small man standing beside him.

'I see you have been busy, my lord,' said the tall man, gesturing to the gag on the floor beside Sir George.

'Damn you, sir,' Sir George spat belligerently. 'You left me a flask of light beer but then gagged me so that I couldn't drink it. It took me hours to work it loose.'

'Did I? Oh yes, so you wouldn't call out. I remember.' There was a flash of amusement in the tall man's eyes.

'I offered my word of honour not to cry out, sir, but you wouldn't accept it. Well, you should know that I have been crying out all night long.'

'And did anybody come, sir?'

Sir George's shoulders slumped. 'No — no one came.'

'And why do you think that is?'

'I can smell the river; we are near the Thames, if I am not mistaken.'

'No, you are not mistaken, sir. And the Thames is a busy river, is it not?'

'It is.'

'Busy it may be, but we have chosen our location carefully. You are in an empty warehouse by Mr Williamson's wharf, and Mr Williamson is recently deceased. There are no houses nearby either — the whole place is deserted. So there is no one to hear you.'

'So why gag me?'

'A test.'

'A test?'

'Yes, to see how resourceful you are.'

'And how have I done, sir?'

'It depends on your point of view. I didn't expect you to spit out that gag; it was tied tight.'

'So will you gag me again tonight?'

'We'll see.'

He turned and nodded at the smaller man, who released the manacles, replacing them at the front. He handed Sir George a new flask of light beer, who pulled out the cork with his teeth and guzzled most of it down. Then, from his pocket, the tall man took a linen parcel and opened it. It was a pie, much better fare than the stale bread and cheese of the previous night.

'Now, this was going to be a reward for behaving yourself, but then you went and cried out.' He broke off a piece of pastry and put it in his own mouth under the black kerchief hiding his lower face. 'It's good, sir,' he said, then paused to judge how his mocking had affected his captive. 'But, I suppose, if nobody heard you…' He waited again. He saw the distress on Sir George's face, then leaned forward and dropped the parcel into his lap.

Sir George picked it up before it was taken back and started to devour it. His cheeks filled with pastry, and he looked at the tall man as he ate. There was no hostility in his face. On the contrary, it was businesslike. Perhaps the best way forward was to work with him, thought Sir George.

'Thank you for this pie, sir,' Sir George mumbled, small pieces of pastry spraying out as he spoke. He tried to swallow, but his throat was dry once more and he started to choke. The tall man picked up the flask and put it to his lips. Sir George swallowed, and the errant piece of pie found its way down.

Sir George coughed. 'Have you heard from Pitt or the Home Secretary, sir?'

The tall man shook his head. 'Afraid not; you will have to spend at least another night here.'

Suddenly the pie tasted sour in his mouth. Sir George chewed the last of it without any gratification. 'If I give you my word not to cry out, will you leave me without the gag, sir?'

'We are quite near a lead pipe factory, but that also belonged to Mr Williamson,' the tall man said, 'and since he died, that factory is also empty. You will find Mr Williamson's wharf a dark and deserted place.'

'So you will, sir?'

'Yes, why not? I will take you on your word.'

'And you will leave my hands at the front?'

'You ask a lot, sir.'

'But you will?'

'Very well, so be it.'

Left alone in the dark, Sir George's spirits rose temporarily. He shuffled back to rest against the wall. He closed his eyes so that sleep could take him, but as he drifted, a nagging thought came to him. These men had murdered two of his Cabinet colleagues. Was he next? The thought kept sleep out of reach. It would be another long night.

THIRTEEN

Father said that he was now well enough to take his free clinic, but Mother would still have none of it.

'Your wounds are healing, Gus,' she said, 'but don't you always say you have to give the unseen wounds inside time to heal? You will mend for two or three more days, if you please.'

I agreed to take his free clinic, and he did not protest. In truth, I think he knew he was not yet recovered enough to return to work. And anyway, I needed the distraction; Edward was taking me to Vauxhall Gardens that evening.

I set off with Grandpa to our new property in Essex Street. It was only around the corner, a matter of yards. Grandpa took the keys from his pocket, shuffling them to find the right one, when he stopped abruptly. I looked up to see what had alarmed him. By the side of the door was a painted symbol.

'Is that the symbol your father described when you investigated the poisonings?' he asked.

'Aye, Grandpa, it is,' I answered. 'It looks a bit like a cloverleaf.'

'Then they've found our new premises, Cully.'

We both knew what that meant. It was a message to us, or possibly to others in the Brotherhood, saying where to find us.

I set about my work with verve; it took my mind off the knot in my stomach. Father had said that symbols were powerful; now I understood what he meant. I didn't want to alarm our new messenger boy, but I told him not to dawdle between the new premises in Essex Street and the apothecary shop at Temple Bar. Rafe Bullimore, the new apprentice, made up the prescriptions and the tinctures, and everything was running efficiently.

One prescription, however, Rafe could not fulfil, and he sent a note saying that he didn't recognise the medication prescribed. I told the patient to return for his medicine later in the day, and at the end of the clinic, I went back to the shop, carrying Grandpa's pistol under my cape; he had insisted. At Temple Bar, Rafe let me in as all the doors were locked.

'Hello, Miss Swift,' he said. I saw his face redden like a pomegranate.

'You can call me Cully, Rafe,' I said with a smile.

'Thank you … Cully,' he answered, but the flush in his cheeks seemed to intensify. 'Why Cully, if it's not too impertinent?'

'It's just a nickname. Father and Grandpa are great believers in the works of Nicholas Culpeper.'

'Ah, Culpeper,' he said, obviously recalling his interview.

'The *great* Culpeper,' I corrected him, teasing. 'That prescription I sent you was one of his. It is made with local herbs. Culpeper believed that herbal medicine should be available to everyone, and that included the poor.'

'Is that why your father gives a free clinic?'

'One of the reasons,' I said. 'Now, let's look at that prescription I sent to you.'

I showed Rafe how to make up the mixture, but he was so keen to learn from me that I spent the next hour in his company, teaching him many of Culpeper's special remedies. Strangely, all thoughts of Edward and Vauxhall Gardens slipped from my mind.

As promised, Edward's carriage picked Mother and me up promptly at six o'clock. It took us along the Strand, then turned south along Whitehall, eventually dropping us at the Huntley Ferry, which took us across the river to the Vauxhall Pleasure Gardens. I knew all about it, of course, though I had never been there and neither had Mother. It was the foremost place of public entertainment in the city. Edward paid the six-shilling entrance fee, which was two shillings for each of us. We started to walk the acres of avenues lined with trees and shrubs. It was a warm summer evening, and there were hundreds of people. Although the gardens were open to all who could pay the entrance fee, the general impression was one of privilege, and everyone appeared to have dressed in their finery.

But it was much more than a place where people came to promenade. There was entertainment at every turn: tightrope walkers, hot air balloon ascents, fireworks, hanging picture displays. We visited the Chinese Pavilion and took supper in an establishment surrounded by elegant paintings and Mr Handel's statue outside. After supper, we went to see a concert. An orchestra played stirring music, and then soloists sang rousing patriotic songs. As the night drew in, to my delight, hundreds if not thousands of lanterns were lit, lighting up the main walks. We walked around a second time to take in the illuminated display.

I took Edward's right arm as we walked. He offered his left to Mother, and we walked three abreast. Father had not brought me up to be frivolous, but at that moment, I lost myself in this scene of merriment. I thought it was magical, the most perfect night of my life.

I then noticed that not all the walks were lit, yet I saw ladies and gentlemen turning from the brightly lit avenues onto these dark paths.

'Why do these couples go along the unlit walks?' I asked innocently. I felt Edward stiffen, and I knew at once I had been I. The reason suddenly became apparent to me.

Edward coughed. 'They are called the *dark walks*,' he said. I could tell he was trying not to be indelicate. 'For couples that are seeking some privacy,' he added.

I felt my face flush, and I was unable to meet Edward's eyes. Fortunately, the elements came to my aid.

'I do believe it is starting to rain,' said Mother, looking up at the sky.

Edward and I also looked skyward. Only a few minutes before, there had been a full moon in the night sky, but now clouds were rushing in to obscure it.

'It'll soon blow over,' Edward said hopefully.

He may have been right, but within seconds, those few spots of rain turned into a torrential downpour.

'We can shelter at the Turkish Pavilion,' Edward said. I put my hand up to hold onto my bonnet and set off at a run with him. After a few yards, I realised that we were leaving Mother behind. I turned to see her also holding onto her bonnet as other people rushed by. She was getting overtaken and lost in the crowd.

'Come on, Mother,' I called, 'we are going to shelter in the Turkish Pavilion.'

She nodded and started to run faster. I lowered my head to keep the rain out of my eyes. Edward took my arm. 'This way,' he said, and I ran alongside him away from the crowd, thinking that he knew a better way around.

Edward pulled me around a corner onto another tree-lined avenue, and suddenly there was darkness, the shrubs obscuring the light from the lanterns on the other side. We were on one of the dark walks.

'Is Mother still with us, Edward?' I said, a little out of breath.

'Don't worry about your mother, Miss Swift,' said a man.

It was not Edward's voice. I knew at once I was in danger.

'Edward?'

'No, not Edward,' the voice said.

'The Brotherhood of the Parole,' I whispered.

'That's right,' said the voice. 'So do as you're told.'

My heart thumped. I knew I needed to act. I opened my mouth and let out a scream. It was so loud it surprised even me. Then a sweaty hand clamped over my mouth; it had a sour smell, a mixture of stale sweat and something else that I couldn't quite place.

The man leaned in and whispered in my ear. 'Now, you come with me,' he said and started to drag me away. As I strained to look back towards the avenues, a figure appeared. He must have heard me scream, because he ran towards us and jumped on the man holding me. I was let go and fell to the ground.

The two men started to fight. They were shouting at each other, and I recognised Edward's voice — he had come to my rescue. Relief coursed through me as I looked on, hoping that Edward would be triumphant. Edward's opponent was holding him by the lapels of his frockcoat. The scoundrel seemed to have the upper hand, but then he released Edward and started to run away, down the avenue.

Edward came back to help me up. We walked back into the light and then found Mother. He took us to an establishment and ordered three large brandies. I had never had strong spirits before; it made me cough, though it did warm my throat as it went down. I decided to tell Edward about the attempt on Father's life, and he listened attentively, realising the strain my family was under.

The evening had started so wonderfully, but we were all subdued on the way home. Nobody spoke in the carriage, the only sound the wheels rolling over the cobbled streets.

Swift's first trip abroad following his assault was a visit to Bow Street; he had two Runners to protect him. He was shown into an office, where Constable Stoll waited. Stoll stood and walked around his desk to shake his hand. They had not known each other for long, but a friendship had emerged.

'Come and sit down, sir,' said Stoll warmly, gesturing towards a seat. Swift obliged, easing his long, lean frame into the chair gingerly. Stoll noticed. 'You are still not fully recovered?'

'It is stiffness more than pain.' This was not an entirely truthful reply. 'Your note said you needed my assistance; how can I help?'

'I have interviewed both Brownlow and Broad, but, to be honest, I am not getting very far with them.'

'I'm surprised, Stoll; you have a fine investigative mind.'

'Good of you to say so, sir, but being a Bow Street Runner gives me little chance to use it. I spend my time policing the streets rather than investigating crime. I keep public order, arrest offenders on behalf of the magistrate, that sort of thing.'

'So this investigation is satisfying to you; can you use your skills?'

'Some, sir, but it's like being promoted from a private to a general.'

Swift smiled at the metaphor. 'Do you have enough to charge these men?'

'Oh yes. With your testimony and mine, they will both go down. I need your formal identification of your attackers, and when I have that, I can take them in front of the court.'

'But that's good, is it not?'

'It is, but I want more from them. I know who the third member of their team is — a man named Jack Broad — and your life and mine are in danger while he's at large. And I want to know who their leader is. This *Première* fellow is damned arrogant, but — well, I also sense something else. I think it's fear.'

'That makes sense. He believes he belongs to an organisation far superior to the Bow Street Runners. But I also suspect he fears the Brotherhood more than you. It's probably to do with an oath he's sworn — never to reveal their secrets.'

Stoll nodded. 'Aye, you're probably right, sir, but that doesn't make me feel any better. If this Brotherhood do for us, then there's nobody to identify them, and the men walk free. Even if we get Jack Broad, their leader can just send more assassins after us.'

Swift sighed heavily. 'There was an attempt to abduct Cully last night at the Vauxhall Pleasure Gardens,' he said.

Stoll's hands clenched involuntarily. 'Is she all right?'

'Yes, she's shaken but unhurt.' Swift relayed the story.

'Jack Broad must be desperate to try something like that with so many people about.'

'Aye, but is that good news or bad? We've taken precautions as a family; we're living behind locked doors, all our food monitored. I suspect Broad's been watching us for days, but we've given him little opportunity to use his skills. We know he's identified our new property because he has marked it with their symbol.'

'He wants to frighten you.'

'Aye, and he's succeeding — yet he's less effective on his own, clearly.'

'True enough; his group of three has been severely weakened. That makes him vulnerable, but at the same time, desperate.'

Constable Stoll sat up straight in his chair. 'Right, our strategy is clear. We catch Broad as soon as we can and get all three men convicted. Once we've done that, their leader cannot save them. Perhaps then he'll have less incentive to come after us.'

'Let us hope so, Stoll.'

Stoll showed Swift down to the cells where Ronald Brownlow and Mickey Broad were confined, for the purpose of identification. Swift took in the acrid smell of sweat and urine and confirmed that he recognised both men. 'That's the one they called *Première*,' he said, pointing at Brownlow.

'That reminds me,' said Stoll, as they turned to retrace their steps back upstairs, 'when we took him, he shouted something to Mickey. Some sort of a warning, I think, because he then ran off. It sounded like *Troisième*.'

Swift's head shot up. 'That's it! It's a codename. *Troisième* is French for third, so Mickey Broad is the third man in their secret group of three. And Brownlow is first — *Première*. Yes, simple, really!' He paused, then said, 'That would make Jack Broad *Deuxième* — the Second. Listen, Stoll, will you be interrogating the two men again this morning? If so, can I sit in with you?'

'Aye, I don't see why not. I'll get extra seats put in the cell.'

'No, interview them in your office, if you will. And one at a time.'

FOURTEEN

Swift sat next to Stoll behind the constable's desk as two Runners brought Ronald Brownlow in, manacled at the wrists. There was still a bruise on his forehead, Swift noticed, caused by Stoll's truncheon in St Giles, but Swift felt no sympathy for the man who had mercilessly beaten him and threatened the lives of his family.

'I've been investigating you, Mr Brownlow,' said Stoll. 'Eight years ago you were an employee of Dunkin's Printers, and then you bought a partnership from your employer.'

'So?' said Brownlow, his face impassive.

'Five years ago, you bought out your partner, and three years ago, you moved to premises on the Strand. Where did you get the money from?'

'I'm a good businessman.'

'Your secret organisation won't save you, if that's what you think.'

Brownlow didn't respond.

'You're safer in *here* than outside, Mr Brownlow,' said Swift. 'You probably know that, of course. The Brotherhood doesn't tolerate failure. They have paid you well, enabled you to prosper, but they expect success, am I right?'

Brownlow remained silent.

'Are you expecting *Deuxième* to save you?'

Brownlow shot a startled look at Swift. For the first time, the mask slipped.

'Aye, *Première* — that's right, *Deuxième*, your second and your brother-in-law Jack Broad.'

Brownlow fidgeted in his seat.

'You think your anonymity keeps you safe, but we know all about the Brotherhood of the Parole. We know that you are bound to the Brotherhood by vowing your word of honour, and there will be severe consequences if you break that vow. We know that there are three members in each select group, and you are the *première*. You control it. Your brother-in-law Jack Broad is *Deuxième*, the second, and your nephew Mickey Broad is *Troisième*.' Swift saw disbelief on Brownlow's face. 'By the way, *Deuxième* tried to abduct my daughter last night. He failed, and Constable Stoll has him in custody.'

Swift paused to let his words sink in.

'You're probably the first *Première* to have his whole group discovered, in what — half a century? You have made quite a mess of things, haven't you?'

He saw Brownlow clench his fists. He opened his mouth to speak, but then closed it again.

'Perhaps you need time to contemplate your predicament. You're facing the hangman, and the Brotherhood cannot save you. Turning king's evidence is your only chance.'

Brownlow glared at Swift, his teeth clenched.

'Very well, Mr Brownlow, you can go back to your cell and think about it.' Swift paused. 'But don't take too long, will you?'

Stoll called for the Runners. 'Bring up Mickey Broad,' he added.

When they were alone, Stoll turned to him. 'That went well, sir,' he said.

'Aye, rhetoric is an ancient art, but still persuasive today. I'll teach you about it in return for those lessons with a cudgel — you'll find it useful in your duties. But something tells me that Brownlow doesn't know the identity of his leader. And even if he does, I believe his fear of the Brotherhood will prevent him from telling us. He's in a classic lose-lose situation.'

'I don't follow.'

'If he keeps his oath to the Brotherhood and doesn't tell us anything, then he hangs. But if he turns king's evidence, then the Brotherhood will eliminate him,' Swift explained.

'Oh, I see, but doesn't that also mean we have the winning hand?'

'A better hand, maybe, but not a winning one. To win, we need Brownlow to lead us to his leader. We need to work out our best options. It's about finding an edge.'

'Is that why you said we had captured *Deuxième*?'

'Aye. It was the best I could come up with at this time.'

Stoll nodded. 'Let's interview Mickey Broad then, see what we can get out of him.'

Broad's arrogance disappeared much quicker than Brownlow's had, though the fear of the hangman still took him like a man plunged into an icy river. He, too, was invited to turn king's evidence, yet his fear of the Brotherhood outweighed his fear of the gallows. But then, Swift thought, Broad had little evidence, anyway, that he could trade. He certainly didn't know the identity of the leader.

Swift changed tack. He would play on the young man's naivety; try to trick him into disclosure. 'Where did you swear your vow?' he asked. 'St Giles, was it?'

Broad declined to answer. Swift returned to this time and again, his intention to convince the lad that to give this information was of little consequence. Eventually, he broke through.

'It was Southwark,' said Broad, and then realised what he had done.

Swift didn't wait for him to find his resolve again. 'South of the river? How did you get there?'

Broad refused to answer. He sighed heavily, and Swift could see he needed to press home his advantage.

'It's all right, Mickey. Brownlow has already told us all about your society.'

'I don't believe you.'

'Brownlow is *Première*. Your father, Jack, is *Deuxième*, and you are *Troisième*. Your father tried to abduct my daughter last night, but he failed, and Constable Stoll has him in custody.'

Broad's eyes narrowed, but Swift also saw despondency there. He asked him the question again. 'Where did you swear your vow, Mickey? It's of little consequence now.'

'There was a building, but I don't think I could find it again,' he said.

'What was it like, this building?' asked Swift.

'There was an extension built onto the main building. It had a hoist with a small landing on the outside for deliveries. The stairs were external — we entered by a door on the first floor.'

'Was it locked, this door?'

'Padlocked, but it had been unlocked. The *Maréchal* was inside, waiting for us.' Broad's eyes widened as he realised what he'd said. He would say no more and was returned to the cells.

Swift turned to Stoll. 'Can you spare some men to find this place?'

'Do you think it's important?'

'Maybe. If we can establish who owns the building, perhaps we can establish a link to the leader. And can you also spare a man to accompany me to the Royal Society? I want to discuss something with a mathematician there.'

Stoll rubbed his chin. 'I'll talk to the magistrate — and may I suggest that *I* accompany you to the Royal Society?'

*

Two days later, Constable Stoll accompanied Swift to the Royal Society at Somerset House on the south side of the Strand. It was an easy route, the Strand running westward from Temple Bar, parallel to the river. Both men carried pistols, and Stoll also had his truncheon. They reached their destination without incident and were shown to the North Wing and Owen Jardine's office, a Fellow of the Society.

His rooms were wood-panelled and lined with bookcases. Jardine gestured for them to sit. His skin had an anaemic pallor, as though he spent his life indoors. He offered them sherry, but they refused.

'This is all very intriguing, gentlemen,' he said, his eyes twinkling with enthusiasm. 'The Royal Society received a letter from the Home Department asking us to assist you with your enquiries.'

Swift handed over his letter of accreditation given to him by the Home Secretary via Mr Hazeldean, and Jardine read it.

'I don't usually get to meet a Bow Street Runner and a Home Department agent,' he said enthusiastically. 'So what precisely can I do for you?'

'I am a physician and apothecary by profession, sir,' said Swift. 'I advise the Home Department on poisons.'

'Wouldn't you be better consulting one of our chemistry Fellows?'

'No, sir, it is a mathematician I need to consult, if you please.'

Swift briefed Jardine on the deaths of the Cabinet members and the secret organisation believed to be responsible. 'I'm pursuing a theory that it was founded on mathematical lines and, in particular, the number three. I wonder what you can tell me about that number that might be relevant.'

'Well, it's certainly a powerful number, Dr Swift, but I can't see how it might be relevant?'

'Then perhaps you can tell me what you know about it, and I'll try to decide if there is anything of significance.'

The mathematician sat back, his forehead furrowed in thought. 'Now, let me see,' he said, 'according to our old friend Pythagoras, the number three, which he called *triad*, is unique in that it is the only number to equal the sum of all the terms below it, and the one number whose sum with those below equals the product of them and itself.'

Stoll took out his notebook and started to write.

'Three is the smallest odd prime number,' Jardine continued. 'It's the only triangular number that is a prime number too, and the only triangular number that is a Fermat number. The first Mersenne prime number, so two squared minus one.'

Stoll glanced up at Swift with a look of confusion.

'A natural number can be divisible by three if the sum of its digits is divisible by three. For example, the number twenty-one is divisible by three (three times seven), and the sum of its digits is two plus one equals three. Moreover, the reverse of any number that is divisible by three or any permutation of its digits is also divisible by three. For instance, 1458 and its reverse 8541 are both divisible by three, and so are 1548, 4158, 4518, and 4815.'

'So, the number three is —' Swift hesitated — 'self-organising?'

Jardine thought. 'Well, I suppose you could put it that way; it's said to have divine symmetry. You can also look at the number three in *scientific* terms. In 1687, Sir Isaac Newton determined that there were *three* laws of motion. A three-dimensional figure has length, width and height, or *three* coordinates. Time is divided into *three* periods: past, present and future. *Three* is the number of dimensions we can perceive. The triangle has *three* edges and *three* vertices and is the most stable physical shape. Is any of this helping, gentlemen?'

'Possibly,' said Swift. 'I can see that arranging an organisation based on the number three will give it stability. The secret organisation we are investigating uses this symbol.' He handed Jardine a piece of paper. 'Do you recognise it?'

Jardine studied the note. 'This is a triquetra knot, sometimes known as the Trinity knot. The triquetra is formed from the interlocking of three equally sized triangles.'

Swift leaned forward. 'It's a religious symbol, then?'

'Oh yes, the three leaves represent the Holy Trinity — Father, Son, and the Holy Ghost. But I believe you can also find it in Celtic, German and Norse mythology.'

'Do you think this one is Christian? Could it be Catholic?'

'Hard to say — it's not my field. But *this* representation has a circle going through the three interconnected loops — see here.' He pointed to the ring in the centre of the symbol. 'Perhaps the circle could emphasise the unity of the three forces? If so, then yes, maybe it is Christian, a Trinity knot.'

'So everything is connected, everything is interwoven, and everything is everlasting?'

'Symbolically, you mean? Well, maybe — but the triquetra also has a mathematical basis to it.'

'Go on,' asked Swift.

'The first theories were only published recently. It's about the geometry of position. For example, in mathematical language, the ends of a knot are joined together so that it can't be undone. So the simplest knot is a ring, and the triquetra is another simple one. The symbol you have shown me is two-dimensional, but the same knot can exist in three dimensions.'

Stoll grunted and put his pencil down, unable to summarise this concept, but Swift thought he had grasped it. 'So, in this diagram, the three loops cross over each other, but in three dimensions they don't. Could you pull it apart to return it to a simple ring?'

'Actually, no. If you attempted to pull it apart in three dimensions, it would knot together.'

'So if one member tried to pull away, the loop would knot around him?'

'Yes, I suppose you could say that — *symbolically*.'

FIFTEEN

Deep in thought, Swift and Stoll returned to the vestibule leading to the Strand. They stopped by a bust of Michelangelo. 'Did you learn something useful, sir?' asked Stoll. 'I must confess to being a little baffled.'

Swift nodded. 'Oh yes, Constable Stoll. We learned that the symbol not only represents the number three but also signifies a knot. So everything is connected, and everything is everlasting — but if you try to leave, the knot will close around you.'

'Yes, powerful stuff indeed, but isn't it all — allegorical? Does it tell us anything about how the Brotherhood operate?'

Swift paused. 'What do we know about this secret organisation? They understand the danger of writing anything down that can be used against them. They understand not to use codes or cyphers either; history tells them they can be broken. Mary, Queen of Scots, found that out to her detriment. So they communicate only by the spoken word.'

'And,' said Stoll, 'if I have this right, then their structure is linear — up to the leader and down again to the three-men squads, never across.'

'Yes, Stoll, and remember the leader wants to be hidden even from his men.'

'But how does he contact his squads? If the leader uses a messenger to call them in for instructions, that messenger makes the leader vulnerable, because the messenger must then know his identity.'

'I agree with you, Stoll, and this man is too shrewd for that.'

'So he must have another way?'

'Exactly, but what is it?' Swift clicked his tongue. 'Mr Jardine said a natural number could be divisible by three if the sum of its digits is divisible by three.'

'Yes, he used the number twenty-one as an example. It's divisible by three, and the sum of its digits is two plus one equals three.'

'And the reverse of any number that is divisible by three, or indeed, any permutation of its digits, is also divisible by three.'

'Sorry, sir, but you've lost me now.'

'What if all the three-man squads know where a principal symbol is located, some random place that only they know? It could be a *call-up* symbol. If he puts, say, the digits two and four below the symbol, that number will refer only to one particular squad.'

'So they add two and four together? It refers to squad six?'

'No, I suspect this man likes the symmetry of mathematics; it will be squad eight. Twenty-four divided by three.' Swift paused as another thought took him. 'And remember, everything has three coordinates. So he can also send directions this way.'

Constable Stoll stroked his chin, but before he could respond, somebody shouted his name. A Bow Street Runner was running towards them.

'Constable Stoll!' the man yelled. 'You have to take cover!' They all crouched down beside the statue of Michelangelo, the Runner panting heavily from his exertion.

Stoll turned to his colleague. 'Report, Constable Oakman.'

'Constable Devlin thought he saw a man following you, sir. He tailed him until he was sure. He dared not blow his whistle, fearing that the man would flee. When you reached Somerset House, Devlin decided he had to do something and approached the man, who pulled a pistol. He grabbed the man's gun, and in the fight the pistol went off; the bullet went through his shoulder, sir. Three of us came running at the sound of the shot, but the man disappeared into Somerset House. We haven't found him yet.'

'Description?'

'About thirty-five, sir, heavy build, wearing a smart black frockcoat.'

'That sounds like Jack Broad. Come on, we'll go back to Jardine's office.'

The three men rose. Stoll drew his pistol. They had only gone a few yards when a figure emerged from behind the plinth of the statue. His pistol was already cocked, raised, and pointing at Swift. Swift reached for his own gun just as Constable Stoll threw himself in front of Swift.

Two cracks rang out in rapid succession.

Confusion and fear seized Swift. He saw the powder in the pans of both pistols flare. There was smoke, and the acrid smell of gunpowder.

When the smoke cleared, Stoll was on his knees, doubled up. He was holding his stomach, blood seeping through his fingers. Broad had fallen backwards, a red hole in the middle of his chest. His eyes were hooded, a faraway look in them.

Swift turned to Constable Oakman. 'Send one of your men to fetch two hackney carriages. We'll take both men to my clinic at Temple Bar. We'll take the other wounded constable, Devlin, as well.'

Constable Oakman gave the instructions to his men as he had been ordered, and before long two carriages, three Runners, and three bloodied victims were speeding towards Temple Bar.

Swift banged on the door. 'Cully, it's me!' he shouted. 'Open the door and prepare the clinic for surgery, please, right away.'

Iona came to the door. She put her hand to her mouth as she too took in the scene. 'Is that Constable Stoll?' she asked, alarm rising in her voice.

'Aye, it is, Iona.'

'I think this man is already dead, Dr Swift,' said Constable Oakman, indicating Jack Broad.

Swift put his fingers to the side of Broad's neck and felt for a pulse. The man's eyes were now vacant. He nodded. 'Aye, he is. Bring him in anyway.'

Swift prepared to operate with Cully as his assistant. Rafe asked to observe. 'You can do more than that, Rafe. You can assist as well.'

Together they lifted Stoll onto the bench and then helped Cully cut away his clothes. Swift asked Stoll if there was pain away from the wound. Stoll shook his head, but he was drifting in and out of consciousness.

'If all the pain is centred around the wound,' Swift explained to Cully and Rafe, 'that may suggest he's been lucky, and the damage internally is not so severe, but there is a lot for the ball to have missed: the large bowel, liver, spleen, pancreas, kidneys, diaphragm…'

Swift looked down at Stoll, saw he had drifted into unconsciousness again, and knew it was a good time to operate. Still, he put a wad of material in his mouth for him to bite on in case he came round, then examined the wound more closely.

'The ball entered through the middle of his abdomen,' he said, 'and it left there.' He pointed to a smaller hole on the left side. 'The trajectory means that it missed the spine, and was too low to have damaged the heart. Let's hope that it missed the liver as well. First, we need to clean the wound and stop the bleeding.'

Swift selected a pair of long forceps. He probed the wound for fragments of cloth ripped from Stoll's tunic by the velocity of the ball. 'I can't leave these,' he said. 'They will cause infection.' When he had finished, he swabbed the wound, leaned in, and smelled the wound.

'What do you smell for, Dr Swift?' asked Rafe.

'A spillage of bowel contents; I can smell blood, but there's nothing to suggest the ball has penetrated the large bowel. Come, smell for yourself, Rafe — do you agree?' The apprentice learned in, sniffed, then nodded.

'What if the ball *had* pierced the bowel, Dr Swift?'

'If it had, I would have to open him up more, and I doubt he would survive that. I'll stitch him back up now, to stop the bleeding.'

As he spoke, the patient jerked violently on the bench as he returned to consciousness. Cully and Rafe took his arms and legs and held him down while Swift began the suturing. Stoll screamed through the wedge of material in his mouth, making the delicate work difficult, but faded into unconsciousness again after some minutes.

They put Constable Stoll on a cot in the clinic, and Constable Devlin was next on the operating bench. Swift assessed the wound. 'There is a large hole in the shoulder, but I can't see an exit wound. The ball is still inside and has made a mess of the deltoid and other muscles — actually the whole of the shoulder muscle mass, but the clavicle bone hasn't been shattered.' He probed with the long forceps until he found the ball, plucked it out from the shredded muscle, and dropped it into a metal kidney dish. Swift then removed the fragments of material that the ball had forced into the wound and cleaned the cavity. 'I'm sorry, Constable Devlin,' he said, looking down at the unconscious patient before him. 'That's the best my knowledge and skill can do for you.'

He supervised as Cully closed and stitched the wound. 'Leave him on the bench, Cully,' he said, looking at the sleeping face, then patted the constable's arm gently. 'If you survive the operation, sir,' he added, 'I'm afraid you will have a lot of shoulder pain for the rest of your life.'

He went over to Constable Stoll and took his hand. His throat tightened. 'We still have to arrange those lessons in logic for you, my friend,' he said, his voice faltering.

SIXTEEN

I opened the door to the clinic and peered in. The morning sun shone brightly, glinting off the metal instruments and glass vessels. It was just before six o'clock, and another bright summer's day had dawned.

Father was sitting in a chair by Constable Stoll's cot. His eyes were closed, but I sensed he wasn't asleep.

'How are the patients, Father?' I asked quietly.

His eyes opened and he looked at me. There was a weariness in his face, and I knew that something had happened.

'Constable Devlin has come through the night well. His pulse is strong, and his breathing deep.'

'And Constable Stoll?'

'His breathing was shallow throughout the night, his pulse weakening. He passed about an hour ago.'

I crossed the room and put my hand on Father's shoulder. 'I fear he may have lost too much blood,' I said.

'You're very clever, Cully,' Father said, then, 'I need to write to his wife, but I don't know what to tell her.'

'You will, Father,' I said. If anybody could find the right words, Father could.

It was just after eleven o'clock when Mr Hazeldean from the Home Department called. Father and I met him in the drawing room. Sampson Wright, the Chief Magistrate at Bow Street, had visited the Home Department to update him on the events at Somerset House the previous day. He now wanted Father's appraisal.

He said the right words about Constable Stoll when Father advised him of his death, but I could see from Father's face that he had doubts about his sincerity. We had both seen first-hand the condescension he'd displayed towards Stoll.

'I know this is a difficult time, Dr Swift,' said Hazeldean hesitantly, 'but there are still lives at stake. So I must rely on you to tell me what progress you and Constable Stoll have made.'

Father let out a long sigh. 'We have taken out one of their three-man squads. *Première*, their leader, and *Troisième*, the number three, are in Bow Street cells. *Deuxième*, the number two, was killed yesterday, after another attempt on my life. Abel Stoll gave his own life to save me.'

'Tragic, Dr Swift,' the Home Department man said, 'but at least it removes the threat to your own life.'

'Unless their leader sends another squad after me.'

'But, with your evidence, the magistrates will get a conviction?'

'I believe so, sir,' said Father.

'Well, that is good news.' There was a pause before Hazeldean spoke again. 'When we last spoke, Dr Swift, you said the fourth circle to penetrate was to uncover their weakness. Have you discovered what that is?'

'I believe so. And in doing so, I think I have also revealed the fifth circle — which is how they operate.'

Hazeldean leaned forward in anticipation. 'Go on, sir.'

'Layer four was to determine how they communicate if the leader never reveals his identity, even when he meets his secret squads. He is always hooded and in darkened rooms. We know they never leave a paper trail; that is part of their code of secrecy. My *valid inference* is that they communicate by way of symbols. And that is their point of weakness.'

'How does he use these symbols?'

'Mathematics, Mr Hazeldean.'

The Home Department man's eyebrows knitted in confusion.

'That symbol left at the scenes of their crimes is called a triquetra, sometimes known as a Trinity knot. The three leaves represent the Trinity. But this symbol also has a circle through it. It symbolises that everything is connected, everything is interwoven, everything is everlasting — but if you try to leave, the knot will close around you.'

'And how does that affect the way they work?'

'By the power of the number three.'

Father told him about the visit to the Royal Society, what he and Stoll had found out about the number three, and his theory that they had squads of three men, and that the symbol was also a calling card, a means of giving directions.

Hazeldean nodded. 'So, if we can find the principal symbol, we may also be able to determine where the next meeting will be. That symbol will be the Brotherhood's weakness, yes?'

'Precisely, Mr Hazeldean. We have to find it.'

'I'll arrange with the Chief Magistrate to allocate you some Runners to scour the streets.' Hazeldean stood up and turned to leave.

Father called him back. 'You are assuming that I want to continue working for the Home Department.'

'Is it a question of money?'

'If my life were a question of money, sir, I wouldn't offer free clinics.'

I saw a muscle in Hazeldean's cheek twitch. He was desperate to have Father on board; they were making no progress at the Home Department. 'As you wish, sir,' he said, 'but may I suggest that you defer your decision? You are upset this morning after Constable Stoll's death.'

'What about the dinner party that Cully and I attended at Henry Lawton's house? I told you that I thought the Brotherhood's leader was there. You were going to have dossiers drawn up for the seven suspects.'

Hazeldean sat back down. 'You were right in your assumption, Dr Swift; the men are all close to the heart of the government. One is an earl, and two are baronets, all with seats in the House of Lords. Two are Whig members of the Commons, but both are connected to influential aristocratic families. That leaves two, and one is Lawton's son.'

'Can I see the dossiers, please?'

'I'm afraid the Home Secretary won't authorise that. These are … influential men.'

Father could not hide his contempt. 'Sir Thomas's logic is seriously flawed, sir. He has the deaths of two Cabinet members on his hands and a third kidnapped. I have given you a list of suspects, but he won't allow me to study what you have found out about them?'

'You can ask me what you want to know, sir, and I will decide what I can tell you.'

'How many of the men are Catholics?' Father asked.

'They all are. You were right about that, sir. But this is about radicals, surely, not religious doctrine?'

'It would seem so, but Professor Margett at Oxford told us he believed it was originally a secret Catholic organisation. It seems he was right.' Father paused. 'What can you tell me about the earl on the list, sir?'

'Charles Harrisbrooke, the Earl of Penistone. He has an estate in South Yorkshire, granted to an ancestor by Henry V, who fought with him in France.'

'What is the source of his wealth?'

'His estate, the rent from his tenants, and coal mining beneath his land.'

'Does he keep a London residence?'

'Aye, sir.'

'Parliament?'

'Yes, active, sits on the Whig benches.'

'And the two baronets?'

'Lords Bastable and Riplington. Small estates in Norfolk and Kent, respectively. Both living off their estate rents, but only Bastable has a London residence. Both sit on the Whig benches, but Riplington is less active.'

'The two members of the Commons?'

'Lawton, you know; he holds a pair of Opposition briefs under the Whig leader Charles Fox. Very active in Parliament and very outspoken. He lives in the West End, but you know that, of course. His background is in banking, which is the source of his wealth. The other is Robert Slade; younger than the others, he took the seat when his father effectively bequeathed it to him. Lives off a generous allowance from his father. He's friends with Edward Lawton.'

'Which leaves just one,' said Father.

'Aye, Stephen Windham. No title of his own but a cousin of Penistone. Not a Member of Parliament either, but a very influential man. He is one of Charles Fox's close advisors; he has his ear, so to speak.'

'And his wealth?'

'Substantial. As much as many a duke.'

'The source?'

'He is a lawyer, but a lawyer to the best of families; they all go to him. And if any of our nobility has a gambling problem, he is the man to go to, the man to borrow money from.'

'And the money is loaned against their property, I take it?'

'You are ahead of me, Dr Swift; he has acquired much property that way. But he also buys real estate for investment. Over the last twenty years, he has bought up many of London's new properties. Many of the new developments are also his.'

'So he will know many people, from the aristocrats, through the gentry to new money?'

'I suppose so,' said Hazeldean.

'Don't you see, sir? Such a man will be party to much information. He is our front-runner.'

Justice came swiftly to Ronald Brownlow and Mickey Broad. I watched from the gallery of the Old Bailey as Father gave evidence against them, and was surprised to find that the law offered no right to a defence counsel. Only the rich could afford someone who knew their way around the pitfalls of the justice system. But then I had no sympathy for these men; they had killed Constable Stoll, assaulted Father, and attempted to abduct me.

Called to give evidence in their defence, they refused, remaining loyal to the Brotherhood of the Parole until the end.

The case was put to the jury to consider their verdict. I saw the foreman call the other eleven men together in a huddle before he informed the clerk to the court that they had reached a unanimous verdict.

The judge asked him to advise the court of that verdict.

'Guilty.'

The word rang out like a bell. The foreman coughed. 'Sir,' he said, 'the jury wish to recommend Michael Broad strongly to His Majesty's mercy.'

Troisième, Mickey Broad, was indeed given the king's mercy and sentenced to transportation for seven years. The judge ordered that he be transferred from the gaol to a prison hulk at Chatham. He was to be held in that old man-o'-war until the next convict ship left for Australia.

All eyes now turned back to Brownlow.

The judge sniffed before he spoke. 'Ronald Brownlow, you have been found guilty of a heinous crime. The citizens of this city must be protected from men such as you.' So saying, he placed a black fabric square on top of his judicial wig, one of the four corners of the fabric facing forwards. There was a sharp intake of breath around the court, and then it fell silent.

'Prisoner at the bar,' the judge intoned, 'it is my painful duty to pronounce the awful sentence of the law which must follow the verdict that has just been recorded; that you be taken to the place of execution, there to be hanged by the neck until you are dead, and may God have mercy on your sinful soul.'

Brownlow was hanged on the first day of August. He was dispatched on his own, which was unusual, for the authorities typically arranged for collective justice, as it made a better spectacle for the baying masses. It was also cheaper to do it that way. It was clear that the Home Secretary had intervened; Sir Thomas wanted no delay.

As a family, we had agreed to continue the temporary clinic at Essex Street, although two of the secret three-man squad were now dead, the third imprisoned on the hulk at Chatham. We had feared that our lives were in danger, and although that anxiety had eased, it was still at the back of our minds that we were vulnerable if the leader of the Brotherhood were to send more men to kill us. So, we would keep our security measures in place.

Mr Hazeldean had been optimistic after the capture of the three men. Magistrate Wright had supplied constables to find the "key" symbol that Father had reasoned must exist. They were dispatched across the city, but had not yet discovered it.

Constable Oakman was now assisting Father. He was a large, generous-spirited man, eager to help, but he was no Abel Stoll; he did not have the same investigative mind that Stoll had. But at least he could act as a bodyguard, which was a relief to Mother and me.

Father was still keen on finding the Brotherhood's place of initiation, believing that it would yield some clues as to the identity of the leader. He always said to *go where the facts take you*, but the problem was that we had so few facts to follow. He had started to go out with Constable Oakman, looking around the streets of Southwark. He had recovered from his beating, but the exertion sometimes proved too much for him. Twice he had to come back after only an hour or so.

After dinner, I suggested that I accompany Constable Oakman instead.

'I don't think so,' said Father. 'Have you forgotten what happened at Vauxhall Gardens?'

'I agree,' said Mother. 'It's far too dangerous, Cully.'

'But I'll have Constable Oakman to protect me,' I pleaded, but they were both adamant.

Rafe coughed nervously. 'May I suggest a possible solution? Perhaps *I* could go out with the constable?'

Father sighed. 'No, my boy,' he said. 'This is a family matter. We couldn't ask you to do that.'

'I don't mind, Dr Swift, honestly. You have invited me into your home and treated me as a member of your family. Let me repay you. I'll be happy to go.'

Father sat back and looked at Grandpa. 'What do you think, Father?'

'It has merit,' said Grandpa. 'You are not back to full vigour yet, and it may be that young Rafe will be less conspicuous than a family member. If finding this place of initiation is so important, it will have to be Rafe or me.'

'Very well,' said Father, turning to Rafe. 'I will gladly accept your offer. You can go out with Constable Oakman tomorrow. But your task is only to identify the building — that's all.'

SEVENTEEN

The following morning, Rafe went out early and returned with a Carrington Bowles' pocket map of London. The new 1795 edition covered both sides of the River Thames, including Southwark. It was, in fact, quite detailed, with the principal churches, individual buildings, estates and gardens noted.

By the time Constable Oakman arrived in the hackney, Rafe had divided the map into grids so that they would not visit the same streets twice. He showed it to Father and asked which areas he had already covered, so that by the time the hackney arrived, he had a clear plan in his mind. I put on my cape to accompany them, expecting Father to stop me. He gave me a stern look, but, surprisingly, just returned to his clinic. I knew what that meant — he would simply tell Mother that I had disobeyed him.

The cabbie opened the door, and I took a seat beside Constable Oakman. Rafe climbed in behind me.

'Should you be accompanying us, Miss Cully?' the constable asked hesitantly.

'Probably not,' I said, grinning at him.

We crossed Blackfriars Bridge and descended onto Great Surrey Street, intending to cover all the streets from there to Blackman Street, leading to London Bridge. We methodically walked the streets in the order that Rafe had mapped out. It took longer than we expected, as we had to go around the rear of each street to look for a building extension built onto the back.

As we walked, Constable Oakman kept a keen eye out, but there was no indication that we were being followed. I turned to Rafe.

'I noticed that you always go out on your half-day off, Rafe,' I said. 'May I ask where you go?'

Rafe looked uncomfortable. 'I go to Mr Samuel Medina's academy every week for tuition.'

'Tuition? In what? Who is Samuel Medina?'

'The pugilist,' Constable Oakman answered for him. 'Good for you, young man.'

'You are learning to be a fighter, Rafe?'

'I'm learning how to defend myself, Cully.'

I said no more, but I was impressed.

It was a hot day, and by lunchtime we were parched. I heard a cry of, 'Hot spiced ginger!' and saw a street vendor on the opposite side of the road. Rafe purchased three refreshing glasses for us to drink. Another vendor saw us and came looking for business, crying, 'Ring bell!' He was the muffin man, and we bought from him as well. It was becoming a pleasant day out.

It was three o'clock when we arrived at Borough Street, where travellers from the south entered the city, including those from Europe via Portsmouth, Dover and other ports. As a result there were many coaching inns, including the Queen's Head, the King's Head, the Catherine Wheel, and others. These were substantial buildings, and we walked up and down the street, surveying each in turn. We then went around the back — several had courtyards and extensions built onto them.

'Dr Swift said we were to look for external steps leading to a door on a first-floor landing,' said Rafe. 'Only one of these inns seems to fit that description. This one —' he pointed — 'the Tabard.'

'And look there, Rafe,' I said, 'by that side window — a hoist with a small landing in front of it.'

He nodded. 'I think we may have found it.'

It was almost six when the hackney dropped Rafe and I back home at Temple Bar. Father's clinic was running late, and we didn't have the opportunity to tell him about our day. I went into the clinic to help him finish up, so it wasn't until we sat down at seven o'clock for the evening meal that I saw Rafe again.

Rafe and I took our seats at the table just as Mother came in with a tureen of soup. She thumped it down on the table.

'You haven't been murdered in the street, then?' she snapped at me, her Scottish accent more pronounced than usual. I knew I was in trouble.

'No, Mother, I was adequately protected by Rafe and Constable Oakman.'

She filled Grandpa's bowl, soup splashing across the tablecloth.

'My cup runneth over,' he said, winking at me.

I managed to contain my mirth, although a smile escaped.

'You can stop smirking, young lady,' she said. 'You defied us both — put yourself in danger.' She turned to Father for confirmation.

'Your mother is quite right, Cully; we may all still be in danger,' said Father.

We were quiet for a while, and then Grandpa spoke.

'Did you have a successful trip, Cully?'

'We did, Grandpa. We believe we have found the building.'

Father put down his spoon. 'Really, on the first day? Where?'

'One of the coaching inns on Borough Street, sir,' Rafe answered. 'The Tabard.'

We told Father all about our day.

'We'll go tomorrow,' said Father. I could see he was anxious to see for himself.

'Can I come, Father? After all, it was Rafe and I who found it.'

'Certainly not,' interrupted Mother. 'Anyway, there is a letter for you on the mantle, from Edward Lawton.'

I jumped up, grabbed it, and broke the seal. 'Edward wants to take me, I mean us, to the circus — Astley's Amphitheatre.'

'When?' asked Mother.

'Tomorrow evening.'

'Well, that settles it; you can't go roaming the streets with your father tomorrow.'

I didn't much mind. I wanted to see Edward again. 'Very well, Mother,' I said. 'We'll send an acceptance note tonight.' But when I looked at Father, there was a frown on his face. 'Do you still not trust him, Father? He did save my life, remember?'

'Aye, and I'm grateful to him for that,' he said.

The following day was unseasonably cold and overcast, the rain falling steadily. Swift, Rafe and Constable Oakman, all wearing their capes, climbed into the hackney. The cabbie wore a great oilskin coat, his hat pulled down to shield his face from the rain. Swift looked out of the window at the dreary view. London's streets were normally filled with its citizens' voices, but today it was as if they were as bleak as the weather.

When the hackney arrived at Borough Street, they all stepped down outside the Tabard Inn and walked around the back.

'Yes, this could well be it,' said Swift when he saw the steps to the first floor, the side window, and the hoist with a small landing in front of it. It was exactly as described by Mickey

Broad. They climbed the steps to the door. It was secured with a heavy padlock.

'How do we get in, Dr Swift?' asked Rafe.

Constable Oakman coughed. From under his cape he produced an iron crowbar. 'I'll prize it off,' he said, slapping the iron bar against his palm.

'Perhaps we should see if we can get in from the inside first, Constable,' suggested Swift.

They entered the inn by the front door. The rain had swelled the custom, despite the early hour, and they were met by loud voices and the aroma of stale beer and cooked meat. As the group removed their capes, all eyes turned to the constable's uniform.

Oakman approached the barman. 'We'd like a word with the innkeeper, my man.'

The barman set his mouth hard. 'He's busy.' He carried on pulling beer.

Oakman leaned across the bar, grabbed the man by his shirt and pulled him close. 'Now!' he demanded. The barman grunted acceptance.

The landlord came, wiping his hands on a towel worn around his waist. He was a rotund man with a red face, his shirt stained at the armpits from the heat of the kitchen.

'We'd like to speak to you, sir,' said Oakman. 'In private, if you please?'

'Now?' said the landlord, looking around. 'The Dover coach is due, and I already have a full house.'

'I can arrange for you to have an empty house if that's what you prefer, sir?' said Oakman.

The innkeeper heaved a sigh and gestured for them to follow him into the kitchen. Inside, the heat from the ovens was intense, while steam rose from numerous pots of boiling vegetables. The innkeeper turned to Oakman. 'Now, what's all this about?'

'You have a room at the back with its own entrance?' said Oakman. When the innkeeper nodded, he continued, 'I want you to take us inside.'

'Can't do that. I don't have access; the room is padlocked from the other side.'

'Who by?' asked Oakman.

'By my tenant; he pays rent for exclusive use and access to the room.'

'How long have you been letting it?'

'I've been here for ten years, and the arrangement was in place when I came. The tenant pays well for it.'

'Who is the tenant?' asked Swift.

'Don't know. I've never met him.'

'So how does he pay you?'

'An envelope is delivered with the rent, paid a year in advance. And the amount increases every three years.'

'So you don't need to negotiate with him?'

The landlord shook his head.

'Who delivers the envelope? Can I see one?' asked Swift.

'It's delivered by a messenger boy. A different one each year — and I don't keep the envelopes.'

'What's inside the room?' asked Oakman.

'I don't know — never been in.'

'We're here on the business of the Home Secretary. I demand that we see inside that room.'

'I've told you I don't have the keys to get in there,' snapped the landlord.

Oakman stood tall in front of him, but Swift put his hand on his arm. The constable looked around and saw him shake his head.

'Thank you anyway, sir,' he said politely.

Outside, they huddled in the rain. It had eased slightly to a drizzle.

'We need to get into that room, Dr Swift. You should have let me force him,' said Oakman. 'I thought this was important work?'

'It is, Constable, and I'm not going to let it go. Your original plan is now the preferred one. Will you force entry around the rear?'

At the back, they climbed the stairs, and Oakman examined the padlock. He put his crowbar under the lever and jemmied the encasement, putting his force behind the long claw. It was a substantial catch and, at first, did not give way. He tried again and then a third time when he felt the resistance failing. The padlock and the encasement came away with a loud snap.

'There you go, Dr Swift,' said Oakman, satisfaction writ large across his features.

Swift pulled at the door tentatively. It opened outwards and he entered, followed by Rafe and Oakman. It was gloomy inside, the day being so dull. Swift looked around. The floor was tiled in a black and white chessboard pattern, with large mahogany cabinets set against the walls. In the centre of the room was a long mahogany table with ornate seats down both sides. At the head of the table, a larger chair was raised higher, as if for a judge to preside over his court. Carved into the back of the wooden chair was the triquetra.

'That will be where the leader sits,' noted Rafe.

Swift nodded his agreement as he continued to look around. The furniture was of good quality but old; perhaps as old as the Brotherhood, he thought. There were four floor-standing wooden candlestick holders, each six feet high, one at each corner of the table. With candles inserted, anyone sitting at the table would be in shadow.

'There's a cape hanging behind the door to the inn,' said Rafe, pointing. He went over and removed it, bringing it back to Swift. It was black, made of a heavy woollen material. He held out another object.

'This is a domino mask worn at masquerades,' said Swift. 'It covers only the area around the eyes, but together with the cloak, it is enough to hide the identity of the wearer.'

'What do they do here, Dr Swift?' asked Rafe.

'I've no doubt this is a place of ritual, a site of initiation. The members probably vow never to reveal their identities or the identity of their leader. Then I suspect they make a pledge. Something along the lines of they come of their own free will, and that they are Christian, or in this case, Catholic.' Swift sat down at the table and frowned.

'What's wrong, Dr Swift? This is the place you wanted to find, is it not?'

'Aye, it is, Rafe — but I can't see that it takes us any further. The leader has covered his tracks too well. His method of payment to the landlord does not lead a trail back to him.'

'What about your method, your *philosophy of reason*?'

'Islamic philosophers say that small facts on their own may be insignificant, but taken together may suggest a valid conclusion. That is what I am trying to do.'

'And have you? Come to a conclusion, I mean?'

'No, I haven't, Rafe. I just can't fathom what they have been doing for the last fifty years, or why they are now killing government ministers in support of a *radical* movement.'

Constable Oakman sat down beside them, and they sat in silence.

'You know,' said Swift at length, 'some Islamic philosophers argue that limited knowledge will not lead you to the truth.'

'So you will have to fill in the blanks before you can establish the truth?' said Rafe.

'Yes, Rafe, and build a strategy; I have to know the *value* of the outcome.'

'I'm not sure I follow.'

'If the leader is identified, he loses everything: his reputation, his liberty, and possibly even his life. If he isn't, then he goes on as before and may even take my life in revenge. Their security has been in place for decades, and it has served them well, but we have discovered the Brotherhood, which should mean the leader's security is weakened — but it isn't. Why?'

'But you *have* frightened him, Dr Swift,' said Oakman. 'He wouldn't have sent somebody to kill you if he hadn't been fearful.'

'True, but is that enough, or does he still hold all the cards?'

'If the innkeeper doesn't know his identity, then he can't warn the leader that we've been here. Shall I watch the building for a few days and see if anybody comes?'

'Will Magistrate Wright allow you the time to do that?'

'I could do it until I'm stopped,' Oakman replied with a wink.

Swift nodded. 'There is one other thing,' he said. 'Mickey Broad called the leader *Maréchal*. It is French for marshal, meaning the officer of the highest rank. So from now on, perhaps we should call him *Maréchal*.'

EIGHTEEN

Mother was busy curling my hair with the hot iron when Father knocked at my bedroom door.

'Doesn't your daughter look beautiful?' Mother said.

'Yes, she does indeed,' Father said with a proud smile. But it was fleeting.

'What is it, Father?' I asked. 'Surely you can't still mistrust Edward? He saved my life, remember?'

'Aye, that is true, Cully. It's just…' He trailed off.

'It's just what?' I pressed.

'Well, if I am right, then the *Maréchal* of the Brotherhood was at the dinner party we attended at Henry Lawton's house.'

'Yes?'

'Well, he may be a friend of Edward's father. So whatever you tell him might find its way back to the *Maréchal*.'

'You think he will betray us?'

'No … well, not knowingly, anyway. But the *Maréchal* is smart. In the guise of a friend, he may be finding out all about us.'

'Then it may already be a bit late. Mother has told Edward all about you and your work for the Home Department.'

'I fear so, Cully, but let's not make it worse. Don't tell him we have found the place of initiation — say that I have resigned my consultancy with the Home Department and that the Home Secretary dislikes me.'

'Very well,' I said reluctantly.

Edward arrived in his carriage at seven o'clock. He looked smart in his frockcoat and waistcoat. He bowed and kissed

Mother's hand.

Father shook his hand warmly. 'I am enormously obliged to you, sir.' His voice caught in his throat. 'You saved my daughter's life.' I could see that his emotions were genuine.

'It was no more than any other man would have done, sir,' Edward said modestly.

'No, I doubt that, sir. We owe you a great debt.'

Edward changed the subject. 'I read in the papers that the man who tried to kidnap Augusta was killed by the constables, and his accomplices hung or transported. That must be a relief to you all?'

'Yes, a relief, but also a great sadness; Constable Stoll was killed in the melee while saving my life.'

'As you say, a great sadness,' Edward said, then glanced down at his hand, still held tightly by Father.

Embarrassed, Father let go. 'You three have a good evening,' he said.

Edward's carriage took us to dinner, and we dined most elegantly. He was as attentive as he had been before, asking Mother all about her life in Egypt, a place that he hoped to visit himself one day. He asked Mother about Father's business with the Home Secretary, but she told him only what Father had said.

The carriage then took us onto Westminster Bridge Road in Lambeth to see Astley's Circus. We were entertained with bareback riding, rope-walking, juggling, acrobatics, and performing dogs, all with musical accompaniment. I was not a horsewoman, but the riding seemed terrific to me. The rider picked up handkerchiefs from the ground while cantering, then performed headstands on his saddle, and even rode astride two horses while playing a pipe. I put my hand to my mouth, as I was sure that he would fall.

The spectator galleries gave us an excellent view of the riders as they performed in a circular pit in front of the stage. I particularly liked the clowns, and the evening finished with fireworks and waterworks, to the delight of everybody present, who cheered Mr Astley roundly at the end of the show. I could not sleep when we returned home; my mind buzzed with wonder.

The cabbie came around and unfurled the hackney steps, and I stepped down onto Greek Street in front of Henry Isherwood's haberdashery. I was going to my music lesson and picking up Jane Isherwood on the way. Mother had insisted that I take a hackney for safety, and I was happy to do so in truth.

I asked the cabbie to wait while I went inside, where Jane was ready for me. Back in the carriage, we settled down and chatted as it took us to Miss Tancred's Musical Academy. As we passed the famous inn known as the Pillars of Hercules, something caught Jane's attention.

'Look,' she said, pointing out of the window. 'There — isn't that…?'

I looked out of her window to see a tall, striking woman with flowing black hair escaping from the back of her bonnet. She was wearing a black cape over an elegant dress and was alone, looking up and down the street.

'Yes, it's Mary Gayle,' I said, 'the woman who poisoned your mother.'

'What do you think she's up to, Cully?'

'I don't know, but I bet it is no good.'

As the hackney passed by, we sat back in our seats so that she wouldn't see us, but then I knocked on the roof and told the cabbie to stop. He pulled up, and we turned and looked out of the back window. Mary appeared agitated, as if she was late for an appointment. She flagged down a hackney, then set off in the opposite direction. I looked at Jane.

'Are you up for skipping our music lesson today?' I asked.

Jane's eyes widened. 'You mean we follow her? I'll get into trouble with Father.'

I looked back out of the window; the hackney was trotting away. There was little time. 'So will I,' I said.

'Yes,' she blurted, 'let's follow her.'

I called up to the cabbie to follow the hackney. He wheeled the horse around expertly, and we set off in pursuit. The hackney turned onto the Strand and followed its entire length. It continued along Fleet Street and then onto Thames Street, following the river.

'I wonder where she's going?' I mumbled, more to myself than Jane.

The hackney turned onto London Bridge, and we followed. I knew then that we were heading for Southwark.

'They're stopping by a coaching inn, Miss!' shouted the cabbie.

'Go past and then stop, please,' I called back up to him.

We came to a stop, and both Jane and I turned to look through the back window. We saw Mary Gayle climb out of the carriage, to be met by two men: one tall, one much shorter. They were talking earnestly. I strained to see the sign of the inn without revealing myself. It was the Tabard.

A knot tightened in my stomach.

'What street are we on, Cabbie?' I shouted up.

'This is Borough Street, Miss.'

I suddenly realised that what had been an impulse, an escapade, was now more serious — and more dangerous. I put my hand on Jane's arm.

'We have to be careful, Jane,' I said. 'Sit back; we mustn't be seen.' We lowered the blinds by our windows, then used our fingers to pull them back just enough to peep out.

I was unsure of what to do, but then I remembered what Father had taught me; *define a problem by logic and reason.* I needed to be rational in my thinking. But first, I had to establish the facts.

We were following Mary Gayle, I reasoned, a woman who earned her living by deception and was skilled in poisons. The value of that deception was absolute to her. If she was found out, everything would fall like a house of cards, and that made her dangerous. But what was she doing here at the Tabard?

Father had established that the inn was the place of initiation for the Brotherhood of the Parole. Was her presence here merely a coincidence? The Brotherhood operated on the rule of three. Mary had met up with two men; together, did that make them one of the secret squads? Was that a *valid inference*?

No, it is not enough on its own, I thought. *I need more facts.*

My thoughts were interrupted by Jane. 'They're going around the back of the inn, Cully,' she said.

I needed to make a decision, but was unsure if I had correctly thought it through. What *was* clear was that to follow them would put both Jane and I in danger, and that was *illogical.* Yet logic suggested that I needed to fill in the gaps; I needed more facts.

'Wait here for me, Jane,' I said and opened the carriage door. As I stepped down, she made to follow me.

'I'm coming too,' she said.

'No,' I said, 'you must stay here. If they come back, and I haven't returned, go and find a constable.'

She nodded and sat back reluctantly.

I walked quickly up the street, past the Tabard. At the corner, I looked down the side of the building, but couldn't see anyone. I took a deep breath and entered the curtilage. At the end, I peeped around towards the rear. Mary Gayle and her two companions were climbing the outside stairs to the room on the first floor of the extension. I had followed the facts, filled in the missing information. Mary Gayle *was* part of the Brotherhood.

I had started to back away when a commanding hand gripped my shoulder from behind. I froze.

There was a fierce whisper in my ear. 'What on earth are you doing here, Miss Swift?'

I glanced over my shoulder to see the large, round face and ginger side-whiskers of Constable Oakman. Relief coursed through my veins, and I exhaled the breath I had been holding.

'We have been following Mary Gayle,' I said in a low voice.

'We?'

'Yes, Jane Isherwood and myself.'

'Mary Gayle is the tall woman? You know her?'

'Aye, Father stopped her poisoning Jane's mother.'

'Look, you and your friend must leave this to me. It's too dangerous for you to be here.'

'He's here, isn't he? The *Maréchal?*'

'I believe so; he arrived about an hour ago and had the key for the padlock.'

'And that must be one of his secret squads that have just gone in.'

'Aye, it would seem so. Now you must go, Miss.'

I was happy to do just that. 'Promise me that you won't go in alone. It will be four against one.'

Oakman gave an uneasy glance towards the place of initiation, then looked back at me. He nodded.

'Come and report back to Father, tonight,' I said as I started back towards the hackney.

Jane and I went to our music lesson. Jane was insistent, as if somehow it lessened her disobedience to her father. I returned home to Temple Bar around lunchtime. Father was still in his clinic, but I caught him before he called in the next patient.

I told him all about Mary Gayle and the Tabard Inn, and that we should expect Constable Oakman to come and brief us about what he had found out. But he hadn't arrived by seven o'clock, when Mother served the evening meal. Mother was chatty, but Father and I were quiet.

'Is there something wrong with the food?' Mother asked, looking at us suspiciously as I pushed my meal around the plate.

'No, Iona,' said Father, and we both made an effort to eat more wholeheartedly, to hide our anxiety.

After dinner, Father and Grandpa took a glass of whisky and even offered one to Rafe.

'It's a bit early for your nightcap, isn't it?' said Mother.

'Aye, maybe,' said Father, looking at the mantle clock. It was five after eight.

'Well, maybe I'll join you,' Mother said.

Father stood and started to pour another glass when there was a loud rap on the door. We all shot a glance in its direction.

'Are we expecting visitors?' asked Mother.

Father didn't answer; he just hurried to the door. We heard him say, 'Ah, Constable Oakman, come in, won't you?' He was safe, and I was relieved.

Father gestured for him to sit. 'You'll take a glass of whisky with us?' he offered.

'Aye, that will be grand, sir.'

'Have you eaten, Constable?' asked Mother. 'I'll get you something,' she added when he shook his head.

Father leaned forward in his chair. 'What have you found out — Jacob, isn't it?'

Oakman nodded. 'I found a good vantage point from which to watch the building at the back of the Tabard Inn. I've spent the last few days there. Then, this morning, a man arrived, climbed the steps, and unlocked the padlock.'

'The *Maréchal*,' said Father. 'Sorry, Jacob, please carry on.'

Mother put a plate with pork pie and pickles in front of the constable.

'I had repaired the lock casing as best I could,' he said, taking a piece of pie. 'I hoped that it would fool the Brotherhood.'

'And did it?' I asked.

'No, I'm afraid not. After unlocking the padlock, I saw the *Maréchal* crouch down and examine it. I'm sure he realised that someone had been inside.'

'He knows that their hiding place is compromised, then,' said Father. 'He will have to find somewhere else.'

'About an hour later, two men — one very tall — and a woman arrived. They climbed the stairs and went straight in. That's when I spotted Miss Swift. I intercepted her and told her to leave it to me.'

'Thank you, Jacob. That was good advice,' said Father.

I could feel Mother's eyes on me and knew I was in trouble.

'Miss Swift told me that you know the identity of the woman.'

'Aye, she's Mary Gayle,' answered Father. 'An entertainer and known poisoner. I hadn't connected her with the Brotherhood, but now that I think about it, she has skills that the Brotherhood can use. This is a piece of good fortune; we know where we can find another member.'

'They were in there for some time,' continued the constable. 'I was beginning to wonder if they may have left through the inn. Then the tall man came out, and I followed him around to the street and saw him enter the inn by the front door. I followed him in and saw that he was talking to the innkeeper. I couldn't get close enough to hear what they were saying, though. He then went back around to the secret room.'

'Presumably to report back to the *Maréchal*,' said Father.

'Aye, that's what I thought. So I waited again, and then the two men and the woman left. I knew I needed to follow them, but I didn't know which one to take. So I decided I would wait for the *Maréchal*.'

'Good man, well done,' said Father enthusiastically.

'He came out about twenty minutes after the others.'

'What did he look like, Jacob?'

'He wore a black frockcoat under a cape, the collar turned up to obscure much of his face. His hair was neat but greying, though he was vigorous in his gait. He hurried down the stairs and walked away.'

'What age would you put him?'

'Mid-forties, maybe fifty, sir.'

'Go on.'

'Well, I followed him for a few minutes, and he turned onto Mint Street. There was a carriage waiting for him. He jumped in and took the reins, and it sped away. I ran back to Borough

Street for a hackney, but by the time I had found one, he was long gone.'

'Not to worry, Jacob. I know where to find Mary Gayle. We can track her down to the theatre where she gives her predictions.'

'I did go back to the Tabard Inn to speak to the innkeeper, though. He didn't want to tell me what they had discussed, but I got it out of him. He had told him all about our visit.'

Father sat back in his chair and steepled his fingers before his face. I knew what he was doing. He was applying his systematic investigation to the problem. He turned to me. 'What do you think, Cully?'

I was taken aback. 'Well, in all the years of the Brotherhood,' I said uncertainly, 'probably half a century, no one has got closer to them than we have. That makes them vulnerable. The *Maréchal* sent the tall man to question the innkeeper; that reveals the tall man's identity. He has never done that before either.'

'I agree, Cully. This man is a careful planner, but we are forcing him to behave reactively. Fortunately, we've had a piece of luck in tying Mary Gayle to the Brotherhood. If we had had the manpower today, *Maréchal* would be in custody. When the tall man reported back, he must have known that and fled. And therein lies our problem.'

'You think we are back in danger?'

Father nodded. 'I do.'

NINETEEN

Sir George Cornysh paced in a large semi-circle, the distance determined by his tether. He was as filthy as the warehouse prison that confined him. His imprisonment had now stretched to nearly three weeks, and he had worked out a daily routine to keep his body and mind active. He walked back and forth, reciting the Latin grammar he had learned during his schooldays — articles, nouns, plurals, prepositions, questions; he repeated them all.

He sat down for a rest and then started to list all the Latin phrases he knew. After a while, he began to feel drowsy, and he allowed himself to fall asleep. He was sleeping more and more, he realised, but that helped break the monotony of his endless days.

When he awoke, the light was fading, and he saw a shadowy figure drop from the high window and open the door from the inside. Lantern light appeared at the far end of the warehouse, and two figures emerged.

'Good evening, Sir George,' the tall man said congenially.

'A good evening to you, sir,' Sir George responded in the same cordial tone.

The tall man sat down before his prisoner, and the small man joined him. Sir George had realised that this man never spoke, except for some whispers in his partner's ear. Now he unfolded a linen parcel and handed it to Sir George. It was a pie and some cheese and bread for the following day, and a flask of small beer to wash it down. As he ate, Sir George made conversation with the tall man.

'The summer heat lingers,' he said between mouthfuls.

'Aye, it does.' The tall man looked around at the toilet area. 'And it doesn't help the stench in here, does it?'

Sir George had become immune to the smell. 'You could bring something to take it away in? Next time you come?' he asked hopefully.

The tall man shrugged his shoulders. Sir George was unsure what that meant. 'What day is it?' he asked.

'It's Thursday.'

Sir George pondered the information. He had believed that as each day went by, the chance of being discovered by government agents or the Bow Street Runners increased. But they had not found him.

'So, what happens now?'

The tall man looked at him. 'I have been given new instructions by my principal,' he said.

There was something about the man's tone that unnerved Sir George. 'New instructions?'

'A final demand will be sent to the Prime Minister. If he doesn't make a statement by midnight this Sunday, the twelfth of August, announcing that he has dropped the gagging legislation, then you will be executed on Monday.'

'Samuel Medina, the pugilist?' barked Father. We were taking lunch, boiled ham with gherkins.

'Yes, that's the man,' I said, glancing over the rim of my cup of hot chocolate. 'Constable Stoll promised to teach you how to use the cudgel. Now that he's gone…' The words died on my lips.

'Well, it's still a good idea, don't you think?' said Mother.

'I'm not sure that I have my vigour back yet.'

'Then the exercise will do you good.'

'I'll need an introduction,' he said. He was finding excuses.

'I've thought about that. Rafe knows him,' I said.

'How on earth does Rafe know him?'

'On his half-day, he goes to Mr Medina's academy to learn the art of self-defence. In fact, he's going tomorrow afternoon. You can go with him, after your clinic.'

I sliced a piece of ham and loaded it onto my fork with a slice of gherkin. Just as I put it in my mouth, there was a rap at the front door. I heard Betsy answer, then Mr Hazeldean entered the dining room.

'Sorry to disturb your lunch, Dr Swift.' He turned to Mother, realising that he had forgotten his manners. 'Mrs Swift.' Then he nodded at me politely.

'Is something wrong, Mr Hazeldean?' asked Father.

'Yes, sir, there is.' He paused, unsure.

'Sit, sir. Take a cup of tea with us and tell us all about it. Do you mind if we continue to eat while you talk?'

Hazeldean took a cup of tea from Mother, but just stirred it endlessly.

'You're causing *quite a stir*, Mr Hazeldean,' said Grandpa, grinning.

'Huh?' he said, then looked down at his cup. 'Oh, yes, very good,' he mumbled.

'What has happened?' Father asked.

'The Home Secretary received an ultimatum late last night.'

'You have something in writing from the Brotherhood? They have not done that before — may I see the letter?'

'No, Dr Swift, there was no note. At eleven o'clock there was a knock at Bradbrook's front door.'

'Sir Thomas's private secretary?'

'Aye, a tall man in a black cape asked the maid if he could speak to him. He was asked to step inside while she enquired. The family had gone to bed, and the maid was on her way too, so Bradbrook let her go and went to see who it was. When he got there, the man was holding a pistol and had pulled up a black kerchief to hide his face. At first, Bradbrook thought it was a robbery, but then the man outlined an ultimatum from the Brotherhood.'

'That tall man must be the *première* of a squad,' said Father.

'Aye, I believe so, and by going to Bradbrook's house, the organisation demonstrate once again that they can strike at the heart of the government. Bradbrook is badly shaken.'

Father nodded. 'What is their ultimatum?'

'It's Friday today,' he said. 'If Pitt doesn't announce by Sunday night that the gagging legislation is dropped, then Lord Cornysh will be executed on Monday.'

'Then Pitt's course of action is quite clear,' said Father. 'He must concede and drop the proposed legislation. Nobody wants it anyway.'

Hazeldean's shoulders slumped. 'You don't know Pitt and the Home Secretary, sir. Two Cabinet deaths have not derailed them, and I don't think a third will either. They are determined to fight sedition.'

'But it makes the Home Department look incompetent.'

'It does indeed, and the Home Secretary is spitting nails. I know you said you didn't want to work for us anymore, but I really would welcome your help.'

'Have your agents not been able to find where Cornysh is being held then?'

'No, we've searched London extensively but can find no sign of him.'

'What is it now, three weeks?'

'Aye, and now we have this deadline.'

'What about Stephen Windham, the lawyer — Charles Fox's advisor — any progress there?'

'Our agents have had him under surveillance for weeks, and one of our spies has infiltrated his office. You were right — he has dealings with many different people: government, aristocracy, lawyers, merchants, businessmen, tradesmen.'

'And have you discovered anything incriminating?'

Hazeldean gave a heavy sigh. 'No, nothing suspicious.'

'If he *is* the *Maréchal*,' Father said, using the title we'd discovered, 'then we know he is a clever and devious man. Has he visited the Tabard Inn in Southwark?'

Hazeldean's forehead creased into a frown. 'The Tabard Inn? Why would he go there?'

Father told him about our discovery, that the *Maréchal* had been seen there, along with another of the suspected secret squads. 'It is likely to have been there that the *Maréchal* gave orders to have Cornysh killed.'

'I've read our agent's reports, but I don't remember a visit to the Tabard. I'll check again when I get back to the office. I'll also have it watched to see if they come back.'

'They won't come back,' said Father. 'The *Maréchal* knows his hideaway is compromised.'

'It would seem *we* have discovered more than the whole of the Home Department,' I put in, '*and* we also think we have identified one of the members of the new squad.'

Hazeldean's eyes widened. 'Do you have a name, Miss Swift?'

'Yes, Mary Gayle. She's a theatre entertainer working as a mystic.'

'Ah yes, I seem to recall Constable Stoll telling me about her when he first suggested that you advise us on the poisonings of the Cabinet members.'

'Father's had dealings with her before. She's a poisoner — ideal for the Brotherhood.'

'I'll have her picked up and questioned.'

Father shook his head. 'It would be better to have her followed to see where she goes, who she contacts.'

'But we don't have time for that; they will kill Cornysh in three days.'

'Twenty-four hours' surveillance would still be my advice.'

'Perhaps,' Hazeldean murmured, then, 'are you getting close to identifying the leader?'

'Aye, that's the final layer, the seventh concentric circle, but I'm not there yet, Mr Hazeldean.'

'What's the difficulty, sir?'

'There is still one thing that I have to establish. A hole I have to fill in.'

'Sir?' enquired Hazeldean.

'This society was formed to support the Catholic cause. But this abduction, the poisonings, well, they don't seem to fit — on the face of it, it's about radicalism, about parliamentary reform, not Catholicism.'

'But we have enough evidence, surely, to confirm we have the right organisation?'

'Oh aye,' said Father, 'but not *why*.' He sighed heavily. Then I heard him click his tongue, and I knew something had fallen into place in his mind.

I leaned forward in my chair. 'What is it, Father?'

'Suppose,' he began, 'you're a prominent Catholic family when James II is overthrown in 1688, the so-called Glorious Revolution. You continue to support the Catholic cause, but you have to keep it secret. Yet as time goes on, the Protestant hold on the crown tightens. The head of this family is a shrewd man, and he understands that, for decades, the country has been overrun by government spies. He knows that messages can be intercepted, incriminating the conspirators. So he sets up a secret organisation, the Brotherhood of the Parole, with secret, independent groups skilled in espionage, surveillance, and murder. They are able to move information, money and weapons securely around the country, eliminating government spies that get too close.

'This society proves to be very effective; the groups are penetrated only once, but even then, the structure holds firm, and remains intact and functioning.

'But what he can't control is the rebellion itself; it fails — a devastating defeat at Culloden in 1745. Now suppose this man, the leader — the *Maréchal* — is safe and undiscovered, but he has helped finance the rebellion with his own money, gambling that the future King James III would reimburse him when he is crowned. But there never is a King James III, which leaves the *Maréchal* impoverished; perhaps he had even mortgaged his estate. He faces ruin. But this clever man realises that he still has one major asset.'

'The Brotherhood!' I exclaimed.

'Exactly, Cully. So, the society is not cast into the pit of history. It carries on, but it is now a criminal organisation, functioning under the noses of the constables, the magistrates, the government itself. So, if your father is gambling away your inheritance, the Brotherhood offers to eliminate him. If you are taken to court for unpaid debts, the Brotherhood will threaten your accuser so he will not pursue it. If money is owed, the Brotherhood will get it back for you, one way or another.'

'But surely that would mean they had to reveal themselves, to get their commissions?' said Hazeldean.

'That was the point I was missing before,' said Father. 'I had assumed that the client would come to them for their services. But revealing themselves, as you say, goes against the mode of operation that has protected them for half a century. But what if the Brotherhood went directly to the client to offer their services?'

'A whisper in the ear, you mean,' said Hazeldean. *'I know a man who can solve your problem.'*

'Aye, that sort of thing. The *Maréchal* will have many acquaintances who can identify, say, a profligate, and the person who will suffer if he carries on gambling. He allocates a squad, and the *première* will make contact with the client.'

'But if you are right, sir,' said Hazeldean incredulously, 'that would mean they have been murdering people for half a century.'

'Yes, it would, sir. It would indeed.'

TWENTY

Just before nine o'clock, Constable Oakman took his seat in the stalls of the Lincoln's Inn Fields Theatre in Portugal Street. At nine-thirty, Mary Gayle came onto the stage. For the first part of her act she promoted her remedies for various illnesses. If you suffered from the black vomit or the bloody flux, she had a tincture for it. If you had an abscess on the back of your neck or canker of the mouth, she could treat that as well. Dry bellyache, gripe, or lumbago, she had a cure. Augustus Swift had told Oakman that she was a fraud, that her remedies were available from any competent apothecary, but, nevertheless, she was impressive.

Mary then brought out her hen, which clucked about on a table until it laid an egg. She presented it to the audience, holding it high so that they could see that it had writing on it. She called a gentleman from the audience up onto the stage, and he read aloud the message — *Christ is coming*. It was a prediction of the end of times, she claimed, and a hushed murmur went round the audience.

She had a commanding presence and held the audience captive; even Oakman felt her aura. At the end, she offered to sell potions to ward off evil spirits and appointments for consultations. A number of people left their seats before the final acts in order to take advantage of this.

Oakman followed but chose a vantage point from where he could covertly observe her. She was making a good living, he thought. It was ten-thirty when she left the theatre and Oakman followed, his task helped by the moonlight of a clear night. Mary put the hen in a wicker basket and walked briskly north to High Holborn, then west onto Broad Street and then Oxford Street. Finally, she turned northwards again onto Wells Street. She stopped outside a house and looked both ways before she went in.

Oakman knew this was an expensive neighbourhood. The elegant terrace of recently built houses were constructed from stuccoed brick, with columns, decorative plaster mouldings, and paned sash windows.

He took up a position across the road, from where he could observe the house. A light appeared at the window as a lantern was lit, which was then carried upstairs. Mary drew the curtains.

It was the best part of two hours before the lantern light went out. Whatever Mary Gayle had been doing, it had been a lengthy task. After another two hours, there was only darkness. Oakman was tired and thirsty, and it was time to report back to Bow Street.

He headed south, across Oxford Street, then towards Covent Garden and nearby Bow Street. The Magistrates' Court offices were almost deserted, but he reported back to the duty constable.

'I'll go back, but I'll need relieving early in the morning,' Oakman said. 'I've been on duty fourteen hours as it is.'

The duty constable simply nodded. 'I'll get somebody to relieve you at eight o'clock, Constable Oakman,' he said, 'at — Wells Street, did you say?'

Oakman nodded. 'He'll need plain clothes,' he added.

'Right you are.'

Oakman looked around. 'Where is everybody?'

'There's a flap on. All the nightshift are out on the streets.'

'What are they doing?'

'The same as you: looking for the gang who've kidnapped Lord Cornysh. Magistrate Wright didn't leave until after midnight himself. The Home Secretary called him in this afternoon; the gang has threatened to kill his lordship on Monday. He's cancelled all leave; finding Cornysh is our only duty this weekend.'

Oakman's belly growled with hunger as he watched the house on Wells Street. He took out his pocket watch — seven-fifty. He would be relieved in ten minutes; he looked forward to a hearty breakfast, and then a long sleep beckoned.

He took a flask from his pocket, swigging the last of the small beer he had acquired on his visit to Bow Street during the night. As he swallowed, the front door opened and Mary Gayle stepped out.

He knew he had to follow her. She set off briskly, heading towards Oxford Street, and he let her get a head start before stepping onto the street. She was a good eighty yards in front of him, but she was distinctive in her black cape and bonnet.

When she reached Oxford Street, she turned left, heading eastwards. Oakman quickened his step. At the end of Oxford Street, she continued onto Broad Street. Then he saw a broad-shouldered man pass her, coming towards him; it was Constable Glenfield.

'Glenfield!' he hissed as the man reached him.

'Oakman?'

'Shh,' Oakman said, putting a finger to his lips. 'Are you my relief?'

'Aye,' the constable whispered. 'But I was supposed to relieve you at Wells Street.'

'I'm following the suspect. That's her ahead of us, the tall woman.'

'In the black cape?'

'Aye, come on, walk with me.'

Oakman briefed his colleague as they followed Mary Gayle from Broad Street onto High Holborn and then to Lincoln's Inn Fields. She stood in front of the theatre, looking tense, as if waiting for someone.

Oakman let out a breath of relief; he could now go to bed and sleep. 'You'll need to follow her. Make a record of her movements and everyone she meets,' he told Glenfield. As Oakman turned to go, he noticed a tall man walk up to Mary. She then handed him a small parcel. Oakman hesitated. He had seen this man before at the Tabard Inn; he had been with Mary Gayle that day. They were both members of the Brotherhood that Augustus Swift had told him about.

As he watched, the tall man put the parcel in a pocket and turned to go. Constable Oakman's shoulders fell; there was to be no sleep for him. They now had two members under surveillance, but they were separating, and both needed to be followed.

'You take the woman, Glenfield; I'll take the man.' Oakman took off in pursuit.

Covent Garden was no longer a gentrified neighbourhood. The bustling market had driven the gentry from their elegant houses to more genteel parts of the city. During the day, the fruit and vegetable market resounded with the business of buying and selling. Horses neighed, donkeys brayed, street vendors sang their wares, trying to get a sale. 'Fresh hot!' 'Penny a lot.' Flower girls, costermongers, peddlers, and nut and orange sellers all tried to outshout each other.

Constable Oakman weaved through the crowd in his pursuit of the tall man. His height helped; he could see his target over the heads of the crowd.

Suddenly Oakman slipped on a squashed damson. Reaching out, he grabbed at the stallholder to catch himself. The angry vendor almost fell too. 'Hey!' he shouted at Oakman, but there was no time to argue. Oakman scanned the market — the tall man had gained ground and was getting away. He pushed through the crowd, shouting when they were slow to move. The tall man emerged at the far end of the market and strode away, increasing the distance between them. As Oakman reached the far end, he looked around. The tall man must have taken one of the two side streets leading off Covent Garden — but which one? He made his choice and ran to the first street. When he turned the corner, there was no sign of him. He ran back to the other street — again, nothing.

'Damn it,' he muttered to himself. He had lost his suspect.

Constable Glenfield's eyes were fixed on the back of Mary Gayle's head. She walked briskly away from Lincoln's Inn Fields towards the Strand, then onto Fleet Street. She turned south onto Bridge Street then eastward onto Thames Street.

As she approached the Tower of London, she turned sharply northward onto Mark Lane. When he too reached the corner, Glenfield surveyed the road ahead of him. It was quieter; he would have to be more circumspect. He crossed to the other side of Mark Lane, putting some distance between himself and the woman. Suddenly, she turned onto Tooley Street.

'Damn, where's she going now?' he grunted. He ran to the corner and peered round. It was a short street, but he couldn't see Mary. Guardedly, he strolled up the street, surveying any possible escape routes. He approached a small church. He knew London like the back of his hand, and this was St Olave's.

It was old and stone-built, with a solitary tower, short and thick. Glenfield approached the arch to the churchyard; it was wreathed with grinning skulls. He entered the grounds and walked the few steps to the main church door.

Inside, the church was as modest as it was outside; it was almost square, with three bays separated by columns and a central aisle. The roof was a simple oak structure with bosses.

Glenfield looked down the central aisle, then left and right, but the church was empty. Dejectedly, he turned to leave, but thought he saw movement further down the church, beside a supporting column. Was there somebody behind it?

He stepped back into the shadows. Then a woman appeared from behind the pillar. It was Mary Gayle. Glenfield held his breath, but she didn't look in his direction. His spirits rose; she hadn't seen him. As she turned her back, he slipped away to the main door and back out into the churchyard.

He found a vantage point across Tooley Street and waited. It was the best part of an hour before Mary Gayle left. He followed her back westward, to Wells Street and the elegant townhouse. Returning to Bow Street, he made his report. He knew his information was valuable.

Constable Oakman was unsure what to do. He had lost the tall man and he was tired and hungry. He spun on his heel and headed towards Long Acre, his destination the magistrate's buildings on Bow Street, two streets away.

He reported to the duty constable that he had intercepted a second suspect, but had lost him in the Covent Garden bustle.

'I'll tell Magistrate Wright,' said the duty constable. 'He's briefing the Home Secretary every three hours for the rest of the weekend.'

Oakman turned to leave, then paused. 'Don't suppose you have anything to eat?' he asked hopefully.

His colleague sighed, then produced a linen-wrapped package from below his desk. 'This is my lunch,' he said, 'but I suppose you need it more than I do.'

Oakman opened the cloth to reveal an eel pie. He nodded a warm thanks and then took a bite from it.

Outside, he set off for home, eating the pie as he walked. He turned onto Hanover Place, adjacent to Covent Garden. He put the last piece of crust into his mouth and wiped his hands on his jacket. Then he came to an abrupt stop.

There was something, a thought — what was it? He turned and looked back at the people who had passed him by. There was a small, slender man dressed in a black frockcoat — now walking away from him. Oakman set off in pursuit.

He couldn't see the man's face as he followed, but he recognised his gait. He was almost certain it was the same small man he had seen at the Tabard Inn. He did not have long to speculate; the man turned into a house on the corner of Hanover Place and Long Acre. It was a lodging house; it had been an elegant residence of the gentry at one time, but Oakman knew what it was now. It was a brothel.

He walked past, but as he did so he saw the front door open. And he saw who had opened the door — it was the tall man he had lost in the market.

'You little beauty,' he murmured to himself. But now he had to return to Bow Street to report this vital information. His bed would have to wait a little while longer.

TWENTY-ONE

Samuel Medina's academy was a swarm of activity. Swift watched as Medina finished up a sparring session with one of his assistants by way of a tutorial. Most of the students were young gentlemen, keen to learn the art of self-defence, yet he knew that professional pugilists were men of the streets.

Medina himself was something of an enigma. He stood at five foot eight, he estimated, was powerfully built, and weighed no more than eleven and a half stone. How could this man possibly be the champion boxer of all England? But as Swift watched, the reason became apparent; Medina was immensely skilled and highly agile. He knew how to strike, parry, and move in and out of range without being hit.

Swift had read about Medina in the newspapers. He knew that pugilism was considered a noble sport, and that all classes were interested in it, from the street ruffian right up to the aristocracy, and even the Prince of Wales himself. Medina had tapped into the belief that it was honourable for an Englishman to strip to the waist and fight for what he believed in, and the country admired him for it.

Not all those present were students; many of the audience had come just to watch Medina train — he was a national champion. Swift watched him spar with Rafe, teaching him to block and parry, to take his opponents' punches on the arms, to protect his face and his chin, to pull in his elbows to cover his midriff. Rafe was a good student.

Afterwards, Rafe introduced him to Medina. The pugilist must have seen the surprised look on Swift's face when he heard his accent.

'Yes, sir, I am an educated man,' said Medina. 'I am also a poet and a published author. I see I am not what you expected.' Swift nodded politely. 'But enough about me. Rafe tells me you were assaulted recently?'

'Aye, sir,' Swift replied, 'but I fear it was much more than that. I believe it was an attempt on my life.'

'Someone with a grudge against you, sir?'

'I believe so, and they will go through my family to get at me if necessary.'

'How many men attacked you?'

'There were three, all young, fit men.'

'Then you were exceedingly lucky, sir. By what manner did you escape?'

'I was disabled by several blows to the solar plexus. A constable saved me. He used his truncheon to disable them long enough for us to escape.'

The pugilist raised a surprised eyebrow. 'Three against one — you should hire him as your bodyguard.'

'Constable Stoll is dead, sir. He died protecting me.' Swift's voice caught in his throat.

'I am sorry to hear that, sir.'

'It was his idea that I learn to protect myself.'

'I agree with your friend, sir.' Medina then called for pads to be placed on Swift's wrists, elbows and knees, and did likewise himself. He handed Swift a cudgel. 'This will be best for you, Dr Swift. Most gentlemen favour a long cudgel, which doubles as a walking staff, but the short cudgel works better as a weapon. It can also be concealed beneath your frock coat when you take to the streets. Feel its weight, its manoeuvrability. It will take time, but you will learn to handle it with consummate skill. At close quarters, this cudgel will even outperform a sword.'

'How long will it take to become proficient, sir?'

'Do you have any fencing skills, Dr Swift?'

'No, sir, I am a physician by profession.'

'Then it will take some weeks of regular practice.'

'That is time I don't have; the danger I face is imminent. I fear that I have wasted your time, sir.'

'No practice is wasted, Dr Swift. I cannot make you into an expert overnight, but I can teach you some tricks. If you are made of courage rather than bluster, I can make you more formidable.'

Swift nodded his agreement, and the lesson began. First, Medina taught him that the cudgel was an excellent defensive weapon, especially in a confined space. Then he taught him how to wield it quickly, with both a forehand and backhand motion, mainly aimed at wrists and knees. He showed him it could expeditiously disable one man, giving time to take out a second.

'The ruffian will use it with merely a clubbing motion, bringing it down from above, like this,' said Medina, demonstrating, 'but that requires a wide arc and will make him vulnerable. So you must use a smaller arc than your opponent, then you will strike first.'

Swift showed himself to be a quick learner, but exhaustion soon took him.

'We will leave it there for today, Dr Swift.'

'Thank you, Mr Medina. I fear I have not recovered my full vitality yet.'

'Please, call me Samuel, and there is no need to apologise. Should you need to defend yourself, you only need do so for long enough to escape. And please take that cudgel as a gift from me.'

Before Swift could thank him, a shout came from the entrance to the academy.

'Dr Swift! Dr Swift!'

Swift turned and saw Constable Oakman and Cully hurrying towards him.

'What is it, Constable? Is it my family?'

'No, they are fine, Dr Swift, but I have important information for you.'

'How did you know where to find me?'

'I went to your house at Temple Bar. Miss Cully told us where to find you.'

'Come and sit down. You look like you have been twelve rounds with Mr Medina here.'

Oakman acknowledged the pugilist, who found him a chair while he caught his breath.

'Last night I followed Mary Gayle from the theatre to her home. This morning she met the tall man, and I followed him. He lives at the corner of Hanover Place and Long Acre with his partner, the small man. The property is known to us; it's just around the corner from Bow Street.'

'Then we know the lairs of all three of them. Keep them under observation, and perhaps they will lead you to where Lord Cornysh is being held.'

'There's something else. While I followed the tall man, Constable Glenfield followed Mary Gayle. She led him to a church — Saint Olave's.'

'Where's that?'

'It's near the Tower, on Tooley Street. It's old — must have survived the Great Fire. I wondered if it was the place you have been looking for, where the marshal leaves his instructions. What did you call it — the key symbol?'

183

'It could very well be so, Jacob. I'll go and take a look with Rafe; you go and get some sleep.'

Medina took Swift's arm. 'I'm sure I can find you a bodyguard if you can give me a few hours.'

'Thank you, Samuel, that is kind, but that's time I don't have.'

Father gave one of his long sighs as we approached the medieval church of St Olave. That meant he was annoyed with me. Once again, I had persuaded him to let me come along.

He slowed as we neared, taking in the stone building before us. 'What do you think? Cully, Rafe?' he asked.

This was my chance to make good on my promise to be useful. 'Well, it's very modest, and there's nothing to distinguish it. But perhaps that was the intention — somewhere unremarkable.'

Father nodded meditatively. Rafe pointed to the arch to the churchyard. 'Look over there, Dr Swift.'

Father frowned as he walked towards it. 'Why decorate the entrance to a church with skulls?'

'Grinning at the church congregation as they enter,' mused Rafe with a grin himself.

'Do you think the name is relevant, Father? Who was Saint Olave?'

'Maybe,' he said. 'We need to know more.'

'I'll go and find the rectory, Father,' I said. 'The parish priest will know all about the church's history.'

'You will stay here with me, Cully; that was our deal.' He turned to Rafe. 'Can you go and see if you can find the priest? Ask him if he can spare us a few minutes — and be careful.'

Rafe rushed off, and I grasped my opening. 'A church as old as this must have been built as a Catholic church, Father.'

'Indeed, Cully,' he said. 'I'm sure that's relevant — but we need more than that to confirm it is the site of the key symbol.'

'We need to go in then, Father,' I said and set off. Surprisingly, he was content to follow me.

We walked through the skulled archway and up to the church door. It opened smoothly. Father followed me in, and we looked around the space.

There was little of significance at first glance. Then I spotted something.

'There.' I pointed to the roof. 'The boss where the rib vaults intersect. It's intricately carved, but it's not an animal or a bird — it's a triquetra knot. This is the place, Father. We've found it.'

'Well done, Cully. It would seem so,' said Father. 'But we still need to know why — why *this* church?'

'Does that matter if we've found it?'

'What have I taught you, Cully?'

'That limited knowledge may not lead to truth.'

'And what does the logic of Aristotle tell us?'

'To consider every possibility, Father.'

'Why?'

'So that we can make a *valid inference*.'

'Which is what, in our case?'

'The identity of the *Maréchal*.'

'Excellent, Cully,' he said.

I twitched a smile. I was still the apprentice.

Rafe arrived with the priest and introduced him as the Reverend John Noble. Father explained that he was working for the Home Department and asked what he could tell us about the church. Reverend Noble needed no further invitation.

'Saint Olave's is a thirteenth-century church,' he began, 'dedicated to Norway's patron saint, King Olaf, who fought alongside the Anglo-Saxon King Aethelred against the Danes in the Battle of London Bridge in 1014. The church is built on the site of that battle.'

'Has there been a prominent family who have acted as benefactors over the years?' asked Father.

'Yes, the Cely family. They bequeathed money to build the steeple and the altar. The Penn family were also benefactors. During the Great Fire of London, William Penn ordered his men to blow up the houses surrounding the church to create a fire break.'

'Anyone else, Reverend Noble?'

'Oh, yes, the diarist Samuel Pepys. His house and the Navy Office were both nearby on Seething Lane. He had a gallery built on the church's south wall and added an outside stairway from the Navy Office to the church so that he could attend without getting wet in the rain. He is buried here along with his wife, Elizabeth.'

'Is it still here — the outside stairway, I mean?' asked Father.

'Yes, but the Navy Office moved to Somerset House some years ago.'

I heard Father click his tongue and knew what he had worked out. The *Maréchal* could come and go without being observed.

'Is the stairway still used?'

Reverend Noble hesitated. 'I should have a key, but I haven't, and I don't know who has. I have my suspicions that somebody uses it, though.'

'Why do you say that, Reverend?' Father pressed.

Noble gave a self-conscious chuckle. 'This is going to sound odd, but it's the hymn board, sir. It contains the numbers from the church's hymnal. But sometimes there are surprising numbers there, numbers that I haven't put up.'

'Are any other notable people associated with the church?' I asked.

'Queen Elizabeth held a thanksgiving service here on the day of her release from the Tower of London.'

I turned this information over in my mind. Queen Elizabeth had returned the country to Protestantism after the Catholic rule of her sister, Queen Mary. We were looking for a Catholic connection, not a Protestant one.

'Anybody else?' I pressed.

'Sir Francis Walsingham lived across the street from here. The church records show his family's baptisms, marriages and funerals.'

I shot a look at Father; I knew we were thinking along the same lines. Walsingham had been Queen Elizabeth's spymaster. Though he was Protestant, Walsingham had been the man to follow if you wanted to set up a spying organisation. Walsingham had been driven by Protestant fervour to oppose a Catholic resurgence, had been in dread of it, determined that the atrocities committed by Queen Mary against Protestants should never again occur in England. So he had set up a network of informers to spy and cryptographers to decipher letters to track down the conspirators.

'Any other benefactors, Reverend Noble? The Windham family or the Harrisbrooke family, for example?' asked Father.

I knew why Father had asked this. He was trying to establish a connection to Stephen Windham, or his cousin Charles Harrisbrooke, the Earl of Penistone, who had both been at Henry Lawton's dinner party and were both prominent Catholics. The priest shook his head, however.

I drew Noble's attention to the boss in the roof. 'What do you know about that, sir?'

'Oh, the triquetra knot. It's a representation of the Trinity.'

'Is there another one in the church?'

'Aye, there is. It's on one of the two columns at the front that separates the church's three bays. The hymn board sits above it.'

'Could you show us, please, Reverend?' Father asked eagerly.

At the front of the church the priest pointed to another triquetra knot and the hymn board above it. 'Are those your hymn numbers?' asked Father.

'No, sir, they're not,' answered Reverend Noble.

Father nodded and wrote down the numbers in his pocketbook.

On the way home, I was elated. 'That's the penultimate layer, isn't it?' I asked. 'We know how they operate now.'

Father grunted his agreement.

'And you know what those numbers mean, don't you, Father?'

'Aye, I think so, Cully. The top line indicates to which squad the *Maréchal* is sending his message. The next line specifies the date, and the third the coordinates. I suspect they are grid references on a map. He's directing them to their next meeting, or the location of their next assignment.'

'Then we have them, Dr Swift,' said Rafe excitedly.

'I think we have enough to close down their organisation, and hopefully catch the group holding Lord Cornysh before they kill him.'

TWENTY-TWO

Father had sent word ahead that he had new information for the Home Secretary about the Brotherhood, so that when we arrived at the Home Department we were expected. Father and I were shown into Mr Hazeldean's office. Samson Wright, the Bow Street magistrate, and Mr Bradbrook, Sir Thomas's secretary, were already waiting.

'Are your plans in place?' Father asked as he sat down.

'Aye,' said Hazeldean. 'Magistrate Wright and I are coordinating the operation. We have operatives watching Mary Gayle's house and the lodging house at the corner of Hanover Place and Long Acre. As soon as they lead us to where Lord Cornysh is being held, we will step in and arrest them.'

'Cornysh's life is our number one priority,' said Samson Wright. 'All my men have been briefed to stay hidden; the last thing we want to do is to alert the kidnappers.'

'Your note said you had new information, Dr Swift?' said Hazeldean. I noticed that he was grim-faced and in need of a shave.

'I have,' said Father. 'I believe I have found the site of the Brotherhood's key symbol.'

Hazeldean, Wright and Bradbrook all leaned forward in anticipation, and Father told them about St Olave's Church and what we had found. Father opened his notebook at the relevant page, showing the sequence of numbers.

Bradbrook was the first to enquire. 'Have you deciphered these numbers, Dr Swift? We have cryptographers working at the Home Department that can help you.'

'Thank you, but I think I have it, sir. There are three lines of numbers; the first line, number forty-five, is, I believe, the squad number. So it is intended for squad fifteen, forty-five divided by three.'

'Surely they do not have that many squads?' asked Hazeldean in astonishment.

'No, I doubt it. But the Brotherhood has been in operation for over fifty years. Personnel change, of course, and I think it merely reflects that the *Maréchal* has not used the same squad number twice.'

Father let this sink in before continuing. 'I think the second line is the date.' He pointed to the number — 8835.

Samson Wright's brow knitted in confusion. 'I don't follow your reasoning, sir.'

'King George III came to the throne on the twenty-fifth of October 1760. So this is the thirty-fifth year of his reign.'

'Ah,' said Hazeldean, 'so 8835 means the eighth day of August in the thirty-fifth year of his reign — that was last week.'

'That's right,' said Father.

'And the third line? 33238?'

'I believe this refers to a location. Do you have a map available?'

Hazeldean called for a clerk, who returned with Carrington Bowles' map of London. Father opened it on Hazeldean's desk and pointed.

'You will see that the grid is notated in letters across the top and numbers down the side. So if we simply substitute the first number three for the equivalent letter, then the first coordinate becomes C3.2. So the location is somewhere down this line.' Father ran a finger from the top to the bottom of the map to illustrate. 'The next coordinate will be 3.8 across this line.' He ran a finger across the map. 'And the two coordinates intersect here.'

Hazeldean leaned in to see where Father was pointing. 'Borough Street! That's where the Tabard Inn is. You're right, Swift.'

'I had hoped that the location would lead us to where Lord Cornysh is being held, but the date doesn't fit. The eighth of August was last Wednesday, when Cully spied them at the Tabard. So this set of numbers is the call-up for that meeting.' Father looked at Hazeldean. 'Would it be acceptable to you gentlemen if Cully and I stayed here until your men report back, and you get confirmation that Lord Cornysh is free?'

The Home Department man looked intently at Father. 'I would be obliged if you would, sir.'

At eight o'clock that evening, the small man emerged from the lodging house at the corner of Hanover Place and Long Acre and turned right onto Long Acre. Then, at Drury Lane, he turned left, heading north-east towards High Holborn. An agent of the Home Department watched him leave. On adjacent streets, north, south, east and west, operatives were posted, ready to pursue.

Twenty-four minutes later, the tall man emerged. He too turned right onto Long Acre, but at Drury Lane he turned right. The street was busy, being so close to Covent Garden, and he walked approximately a hundred yards before stopping.

The small man continued northward, turning right at High Holborn. He followed the road until he arrived at the Cittie of Yorke public house, going round the back to the stables and harnessing a horse to a carriage. He climbed up to the driver's seat and clicked his horse forward, trotting back down Drury Lane, where he stopped to pick up his companion, the tall man. The agents had anticipated the use of a carriage and had planned for it. Signals were sent up the roads and relayed back to their own transport, a commandeered hackney. Two agents set off in pursuit. By the time they passed the pickup point on Drury Lane, they had some catching up to do.

They followed onto Fleet Street and then onto Thames Street, and had caught up as they crossed south of the river by London Bridge. The carriage turned left down Rotherhithe Street after the bridge. They were soon in a place with few houses, and the light was beginning to fail. The agents had to decide whether to remain close and risk detection, or pull back. They chose the latter. They tracked slowly but determinedly down Rotherhithe Street, past wharves and warehouses, all in darkness.

By the time they reached the end of the street, they had lost their quarry. In the darkness, one of the agents cursed.

Hazeldean's office smelt of candlewax and coffee. The five of us sat around his desk, the candlelight dancing over our weary faces. We were all tired of waiting. Bradbrook played with a loose thread on his sleeve. The magistrate snorted snuff from the back of his hand and then wiped away the excess from his nostrils with a well-used kerchief. Father's eyelids were half-closed as he fought off sleep.

I became aware of something happening outside in the corridor. All eyes shot to the door as a Bow Street constable was shown in. I could tell immediately that he was not bringing good news.

'Report, Constable,' Samson Wright snapped.

The man shuffled from foot to foot, then reported the sequence of events. When he had finished, a deflated silence fell.

'This is not all bad news, gentlemen,' said Father. 'I think the constables' decision to fall back in their pursuit was the correct one. Lord Cornysh would probably be dead by now if they had been spotted.'

'But we now only have a day to save his life,' protested Hazeldean. 'And we still don't know where he is.'

The constable coughed. 'One of our constables was set down near the warehouses on Rotherhithe Street, while we took the carriage back towards London Bridge. The man left behind heard a carriage leaving in the darkness, but he wasn't close enough to identify exactly which warehouse it was departing from.'

'So you think that Lord Cornysh is being kept in some warehouse on Rotherhithe Street?' asked the magistrate.

'I do, sir,' answered the constable.

'So we can narrow it down to a section of this road. How much, do you think?'

'Perhaps a quarter-mile, sir, maybe less.'

'Then we have a full day to come up with a rescue plan,' said Father. 'But for now, I think the best thing we can do is to go home and get some sleep.'

I looked around the room at the candlelit faces. Those darkened expressions had begun to ease.

Troisième pulled his reins to the right and the hackney he was driving turned onto London Bridge. His only passenger was his *première*, the tall man. Two Home Department agents were trailing them, but when they crossed the bridge, they drove straight on to Borough Street, their job done. *Troisième* turned left onto Rotherhithe Street.

They headed into the night, past deserted wharves, leaving the bustle of the city behind. From his position atop the hackney, *Troisième* looked back nervously, but saw no one. He relaxed. Their hiding place had been carefully chosen and undiscovered for almost three weeks; why should it be discovered now?

He turned into Mr Williamson's wharf, reassured by this dark, deserted place, without people or houses. He drove past the abandoned lead pipe factory and pulled up by the warehouse. The horse snorted and jumped from hoof to hoof until it settled.

Sir George's eyes opened. Tonight he was alert, fear driving his vigilance. It was Sunday the twelfth of August; he knew the significance of that. He saw the shadow of the small man come in through the upper window then drop to the ground. He heard him shoot the bolts that locked the warehouse from the inside and open the door, a flicker of lantern light appearing in the gloom. It came towards him, followed by two shadowy figures. As they emerged from the darkness, he could see their black frockcoats, the black kerchiefs covering the lower halves of their faces.

He stood to face his two captors.

'Has Pitt relented?' he asked. 'Has he said that he'll drop the gagging legislation?'

'No, sir; there has been no response from Pitt or his government.'

'Damn the man,' Cornysh cursed. He slumped back to the ground.

The small man put a linen cloth containing an eel pie on his lap. Sir George took a bite, but it tasted like sawdust in his mouth. He pushed the parcel to one side.

'Will it be tonight?' he murmured.

'No, sir,' the tall man replied. 'The Prime Minister still has until midnight to announce he is dropping the legislation.'

'Tomorrow evening then?'

The tall man nodded.

The following night, two constables crept cautiously onto the darkness of Mr Williamson's wharf. They had been posted nearest this point on Rotherhithe Street, and had seen the hackney pull off the road. They approached the warehouse cautiously. Another constable followed them a few moments later. Magistrate Wright had planned the rescue by posting men at intervals of fifty yards. Their brief was that as the hackney passed any one of them, they would walk in pursuit of it down Rotherhithe Street so that they would meet up at the place of incarceration to form a collective force. Those posted further down the street would be called by messenger, it being too dark for signals. Whistles would only alert the kidnappers.

The first constable had a decision to make as the hackney passed him. Should he wait for his colleagues to arrive, or should the three of them go in now before the suspects had the opportunity to kill Sir George? They only had truncheons; four pistols had been pulled from Bow Street, but fate had determined that the armed constables were placed elsewhere. Should they wait for an armed colleague to arrive?

He looked up at the sky; it was a cloudy night, and there was little moonlight.

'Shall we go in?' he whispered into the gloom.

There was a grunt from one of his colleagues, which was enough for him to make his decision.

He whispered for one man to go to the left, while he and the other constable would go to the right. They crept forward in the darkness, passing the hackney. Carefully, the first constable drew closer and heard the horse paw the dirt ground with its front leg. 'Shh, boy,' he whispered as he heard it swishing its tail from side to side. He reached out to stroke its neck. 'There, there, boy.' With relief, he felt it calm beneath his hand.

TWENTY-THREE

Inside the warehouse, three pairs of eyes darted round at the sound of the agitated horse. The tall man looked at the small man, jerking his head in the direction of the noise. His colleague ran to the wall, expertly scaled it, slipped out of the high window and scampered onto the roof. From this vantage point he could view the yard below.

Looking down, he watched as three dark shadows met up at the side door to the warehouse. They were trying to find a way in, he realised.

He saw them whispering, then one reached out for the doorknob.

But the door didn't open. He put his shoulder to the door, but it still didn't give way. He stepped back and thrust his heel at the middle of the door, where the locking mechanism should have been — but it merely flexed.

'The damn thing's held at the top and the bottom,' he cursed, knowing he'd given away their presence.

He stepped back and waved his two colleagues forward. They met it together, their shoulders simultaneously thudding against the wood, and there was a splintering sound. They repeated the manoeuvre, and then the door gave way at the top, the bolt housing ripping free. Now they kicked heavy boots at the bottom until that broke loose, and they tumbled inside as the door swung open.

'That's far enough, Constables,' said a tall man, as the constables drew their truncheons. He was standing behind a dishevelled figure, holding a pistol to his head.

'Lord Cornysh?' asked the first constable. The man nodded, and the constable looked back at the tall captor. 'There's no escape; we have the warehouse surrounded,' he said. *Well, we soon will have*, he thought to himself.

'I am sure you have,' said the man, 'but surrounded or not, I have Sir George here at gunpoint. It's a stand-off. If anything, I believe *I* have the upper hand.'

For a moment, the three constables stood there, unsure what to do. Then another constable arrived at the broken door. It was Constable Oakman.

'I see *Première* here has got the jump on you, boys,' said Oakman to the constables as he drew his pistol. He saw the tall man's eyes widen. 'Constable Oakman at your service, and yes, *Première*, I know who you are. You can take off your kerchief; I have seen you before at the Tabard. Where is your colleague?'

Suddenly, the tall man wrapped his arm around Sir George's throat, looked up to the roof and yelled, '*Troisième*! Bring the hackney to the side door.'

Outside, they heard the sound of movement as the small man climbed down the outside wall and sprinted across the yard, followed by the horses' hooves as the hackney was wheeled round to the side door.

'Ready!' yelled the small man.

This was immediately followed by another voice shouting, 'Hands up, mister! I have a gun!'

Oakman smiled to himself. It was Constable Glenfield.

Another constable entered the warehouse and reported to Oakman. 'We have ten constables surrounding the building, sir, and we have that small fella at pistol point.'

'Send messengers up the road to call the rest of our men here,' directed Oakman. He turned back to the tall man. 'There is no escape, *Première*. It's time to give up. Please give me your pistol.'

The tall man looked coolly at Constable Oakman. 'Do you play chess, Constable?'

'A little,' replied Oakman. Abel Stoll had taught him.

'Well, this looks like a stalemate to me.'

'I think I have your king under threat, have I not?' said Oakman.

'But the king's escape is still possible.'

'How so, *Première*?'

'Why, simply with my pistol.' He raised it in the air to emphasise its importance. 'And I still have a man active outside.'

'I think you'll find that we have taken him.'

'I think not. Now, this is how the game is going to play out. I am going to slowly back out of the warehouse, taking Lord Cornysh with me. If you attempt to apprehend me, I will put a ball in his head. If you fire at me, I will still have time to get off my shot, and again, the result will be the same, the death of our good lord here.'

He tightened his arm around his captive's throat and started to back away, dragging Sir George with him. He stopped by the broken door.

'Tell your men outside to back away, Constable,' he barked.

'Let them out!' Oakman shouted.

He continued to back away, dragging Sir George the short distance to the hackney. Oakman followed and watched as the tall man used his foot to unfurl the steps. But he had no free hand to open the door.

'Don't you think it's time to give up, *Première*?' asked Oakman.

'*Troisième*, come down here and open the door for me!' he shouted up.

The small man made to move, but Constable Glenfield cocked his pistol and pointed it closer to his head. 'You're going nowhere.'

The tall man took a deep breath. 'Constable Oakman,' he said, 'perhaps it's time for an exchange of pieces?'

'But you have nothing to exchange, sir.'

'I have Sir George here,' he said, putting his pistol against the Cabinet minister's temple.

'Do you take me for a fool, *Première*?'

'On the contrary, I see you are holding a powerful position. That's why I am offering an exchange.'

'And how exactly will this exchange work?'

'I let Lord Cornysh go, and you let us drive away.'

'That requires a lot of trust, *Première*.'

'Aye, it does, Constable Oakman, on both sides. And remember, I have nothing to lose by putting a ball in his head. If I'm captured, I will hang — whether he lives or dies.'

Oakman recognised the truth in what he said. Saving Lord Cornysh's life was his prime objective.

'Very well,' he said.

'Tell your men to move away from the hackney, and not to shoot as we drive away.'

Oakman gave the command. 'And when will you release Lord Cornysh?'

'As soon as we are moving. I will need my hands free to hold on, as you can see.'

Oakman nodded his agreement, and the tall man again shouted up to the small man, 'Come down here and open the carriage door for me!'

The small man did so, unfurling the steps at the same time. Then he clambered back up to the box seat at the front of the carriage and took the reins.

The tall man climbed onto the steps. 'Go!' he shouted up. 'Now!'

'There's a constable on the shaft holding a pistol on me!' the small man shouted back.

'He stays,' said Oakman forcefully.

The tall man considered for a few seconds, then shouted, 'Just go!'

The small man flicked the reins. 'Trot on!' he said, and the horse moved forward.

'Faster!' shouted his accomplice.

The small man cracked the whip, and the horse responded. The carriage lurched forward violently. The tall man released his hold on Sir George in order to grab hold of the door housing, and in so doing, the lord fell from the carriage.

At the same time, Constable Glenfield, up top, was forced to let go. He jumped back as hard as he could to avoid the rear wheel. Hitting the ground, he raised his pistol at the swerving carriage and released a shot at the driver. The powder in the pan flared, and the pistol went off with a crack.

He saw the shot hit the small man on the back of his left shoulder.

Oakman rushed to help Lord Cornysh, who lay prostrate on the floor. Others ran forward to try and stop the carriage from escaping, but it had a few yards' head start, and that was increasing with every second.

'Are you all right, my lord?' asked Oakman.

'Yes, I think so.' Cornysh looked up at Oakman. 'You and your men saved my life.'

'You're welcome, my lord,' said Oakman. 'But there's someone else you should thank, sir.'

At the top of Borough Street, two agents waited in the commandeered hackney. They saw what they had been waiting for; another hackney emerged from the darkness of Rotherhithe Street and swung wildly onto London Bridge. They set off in pursuit.

TWENTY-FOUR

I was assisting Father in his clinic when we heard a loud banging on the front door. We looked up at each other, but we knew Betsy would answer it. A few moments later, she peeped around the clinic door.

'It's Mr Hazeldean from the Home Department,' she said. 'I think it's urgent. He has a constable with him and an injured man. He doesn't look at all well.'

When we entered the drawing room, Hazeldean and Constable Glenfield were standing, exhaustion etched on their faces. For the first time since we had met him, the stock at Hazeldean's collar was not freshly laundered. A third man was slumped on the divan. Mother was fussing over him, as he appeared to be bleeding.

Father crouched down beside him and lifted his eyelids, noting that he was on the cusp of unconsciousness. 'Cully,' he said, 'prepare the clinic for surgery, and get Rafe to help us.'

Together, Rafe and Constable Glenfield carried the injured man through to the clinic and laid him out on the bench. I cut away the injured man's frockcoat and linen shirt, and Rafe helped me clean the wound to his shoulder. Father then assessed it.

'What do you think, Rafe?' he asked our apprentice.

'Er — the ball entered the back of the shoulder, but there's no exit wound, sir,' he answered.

'Which means what?'

'The ball is still in there.'

'Do you agree, Cully?'

I hesitated. I did not want to embarrass Rafe. 'No, Father,' I said hesitantly.

'Why not?'

'The size of the wound. If the ball had made such an impact, it would have destroyed the shoulder muscle mass, the clavicle bone, but the damage seems to be only at the point of the entry. It's extensive, but not deep.'

'Good,' said Father, then turned again to Rafe. 'I think Cully is right, Rafe. So what do you think has happened?'

Rafe looked thoughtful. 'If he was turning to his right when he was shot, the ball may have entered his shoulder obliquely.'

'Which means?' Father prompted.

'The entry and exit would be at the same place?'

'Let's see if you are right,' Father said, taking up his forceps. He put a wedge of material in the patient's mouth for him to bite on, then probed into the wound. The injured man didn't respond, suggesting he was unconscious. Father removed fragments of material that the ball had forced into the wound and held them up.

'No ball, just these,' he said. 'The entry and exit wounds are *not* at the same place, Rafe, but very close, here and here, just four inches apart —' he pointed with the forceps — 'and this material fragment has torn open the flesh between them.'

'So we just have a flesh wound?' asked Rafe.

'Yes, if rather a nasty one.'

'So, he'll survive?' asked Hazeldean from the doorway.

'I would have been confident had I seen him earlier. But he has remained unconscious throughout my examination. He must have lost a lot of blood. When was he shot?' He looked up at the observers.

'Just before midnight last night,' Constable Glenfield replied.

'You'd better tell me all about it — but let me suture this wound first.'

Back in the drawing room, Mother served us some tea. Hazeldean told us about the rescue of Lord Cornysh, how his life had been exchanged for the escape of his captives.

'But their freedom was short-lived,' said Hazeldean. 'We had two agents in a hackney on Borough Street. They followed them back to Covent Garden, to the house on the corner of Hanover Place and Long Acre. Two more constables were waiting there. They watched the small man leap down from the front of the carriage, but this time his agility failed him. He was off-balance as he hit the floor, and he fell backwards onto his wounded shoulder. The tall man jumped out of the carriage to help him. The constables took advantage of the situation and challenged them, one with a pistol drawn, the other with his truncheon. Then our hackney arrived with the two agents, but the tall man drew his pistol from beneath his frockcoat and discharged it. He missed, but the constable didn't; the ball hit him in the neck. He died at the scene.'

'What did you find out from the small man — *Troisième*?'

'He hasn't told us anything.'

'And Mary Gayle?' I interrupted.

'She was picked up as soon as we found out Lord Cornysh was safe.'

'And has *she* told you anything?' asked Father. 'Has she admitted to being *Deuxième*?'

Hazeldean shook his head. 'Not even that.'

'I take it the Home Secretary is pleased?'

'Aye, he's ecstatic. His blessed gagging legislation can now go ahead.'

'Is he sure of that? We still don't know the identity of the *Maréchal*.'

'But the Brotherhood is severely damaged — surely he is no longer a threat?'

'It is, Mr Hazeldean, but it can be repaired; the *Maréchal* still has other squads he can call on.'

'But we now know how he contacts them — through the hymn board at Saint Olave's. It'll take time to set up an alternative.'

'You are assuming he knows we have discovered his method. Let's start by supposing the opposite,' said Father. 'You need to keep the church under surveillance. You also need a locksmith to get you into that covered gallery he uses.'

On Father's insistence, Hazeldean left *Troisième* in our care. When he regained consciousness, Father sat beside his cot and tried to gently question him. The man was amazed that Father knew so much about the Brotherhood, but his loyalty to his secret pecialized was still strong, despite his weakness. He wouldn't say anything.

He had lost a lot of blood, and I encouraged him to take liquids and a little food to build up his strength. I cleaned the wound regularly and applied one of Father's special poultices he had brought back from Egypt. However, within a day, he started to display signs of a fever, and we feared blood poisoning was setting in. But he was a young and energetic man, and Father thought he could fight it off.

By Wednesday, the fever was worse. I listened to his heart; it raced intermittently and at times, he became delirious. When he started to have trouble breathing, we both feared the worst. Father sat him up to help clear his airways, and he seemed grateful for that.

'Am I going to die?' he asked Father, his voice little more than a whisper.

'I fear so,' Father answered honestly. 'Your lungs are filling up with fluid. It will probably infect your kidneys before long.'

He seemed resigned. 'It will save me from the hangman.'

'Won't you tell me your name? The name of your *première*?' asked Father. 'His family needs to know of his death. Surely you can at least tell me that?'

'No, the *Maréchal* will take care of that. As it no longer matters, my name is ... Isaac Giles.' Then he drifted into an unconsciousness from which he never again awoke.

For the rest of the day, Father was withdrawn. After he had completed his clinic, he sat staring out of the window, in his hand a note he had received from Hazeldean.

I sat next to him. 'What is it, Father?' I asked.

He handed me the note, and I read it. Father had suggested that the Home Department place St Olave's Church under surveillance and have a locksmith gain access to the covered gallery used by the *Maréchal* as a secret entrance. Hazeldean explained in his note that he'd sent agents down to the church immediately, but they were already too late. The *Maréchal* had already been there, and there were new instructions on the hymn board — the date being Sunday the nineteenth of August at ten o'clock in the evening. Hazeldean saw it as encouraging; they could mount an operation to catch the *Maréchal*.

'But this is good news, Father, surely? Why does it concern you so?'

'Good news? Well, possibly,' he replied. 'But it also indicates that he is rebuilding. I suspect that he has already established a new place for the initiations.'

We both sat in silence for some minutes. Then I asked, 'How old do you think the *Maréchal* is, Father?'

I saw him considering this, then he clicked his tongue.

'Well done, Cully,' he exclaimed, sitting up. 'Do you remember that I made a *valid inference* that the Brotherhood was set up during the second Jacobite uprising but was defeated along with Bonny Prince Charlie in 1745?'

'Aye, Father; your logic was that the *Maréchal* changed it into a criminal organisation to rebuild his finances and pay off his debts.'

'Exactly, but that was fifty years ago. That would make him an old man — well into his eighties, if not older. Yet what little we know of him suggests he's a vigorous man. So what does logic tell us, Cully?'

'That he is not the original *Maréchal.*'

'And?'

'And that there must be some succession in place. If the *Maréchal* were to die unexpectedly, the successor must be ready to take over. They must know how the organisation works. And this succession must be built into its structure.'

Father nodded. 'I think *our Maréchal* is possibly the second *Maréchal*, but more likely the third.'

Logically, that seemed right to me, but I was unsure if it took us any further. 'Does that enable you to break through the final concentric circle? To reveal *Maréchal*'s identity?'

'Not on its own, Cully, no, but let's see if we can extract a *valid inference* from what we know already.'

'Well,' I mused, 'we know that the *Maréchal* guards his identity closely, even from his squads. So that hidden identity — well, it must be of three people. *Maréchal* past, present and future.'

'Aye, I think so too. Let's stick to the French: *Maréchal Passé*, *Maréchal Actuel*, and *Maréchal Futur*.'

'So at any time, his successor has to be in place,' I said.

'Aye, and what is the best way to recruit his successor?'

At first I was unsure, then the answer came to me. 'Family, Father,' I said. 'The loyalty of family will overlay the allegiance to the Brotherhood.'

'Good, Cully. I think we are looking at one family line.'

'But does that inference break through the final circle? If it does, I can't see it.'

'No, it doesn't, but remember, we have to consider all the facts. It gets us a lot closer, though.'

'You think it's Stephen Windham, don't you?'

'Aye, I do, but if it *is* him, then he's covered his tracks exceptionally well. The Home Department has had him under surveillance, yet they have not tracked him to the Tabard or Saint Olave's.'

'We don't know much about Windham at all, do we?'

'Hazeldean tells us he has no title of his own, but he is a cousin of the Earl of Penistone, Charles Harrisbrooke. He's married and has two daughters. One of them could be in line to take over, but it's more likely he has a man in mind.'

'So we are looking at the Windham or Harrisbrooke lines?'

'Yes, I think so.'

'So, what next? Is there something we can do?'

'I think another visit to the Royal Society might prove useful.'

TWENTY-FIVE

The next day I accompanied Father on the short walk from Temple Bar to Somerset House. Father had sent a note ahead, and he received a reply via the same errand boy. Owen Jardine had agreed to see us at two o'clock.

We were taken to the North Wing and shown into Jardine's office. Mr Jardine stood as we entered and held out his hand to Father, who then introduced me.

'Thank you for agreeing to see me at such short notice, Mr Jardine,' Father said.

He gestured for us to sit. 'I've read of the rescue of Lord Cornysh in the newspaper. Were his kidnappers part of the secret organisation that you were seeking? If I remember correctly, you were pursuing a theory it had been set up on mathematical lines, in particular the number three.'

'That's correct, sir.'

'And did your theory prove to be correct?'

'Aye, I believe so. They have remained hidden for over fifty years and are structured around autonomous squads of three people.'

'Remarkable,' said Jardine. 'Mathematics structuring a secret organisation.'

Before Father could respond, there was a rap at the door. 'Come in,' Jardine called.

The door opened and an older man entered, carrying a substantial ledger.

'Your note, Dr Swift,' said Jardine, 'includes an unusual request — permission to see our record of Royal Society

Fellows. This is Mr Shone, our secretary. He is responsible for the ledger.'

'Good afternoon, sir.' Shone paused. 'And lady,' he added, bowing his head at me. 'Our records go back to 1660, when we were founded. Given the letter of introduction from the Home Secretary, we are prepared to open them up for your inspection.'

'Obliged, sir.'

'I understand that you are investigating a secret organisation. That's coincidental — before the establishment of the Royal Society, there was a predecessor run by Robert Boyle and other natural philosophers. It was known as the Invisible College because of its secrecy.'

I looked at Father and saw his brows rise at that information. If the *Maréchal* was an early member, the Invisible College could have inspired him.

Shone continued. 'For what date are we looking? And what name?'

'From the second Jacobite uprising. Shall we say from 1740? The family names of Windham and Harrisbrooke.'

Shone opened the extensive ledger on the desk. He turned the pages to 1740 and ran his finger down the list of Fellows. When he came to the bottom of the page, he shook his head and then turned over. As the pages turned, Father's expression grew darker. His theory was at stake.

Shone looked up at Father. 'I'm up to 1770. Shall I continue?'

'Please,' said Father, his voice little more than a murmur.

Shone continued. Page after page was completed until he came right up to date. Finally, he looked up at Father. 'I'm afraid it seems that we have never had a Fellow of either name, sir.'

Father sat back in his chair with a sigh.

'If,' I began, 'the person we are looking for had a title, could he be registered under that title?'

'Aye, that's quite possible.' Shone leaned forward. 'Shall I start again?'

'If you would be so kind,' I answered, then added, 'Would it be possible for me to examine the ledger? I might also recognise a name.'

Shone looked at Jardine for confirmation, who nodded. Shone turned back the pages to 1740, then swung the ledger around so that I could see it. I started to run my finger down the page; Father stood and looked over my shoulder as I did so.

On the third page, I came upon an entry for a Baron Syston. I looked at Shone. 'Syston?'

'We've had several Lord Systons over the years, but I think the family name is Stourton.'

Father took out his notebook and made a note. The next name was Baron Ompton. Shone could not remember the family name, but remembered that he was a mathematician. When I had finished, we had a list of seven baronets and one earl. Neither Father nor I recognised any other names, however.

At dinner that night, Rafe was keen to know all that we had discovered, and I took it upon myself to tell him all that had happened. Our visit was a dead end, it seemed, and it had affected Father's mood. I knew that, in his mind, he was re-examining all the facts. He thought he had reasoned a *valid inference*, but somewhere along the way, he must have taken a wrong turn.

Grandpa, Rafe and I tossed around various possibilities, but we didn't reach any conclusions.

'The trouble with mathematicians,' said Grandpa, 'is that they will stop at *nothing* to avoid negative numbers.' He wheezed that laugh of his.

'Is this all we are going to talk about all night?' asked Mother. We were to dine with Edward Lawton the following evening, and she had gowns and hairstyles on her mind. I allowed her to change the subject.

The following day we had already started lunch — cold meats and pickles, accompanied by small beer — when Rafe arrived with a large leatherbound book under his arm. I could see that he was eager to tell us something. He opened his mouth to speak, but Mother cut across him.

'Whatever it is, Rafe, it can wait until we have finished eating.'

'My apologies, Mrs Swift,' he said with a blush.

As Betsy removed our plates, Father looked at Rafe. 'What's that book you have there?' he asked.

'I've been to the booksellers this morning, Dr Swift. It's called *The New Peerage; or, Ancient and Present State of the Nobility of England, Scotland, and Ireland*. A Mr Debrett edits it. I've been establishing the family names of those baronets you listed yesterday.'

'And what have you found?'

'Not much at first, but something is interesting about Baron Ompton.' Rafe opened the book. 'Born 1707, died 1765. It lists one of his interests as philosophy, in particular mathematics.'

'What is the family name?' asked Father, his interest tweaked.

'The family name is Royd; Baron Ompton was Evelyn Royd.'

Father shook his head. It was not a name he recognised.

'I know, Dr Swift,' said Rafe, reading his expression, 'but as I read further, I noticed he had a son, Robert Royd, 1730 to 1760. So he died five years before his father. He left a son, Jonathon Royd, born in 1758. So it was Evelyn Royd's grandson, Jonathon, who inherited the title after Evelyn died in 1765.'

'But that would make him only seven at the time,' I said. Then a thought struck me. 'You mean that if Robert Royd was *Maréchal Futur* when he died, Evelyn Royd, as *Maréchal Actuel*, had to find someone else to be his successor?'

'Exactly,' said Rafe. 'Now, Evelyn Royd had a sister, Margaret, 1704 to 1780. She married in 1724 and had several children, the eldest being a son, Benjamin, 1724 to 1786. So he was forty-one when Evelyn died.'

'The dates certainly fit, Rafe,' said Father, 'but we need more than that.'

'I agree, sir,' Rafe replied. 'But I think I have it. Margaret married a William *Lawton*. If I am right, Benjamin Lawton became *Maréchal Futur* in 1760 and *Maréchal Actuel* in 1765. And listen to this, Benjamin's son is Henry Lawton.'

Father suddenly sat forward in his chair. 'And Henry Lawton became *Maréchal Futur* at the same time, in 1765. So it's been Henry Lawton all along — he is the *Maréchal*.'

I stared at Father in disbelief. 'But that would mean that Edward is the *current Maréchal Futur*. I am dining with him tonight.'

I turned to Mother, but she seemed less concerned. 'You're jumping to conclusions, all of you,' she said. 'Think back to our visit to Vauxhall Gardens, when that awful man tried to abduct you, Cully — what did you call him?'

'He was a *deuxième*, Mother.'

'That's right, and who was it that rescued you?'

'It was Edward, Mother,' I said.

'There,' said Mother. 'Now, he wouldn't have rescued you if he had known his father had given orders to kidnap you, would he?'

'I suppose not.' My heartbeat started to return to normal.

'Nevertheless,' said Father, 'I don't think you should go to dinner with Edward Lawton tonight.'

'Nonsense,' said Mother. 'He is an honourable young man and we are only going to dinner.'

'Iona,' said Father, 'until we know for sure, Cully should be cautious.'

'But I will be there to protect her. What can possibly happen at a restaurant?'

I looked around the room; Rafe was staring at me, and Grandpa looked uneasy.

'You are always concerned about my welfare, Father,' I said, 'and I love you for that. But we have now broken through that final concentric circle, have we not? We now know who the *Maréchal* is, and the constables will arrest them shortly. I don't believe that Edward is involved, but I need to find that out for myself.'

My words were positive, but my stomach churned. If Edward *were* involved, my world would be turned upside down.

I smiled at Mother. 'We'll go to dinner with Edward tonight, as planned — but we need to be on our guard.'

After lunch, Swift sat contemplatively in his clinic, looking out of the window. There was a knock on his door. Rafe entered and sat down beside him.

'Dr Swift,' he said tentatively, 'I couldn't fail to notice at lunch — well, you were uneasy about Cully and Mrs Swift dining with Edward Lawton tonight.' He paused. 'You still are, I can see.'

'Aye, Rafe, that's very perceptive of you,' Swift answered.

'Well, sir, I have a proposal. Will you allow me to follow them? Tonight, I mean?'

'I had thought of doing so myself, Rafe, but…'

'He would recognise you. But Edward Lawton has never met me.'

'Has he not? What's your plan?'

'I'll hire a hackney carriage and be waiting down the street. I'll follow Edward's carriage when they leave, then wait outside the restaurant and see if any accomplices are skulking about.'

'It might be better to go inside after that, Rafe. See if he signals to anybody in the restaurant.'

'Aye, that's true. I'll put on my best frockcoat, sit as close as I dare.'

'You're a good lad, Rafe. It would be reassuring if you could do that.'

TWENTY-SIX

Edward arrived punctually at seven o'clock as arranged. His carriage took us to Wigmore Street, where he had made a reservation at Parmentier's restaurant. It was an establishment that pecialized in confectionery. The choice was perfect, everything inspired by Parisian finesse.

We ate dried fruits soaked in brandy, then *pâte de guimauve*, which was a marshmallow confection. Edward chose a sweet white wine to accompany the delights, which, it transpired, was quite potent and Mother quickly became quite tipsy. I was on my guard, however, but when he ordered papillotes — small candies wrapped in paper containing jokes or mottoes — I joined in with the merriment. We finished with ice cream covered in orange syrup.

It was clear that Edward was a natural conversationalist, educated, well-read, and naturally witty. He seemed to have such an open personality; there was no hint of perfidy. As the evening progressed, my anxieties about him started to wane. Perhaps Mother was right after all; Edward couldn't possibly be involved in murder and kidnapping.

Edward caught me staring at him and smiled. 'Now, you must tell me all about your father's brilliant methods of detection. How on earth did he manage to track down those rogues that kidnapped poor old Cornysh?'

I was suddenly on my guard once more. I glanced over his shoulder as I considered what to tell him. A man was sitting alone in the far corner of the restaurant, looking at me. It was Rafe. He had followed us. He had positioned himself behind Edward so as not to draw attention to himself.

My first reaction was annoyance; I knew Father was behind this, but then I knew he was only trying to protect me. Somehow, Rafe's presence seemed to encourage me. I turned back to Edward.

'You overestimate Father's involvement, Edward,' I said as flippantly as I could. 'It was all down to the constables and the Home Department's agents.'

He smiled and turned to Mother. 'Is your daughter making light of Dr Swift's involvement? I heard that he was the mastermind behind the rescue.'

'Oh yes,' said Mother, sensing no danger in the question. 'The Home Secretary should thank him for the rescue.'

Edward nodded. 'I don't know Dr Swift that well, but his intellect is without question.'

'It will be good to return to normal, though, will it not, Mother?' I cut in, before Mother could say any more. 'It feels as though the house has been under siege for weeks.'

Edward turned back to me with a gentle smile. 'Were you at the Home Department when the rescue took place, Augusta?'

It was at that moment that I knew Edward was *Maréchal Futur*. There was now no doubt in my mind that he was using Mother and me as a source of inside information. I wondered how much else I had failed to notice, how much else I had missed that was right in front of me.

I had succumbed to Edward's lies. It wasn't me he wanted; it was the information I could provide. My heart sank — he had never had feelings for me.

The rest of the evening became stilted. I answered Edward's questions with evasion, and his interest in me waned as he realised he was getting nowhere. Before long, he called for the carriage to take us home.

*

Father was anxiously waiting when we returned. I hadn't even knocked on the door when it opened. Edward was impeccably mannered in his farewells, kissing Mother's hand and bowing to Father. Father's worried appearance at the door had provided Edward with at least one piece of information. He must have now known that Father suspected him.

Once inside, Mother let go of her anger before anybody could speak. 'Well, that will probably be the last we see of Edward Lawton. Cully, what on earth was the matter with you? You hardly said a word; it was verging on rudeness.'

'Hang the man,' Father said venomously.

Mother's mouth gaped. 'Gus, don't you want Cully to find a good marriage?'

'I want her to be safe, Iona.'

'I told you we were perfectly safe dining with Edward tonight, and I was right; you are making too much of your suspicions.'

Tears welled in my eyes as I turned to Father. 'I am convinced now that Edward is *Maréchal Futur*,' I said quietly.

Mother's eyes widened. 'What is this nonsense, Cully?'

'Can't you see, Mother? He doesn't want me; he only wanted what I knew. We were a source of information to him, that's all.'

Mother didn't want to let go of her dream of a good marriage for me. She looked at me, then Grandpa, and finally at Father. Then her shoulders dropped and her tears flowed unrestrained.

We did not retire to bed; instead, we waited for Rafe to return. We expected him to be a few minutes behind us, but nearly two hours passed. Father poured a large whisky for himself and Grandpa, and Mother asked for one too. We were becoming a little anxious when Rafe turned up shortly after midnight.

Father gestured for him to sit down and poured him a whisky. He took too large a gulp, and coughed after swallowing. We gathered around him, and he knew he had to give his account.

'I followed Edward's carriage in my hired hackney to the Parmentier restaurant. I looked around Wigmore Street, but there didn't seem to be any suspicious characters hanging around. I asked the hackney driver to wait, then went into the restaurant to observe. Edward never once looked around; all his attention was given to Cully or Mrs Swift. I am confident he didn't have an accomplice in the restaurant either. When I followed him back here and saw that you were safe, I decided it might be good to take advantage of the cabbie, and I followed again, just to see where Edward went.' He looked at us all before continuing. 'He went to the family home in the West End, but after he went in, his carriage remained outside, as did his driver.'

'You think he was reporting back to his father?' Father asked.

'I do,' said Rafe. 'He left again after only a few minutes; this time he went to a very high-class establishment in the West End. It is a members-only club, so I couldn't go in. I wasn't sure what to do, so I asked the driver if he knew the place. It turned out that he knew it well; he said it was famous. It's known as Hooks' Club. I could see a large, powerfully built man on the front door. The driver told me that the footmen inside were likewise heavily muscled, yet the attendants dressed in the most elegant livery — gold braid, epaulettes, white stockings, white gloves, even powdered white wigs.'

'And what goes on there?' I asked.

Rafe coloured. 'Well, it's a gentleman's club, but the most notorious one in London.'

'So young gentlemen go to drink and dine there?'

Rafe paused. 'Yes, they can dine well — but they also offer women. Its main draw, though, is gambling. High stakes, and the management guarantees that any debt will be collected. A gentleman doesn't renege on a wager at Hooks.'

Mother sighed. 'So it's a brothel and a gambling den.' She had finally let go of her illusions regarding Edward.

'So you were right all along, Father,' I said. 'Edward is no different from the others.'

'In some ways, no,' said Father. 'These places are for gentlemanly pursuits, but that doesn't mean gentility. On the contrary, it means gambling, the curse of the elite; it means a place where restraint is left at the door. But there is more to Edward than that. He is *Maréchal Futur* — he has a purpose in life. We must not underestimate him.'

'So why did he rescue me from Jack Broad — the *deuxième* — in Vauxhall Gardens?'

'I don't think he did, Cully. I believe he overrode *Deuxième*'s orders. Brownlow, the *première*, and Mickey Broad, the *troisième*, were in custody, and this man set out to kidnap you as a bargaining tactic. But in doing so, he was interfering with Edward's mission — to use you and Iona as a source of information. So what looked like a tussle to you, what looked like Edward trying to overpower him, was probably Edward giving him new orders.'

I knew Father was probably right. It didn't help, though, and I found it difficult to sleep that night.

Father sent Hazeldean a note first thing the following morning, asking for a meeting. He received a reply, and we arrived at

Hazeldean's office at the Home Department at eleven-thirty. He offered us tea, and I could see that he was once again elegantly turned out, cleanshaven with a freshly laundered stock at his throat.

'We weren't sure whether you would be working today, Mr Hazeldean,' I said as I sipped my tea, 'it being Saturday.'

'Oh, yes, I am coordinating tomorrow's operation at Saint Olave's with Magistrate Wright.'

'You may not need to go ahead with that, sir,' said Father. 'I think I have broken through the final concentric circle.'

Hazeldean put down his cup of tea. 'You have identified the *Maréchal*, Dr Swift?'

'I believe so.' Father proceeded to tell him about our visit to the Royal Society and the connection we had found to a previous Fellow. 'I believe it to be Henry Lawton.'

'The Whig politician?'

'The very same. You may recall that I told you I suspected that the *Maréchal* was at Lawton's dinner party, but I am surprised that it is Lawton himself.'

Hazeldean sat back in his chair. 'Are you sure it's him?'

'Logic would suggest so, sir. It's a valid inference derived from all the facts before us.'

'But that won't count as evidence in court; we need more, Swift.'

'Like being caught in the act, you mean?' I asked.

'Exactly.'

Father's forehead furrowed. 'He directs operations from a distance, behind a mask. Be careful with this man, sir. You mustn't let him slip through your fingers.'

Hazeldean nodded. 'We'll never get a better chance than tomorrow. He has called a meeting, so he must turn up in person.'

'That's true,' agreed Father. 'And he's never been more vulnerable.'

'Aye, sir. When my agents arrived at the church previously, they were already too late. The *Maréchal* had already been, and there were new instructions to meet him tomorrow night — Sunday the nineteenth of August at ten o'clock.'

'And what were the three lines of numbers?' asked Father.

'The first line was 2736394248.'

'But that can't be right,' said Father. 'It should be only two numbers.'

'I know,' said Hazeldean. 'The second line was 1983522, meaning the nineteenth of August this year. Twenty-two indicates ten o'clock in the evening.'

Father nodded. 'And the third line?'

'42529.'

'The map reference. Which refers to where?'

'Saint Olave's Church itself.'

'Saint Olave's?' Father raised a surprised eyebrow. 'That must mean he believes St Olave's is safe.'

'Aye, but why would such a cautious man believe that? He's always played his cards close to his chest before.'

'He's assessed the risks but simply got it wrong,' I said. 'He's shown his hand, but he doesn't know he's done it.'

'Aye, I think you're right, Cully. But his hand has been forced, don't forget. Perhaps he's been trying to find a new place of initiation, but it's not yet ready, not yet functional.'

'Maybe,' I said, 'but whatever the reason, if all goes right tomorrow night, the Brotherhood will be smashed wide open. But what do you think that first line of numbers means, Mr Hazeldean?'

'We've been puzzling over that for a week,' Hazeldean replied. 'We wonder if he is calling several squads at the same time.'

'That would be a departure from his normal way of working. His squads are not supposed to know the identity of each other.' Father suddenly clicked his tongue, signifying that something had fallen into place. 'Nevertheless, I think you are right, Mr Hazeldean. If we break those numbers down into pairs, then twenty-seven divided by three gives us squad number nine, and thirty-six divided by three gives us squad twelve. The rest give us squads thirteen, fourteen and sixteen.'

'It's risky, Father, and he's not normally a risk-taker,' I said.

'No, he's not, Cully. But I think we've forced him into taking a risk. He is putting his squads at risk, but I doubt he'll put himself at risk. He believes he has an escape route.'

'Samuel Pepys's gallery, the covered stairway?'

'Aye,' said Father, then looked at Hazeldean. 'You need to have that exit covered as well, sir.'

'Noted,' said Hazeldean. 'I will be there tomorrow night to coordinate the operation, and Magistrate Wright will be with me. It would be good if you were also there.'

I looked at Father. 'It's too dangerous, Father,' I said. 'These men are dangerous, probably armed, and there could be a lot of them. Five squads and the *Maréchal* would make sixteen. Remember, you are an advisor on poisoning, not a constable. And besides, Mother will kill you herself if you agree.'

Father turned back to Hazeldean and just shrugged his shoulders.

TWENTY-SEVEN

By six o'clock on Sunday evening, Hazeldean and Magistrate Wright had men positioned all along Mark Lane and Tooley Street leading from the Tower of London to St Olave's Church. Constable Glenfield and two other constables were positioned at the rear of the church on Seething Lane, monitoring Pepys's gallery built on the church's south wall and in particular the outside stairway from the Royal Navy offices.

At nine o'clock a carriage drew up. Constable Glenfield, from his vantage point, watched as Henry Lawton stepped down, swung a cape around his shoulders and pulled up the expansive hood. From his pocket he took a half-mask and slipped it on.

Lawton strode onto Seething Lane. When he arrived at the Royal Navy offices, he paused at the entrance to the covered stairway that led to St Olave's Church.

Glenfield watched him take a key from his waistcoat pocket and let himself into the passage. The constable looked at his pocket watch; it was five after nine. The *Maréchal* was early. Another constable joined Glenfield. He sent him around to the front of the church to update Hazeldean.

Hazeldean and Magistrate Wight were stationed inside a house at the corner of Mark Street and Tooley Street. The constable sent by Glenfield made his report. Hazeldean's pulse quickened; the operation was starting sooner than he'd expected. He sent word out to his constables and agents. They must follow their instructions, be on their guard.

*

At nine-twenty, the *Maréchal* emerged from the front of St Olave's Church, looking around the grounds. He walked through the skull-decorated entrance arch, onto the street, then up and down, cautiously taking all in before him. Constable Oakman spied him from his vantage spot, but he had chosen well; he was well hidden. He hoped his colleagues had done the same. He watched the *Maréchal* return to the skull-decorated archway, look down the street one more time, then disappear back into the church.

At nine-fifty, a solitary man arrived. The man looked about him as if he sensed danger. Two minutes later, a second man arrived. Three more men came in quick succession. At nine fifty-seven, Oakman sent a message to Hazeldean saying that only five squad members had arrived.

In his command centre, Hazeldean knew what that meant. They were not now expecting the full squads — fifteen men; only the *premières* had been called. He had planned for fifteen, but five — six with the *Maréchal* — would make it so much easier. A sense of relief washed over him.

Inside the church, the *Maréchal* had chosen the pulpit to address his men. It was a position of leadership and reinforced his superiority. As each man entered, he directed them to a different part of the small church, so they all sat on a separate pew.

'You are all *premières*,' his voice boomed out. 'Your identities are not known to each other. That been for your protection. Keep it that way; do not attempt to speak to each other after this meeting.' He paused as he looked at them. 'You may wonder why I have called you here together.' He saw heads nodding. 'The initiation room at the Tabard Inn has been compromised. The Home Department agents have discovered it. It is no longer our safe place.'

There were some mumbled words, but the *Maréchal* continued, 'I have been searching for a replacement, which has not been easy. The Tabard has been our safe place for over fifty years. I have found such a place, however. When next you are called, you will go to the Middle Temple off Fleet Street. It is where gentlemen studying the law have their lodgings, and the occupancy changes regularly. I have taken a lease on a top-floor room. One of your comrade squads are builders by trade, and I have instructed them to provide a private entrance from the outside so that you do not have to enter the building itself. This is currently under construction.'

The messenger sought out Constable Oakman and handed him a note from Hazeldean. He scanned it. It contained just one word: *Triquetra*. It was the Brotherhood's symbol and the codeword giving the order to enter the church.

Oakman waved his men forward. Sixteen men assembled before him, ten constables and six Home Department agents. They knew their roles; Oakman was to lead the constables inside the church and flush out the suspects. Once outside, they would be arrested by the agents. It was Hazeldean's strategy to avoid, as far as possible, bloodshed inside the church.

'Are there any questions?' the *Maréchal* asked.

A hand rose. 'You say that the initiation room is compromised. Are *we* compromised? Are *we* in danger?'

'Two of our squads have been eliminated by the Home Department. But the strength of the Brotherhood is in our

227

structure. Each squad is independent, unknown to the others. The Brotherhood is secure. You are all secure.'

The *Maréchal's* words were said with conviction, but this security was to vanish immediately.

Constable Oakman and the ten Bow Street Runners burst into the nave. 'Armed constables!' he yelled.

The *premières* were briefly stunned, then panic took them. Two immediately drew pistols; the other three drew cudgels from beneath their frockcoats. The constables fanned out down each side of the nave, then a pistol was discharged. The distinctive smell of gunpowder filled the little church and a constable fell.

Then another pistol shot rang out, this time from a constable, and the *première* who had fired was himself hit. He fell, letting out a shrill cry.

Gunpowder smoke filled the nave, and the *Maréchal* jumped down the pulpit steps and crossed the short distance to Pepys's gallery. Oakman saw him, raised his pistol, and aimed. The shot rang out, but the ball smashed into the door housing, splintering the wood. Now it was up to Glenfield to catch him.

Through the smoke, the four remaining *premières* watched their colleague fall. Collectively, they made for the main church door left deliberately open, emerging into the night. There they were met by the six Home Department officers, their pistols drawn and cocked. The Bow Street constables followed them out to complete the pincer movement. The *premières* came to a sudden halt. They were hunters, predators, but now they came to realise they were the prey.

An armed *première* looked over his shoulder at Oakman. He saw the hopelessness of his predicament, dropped his pistol, and held up his hands. The others followed his lead, throwing down their cudgels. Surrender was their only option.

Constable Glenfield stood with his pistol drawn at the old Royal Navy offices, the exit point from Pepys's covered tunnel. His two colleagues stood shoulder to shoulder with him, their truncheons raised. They all braced as they heard footsteps running up the stairs.

'That's far enough —' Glenfield began as the *Maréchal* burst out, but seeing the constables, the *Maréchal* aimed a double-barrelled pistol and fired without breaking step. The three constables hit the ground as the ball whizzed past them. As the *Maréchal* took flight up Seething Lane, they took off after him.

'Be careful, lads — he's still got a shot left!' Glenfield yelled as they gave chase.

The *Maréchal* sprinted to the end of Seething Lane, his cape billowing behind him. He had opened a gap as he turned the corner onto the adjacent street, and was briefly out of sight. When his pursuers rounded the corner, the constables found his cape discarded on the ground. Looking up the street, they saw the *Maréchal* come to an abrupt halt beside his carriage; his pair of horses had been unhitched. A quick-thinking constable had disabled his escape route.

The *Maréchal* turned and raised his pistol as the three constables slowed before him. He was out of breath, however, his aim unsteady, the pistol shaking in his hand.

'One of you, hitch up my team,' he demanded.

'Not going to happen, Mr Lawton,' said Glenfield.

The *Maréchal*'s jaw dropped.

'Oh yes, Mr Lawton, we know who you are. We know all about the Brotherhood.'

The *Maréchal* took off his mask and stared at Glenfield. He turned the pistol around in his hand and handed it to him.

The following morning dawned bright and sunny. It came as a relief after a restless night full of anxious dreams. I rose early, coming down just before six o'clock, but Father was already up when I entered the dining room.

'You didn't sleep well, either, Father?' I asked sleepily.

'No, Cully,' he replied. 'My mind was too busy.'

'Last night's operation?'

'Aye. I hope it went well, and that this is an end to it all.'

Mother came into the room. She had heard us both get up and had followed us down. 'Right,' she said, 'bacon and eggs, I think? No need to wait for Betsy.'

'That would be lovely, Iona,' said Father.

I could hear Mother singing in the kitchen and then the sound of sizzling as the bacon hit the pan. A few moments later, the delicious aroma drifted in to us. Suddenly, a heavy knocking at the front door disturbed the peace. I darted a look at Father, then held my breath as he stood to answer it.

When he returned, he was holding a letter. Mother came and stood by the door, wiping her hands on a cloth. We both watched as Father broke the seal and opened it.

'It's from Mr Hazeldean,' he said. 'The operation went well; Henry Lawton has been apprehended, along with four of his *premières*. They are being held in the cells at Bow Street. A fifth *première* was shot dead, along with one of our constables. They are confident that the Brotherhood has been disbanded.' Father looked at us. 'I do believe it's all over,' he said, relief in his voice.

'Thanks to you, Father,' I said with a smile.

He glanced back down at the letter. 'Hazeldean wants me to come down to Bow Street this morning to assist with Lawton's questioning.'

Mother sighed. 'Haven't you done enough for that man?'

'At least it will mean more fees for us.'

'Can I come with you, Father?' I asked.

'You can come with me to Bow Street, Cully, but I doubt that they will let you sit in on the interview.'

We arrived at Bow Street later that morning and were shown into Magistrate Wright's office. He was waiting with Mr Hazeldean. Neither of them looked as if they had had any sleep.

Father held out his hand to Hazeldean. 'I believe congratulations are in order,' he said enthusiastically.

Hazeldean stood and shook Father's hand. 'Thank you, Augustus,' he said, gesturing for us both to sit.

'Is something wrong, Mr Hazeldean?' I asked. 'Surely this is what we all wanted?'

'Aye, that's true enough.'

'So what's wrong?' asked Father.

'Lawton is very — canny.'

'I'd expect nothing less from him. He's an insightful, intuitive man. So what's he been saying?'

'That's the point; he's not saying anything, and we can't connect him to the murders of the Cabinet members or the kidnapping of Lord Cornysh without a confession. Nor can we connect him to the other crimes committed by the Brotherhood.'

'What about the four *premières* you have in custody?' asked Father.

'They've been questioned throughout the night, but they won't even give us their names, let alone the names of their squad members.'

'And even if they could be persuaded to talk, they have never known the *Maréchal*'s identity, so they can't incriminate him.'

'Precisely,' said Magistrate Wright. 'But we can charge them all with the murder of the constable killed last night, and that includes Lawton.'

'But wouldn't that leave the members of the Brotherhood still at large?' I asked.

'Exactly, Miss Swift. I don't want this organisation damaged; I want it destroyed. I want to make sure there is nothing left of it.'

'Do you have Edward Lawton?' asked Father. 'I believe he is *Maréchal Futur*.'

'No, he's nowhere to be found.'

Father sat back in his chair. 'That's a pity. As *Maréchal Futur* he's a dangerous man. So, if no one is talking, how can I help you, gentlemen?'

'Lawton has refused to talk to us, but he says that he will talk to *you*, sir. We'd like you to sit in on the next interview.'

Suddenly, Father clicked his tongue. He turned to me, expecting me to have similarly worked it out, but I just shrugged my shoulders.

He looked back at Hazeldean. 'Blackmail,' he said.

'Blackmail?'

'Aye, blackmail. That's why he is refusing to speak; he has an escape strategy.'

'But what has he got to blackmail us with?'

'Names, sir, names. Lawton is going to negotiate for his freedom.'

TWENTY-EIGHT

Henry Lawton was led into Magistrate Wright's office. He shuffled forward, his wrists and ankles shackled, and took a seat before the magistrate's desk. Behind it sat Wright, with Hazeldean and Swift on either side.

Lawton inclined his head politely towards Wright and Hazeldean, then his face lit up when he saw Swift. 'Ah, Dr Swift,' he said enthusiastically, 'so good to see you.'

'You wanted to tell me something, Mr Lawton?'

'I wanted to *ask* you something, to be more precise.'

'It does not work that way, Mr Lawton,' interrupted Magistrate Wright. 'You will tell *us* what *we* want to know.'

'It's all right, sir,' said Swift. 'Let him ask his question. If he wants to trade information, I have no problem with that.'

Lawton nodded. 'How did you identify me as the *Maréchal*?'

'It wasn't easy, Mr Lawton. You have embedded your identity deep within the Brotherhood.'

'Too deep, I had thought.'

'I am a physician, sir. Therefore, I need to be a diagnostician. That requires logic, it requires me to consider every possibility.'

'Ah, the *philosophy of reason* you told me about at my dinner party. And what exactly did that philosophy lead you to?'

'It led me to believe that the *Maréchal* was at your dinner party.'

'I thought I played my cards well that evening, but I see now that it was a mistake on my part. But surely that was just an inference; it wouldn't lead you directly to me.'

'No, sir, you are right. You have surrounded yourself with layers of protection, and I had to break through each one.'

'Such as?'

'Your motive; what the triquetra symbol represents; why you revealed your existence; how your organisation functioned; why you changed your method of working.'

'Ah yes, it was a mistake, it seems, to involve the Brotherhood in politics. I thought the radical organisations would pay well to be rid of this government's proposed new gagging legislation.'

'So they were your clients?'

'No, they shied away, having already faced the spectre of treason. They were content to live a quiet life after their ordeals in court.'

'So who were your sponsors?'

'I decided I would be my own client. I'm a progressive Whig standing for reform of the voting system.'

'Or was it your hatred of Pitt and his government?'

'Aye, that as well. This country needs reform, and Pitt's government stands in its way.'

Magistrate Wright cut in. 'So you confess to your crimes, Mr Lawton?'

'Do you take me for a fool, Magistrate? I'll sign nothing, confess to nothing.'

'But you have just —'

'Let him ask his questions, sir,' Swift cut in. 'We can come back to that.'

'I have admitted to my mistakes,' said Lawton, 'but even so, the safeguards in place should have protected me.'

'They did, sir — but I broke through them.'

'Prey, sir, tell me how.'

Swift sat back in his chair and studied the man before him. This was a man who could impose his will on other people:

was he attempting to do the same to him? He knew he was playing a dangerous game, but he decided to play it anyway.

'Your organisation was a well-oiled machine. That meant that it had been in existence for a long time to establish such expertise. Yet you were unknown. That suggested that you were not originally a criminal organisation. I inferred that you were initially formed to hide from a network of government spies. And the last time such conditions applied was the second Jacobite revolt, put down at Culloden in 1745.'

'Ah, so you reasoned that I must be Catholic. In that regard, yes, your inference was right.'

'You also knew about the proposed gagging legislation and where Cabinet members could be found. So you had to be close to the government. I also concluded that the position of *Maréchal* must be passed down a family line.'

'You were right. But did that get you any further?'

'It did when I saw the connection to mathematics, the power of the number three. That is quite wonderful, if I may say so. An organisation predicated on the number three, all coordinated but acting independently. Simplicity and security.'

'It is, Swift, but I can't see how that helped you.'

'Oh, it did — your founder was a mathematician.'

'That's speculation, not one of your *valid inferences*.'

'On its own, no, but in considering all the possibilities, that was one of them.'

'I still don't see how that led you to me.'

'The Brotherhood protected itself by never writing anything down, never leaving evidence to be found — but other people did. I went to the Royal Society and asked to look at their register of Fellows.'

'And you found — what?'

'That there was an entry in 1742 for a Fellow by the name of Evelyn Royd, Baron Ompton, whom I believe is your great-uncle. He founded the Brotherhood as part of the Jacobite revolt, didn't he?'

'Bravo,' Lawton said in a mocking voice. 'So you added Evelyn Royd and completed the equation. *Maréchal* equals Henry Lawton. So it was my brilliant great-uncle's error all those years ago.'

'It would seem so,' said Swift. Now it was his turn to ask the questions. 'Your family fortunes have been restored, Mr Lawton; you are a wealthy banker — why continue with the Brotherhood?'

'My father founded Lawton's Bank with capital derived from the Brotherhood — that is true. That capital was put to good use; our increasing wealth and influence make my job as *Maréchal* easier.'

'Even so, is it more financially rewarding than banking?'

Lawton smiled roguishly. 'I enjoy the chase, I suppose,' he said. 'It's always exciting, running with the hounds.'

'And look where it has got you.'

'Folderol,' said Lawton, as if it were now of no consequence. 'None of your deductions will be admissible in court.' He turned and looked at Hazeldean and Wright. 'But you won't charge me anyway, will you?'

It's an attempt to provoke them, Swift thought. He saw it succeed immediately. The magistrate's face turned beetroot with anger. 'You arrogant cur!' he shouted. 'I'll see you dancing to the hangman's jig!'

'No, you won't, sir,' replied Lawton, his tone cold. 'The Home Secretary will stop you.'

Wright stared at him in disbelief.

'If you are intent on blackmail, *Maréchal*, then let us hear your demands,' said Swift.

'If you charge me or any of my *premières*, I will stand up in court and give the names of all the people who have been clients of the Brotherhood, and that includes the gentry, the aristocracy, members of the government, even some minor royals.'

'And you think a jury will believe you?' Hazeldean's words were cautious.

'May I borrow a pen and a sheet of paper, Magistrate?'

Wright pushed his inkstand across his desk. Lawton took a pen from the stand, wrote down four names, then passed the sheet back to him. Wright picked it up and read the names, his eyes widening. He showed it to Hazeldean, then Swift.

'Just four names to start with, sirs, but there are many others.'

'This list might persuade the Home Secretary that you must not be brought to trial,' said Hazeldean, 'but it also signs your death warrant. Ironic, isn't it? After all these years you now write something down, and you will die for it.' The threat was undisguised.

This troubled Swift, a man of high principles; the threat was judicial murder to avoid the matter coming to court.

Lawton made a disdainful sound. 'Do you think I haven't considered that possibility? I know how to make a death look natural. It's my trade, sirs — and so is intimidation. You have much to learn in that respect, Mr Hazeldean.' He cast him a withering look.

And there it is, Swift mused. *The mask has slipped to reveal his true nature.*

Swift realised that his assessment had been correct; this was a man who could impose his will on other people. He was doing just that.

'So,' said Swift, '*Maréchal Futur* will cover the risk to you. He is the one to protect you.'

'Ah, you have not let me down, Swift. Perhaps you will explain it to your colleagues.'

'If Mr Lawton is not released, then Edward will reveal the names of those incriminated.'

Lawton smiled at them. 'You see, gentlemen? Simple, isn't it?'

Swift sighed deeply. 'You are a strange man, Mr Lawton. You seem to follow the honourable cause of reform, but your methods are dishonourable in the extreme — shameful, even murderous.'

Lawton shot Swift an angry stare. 'At least I'm not a hypocrite working for a government who opposes everything I stand for.'

The words stung Swift like a hornet. He had tried to justify it by telling himself he was saving lives. He had succeeded in the release of Lord Cornysh, but he knew there was truth in Lawton's goading.

'My morals are my concern, sir,' Lawton continued, 'and it would seem that I am more content with them than you are with yours. How will you feel when this gagging legislation is enacted? When the first innocent man is hanged?'

Swift's thoughts were conflicted; he tried to rationalise them. He had already gauged this man; he knew he could impose his will on other people. He should have been on his guard, yet he had allowed him to do exactly that to him. But he was right. Cause and effect: the principle was fundamental to his own philosophy. Saving Cornysh and exposing Lawton would have consequences, and those consequences offended his moral code.

He looked at Lawton, and for the first time realised just how sagacious he was.

'So, Mr Lawton,' he said, 'let us negotiate.'

Magistrate Wright opened his mouth to speak, but Hazeldean placed a hand on his arm to stop him.

'I want freedom for myself and my *premières*, and a written statement that we will not be charged,' said Lawton.

'It's hardly likely the Home Secretary will sanction the release of the *premières*,' said Swift.

'You think not? He will when he sees that list of names I've given you. My *premières* are all educated men; some of them are gentlemen. They don't deserve to be hanged.'

His words offended Swift. That double standard was at the heart of Lawton's ideology — but not his.

'That would leave the Brotherhood of the Parole intact,' Swift said, 'but you can only play the hand you have been dealt, and you don't have that card to play.'

Lawton sat back and breathed deeply. 'That list of names is a trump card; you can't beat it.'

'Your logic is flawed, Mr Lawton. If you play it, you embarrass the government, but you and your men still hang, so it hurts you as much as the Home Secretary. If you don't play it — you still hang.' He leaned forward. 'No, sir, you do not hold a trump card. It will not give you *everything* you want.'

'So what card will *you* play?'

'This one,' said Swift. 'Your release is subject to the names of all the people in your organisation. The Home Secretary must be sure that the Brotherhood is no more.'

TWENTY-NINE

The long summer was finally over and the leaves on the trees were beginning to turn the beautiful colours of autumn: reds, yellows, oranges, golds and browns. In Temple Bar, the air hung with a hazy mixture of mist and the smoke from ten thousand fires from the tireless city. The good people of London were their usual busy selves.

We were taking breakfast. The stresses of the summer were over, and our spirits were not depressed by the grey day outside. The temporary premises in Essex Street was closed, and the business had moved back to Temple Bar. The apothecary shop had now reopened for Grandpa to run, as had Father's daily clinic.

Grandpa was hidden behind his morning paper, as usual. 'It says here that Pitt got his gagging legislation through Parliament yesterday,' he said. 'It'll become law in the next few days, when it receives royal assent.'

'So he's got what he wanted after all,' said Father, his face souring.

'It's not your fault, Gus,' said Mother, patting him on the arm.

'But this legislation is outrageous, Iona. It states that any alternative discussion is treason. The only place where debate is tolerated is Parliament, and that's a place unrepresentative of the people. These Acts effectively stop any form of reform in its tracks.'

'But it's foolish to think you can stop them, Gus; you are only one man.'

'Fate put me in a position to do just that, Iona, and all I had to do was — nothing.'

Grandpa put down his newspaper and stared at his son. 'You saved a man's life, my boy,' he said. 'You shouldn't let guilt consume you like this.'

'And you must watch what you say from now on, Father,' I interrupted, a knot tightening in my stomach. When it came to injustice, I knew he would speak out. 'You've already upset the Home Secretary once; don't allow him to put you on trial for treason.'

Father looked at Grandpa and me, then smiled and nodded. 'I know I need to be more careful.'

'Talking of trials,' said Rafe, 'when will they bring Henry Lawton to trial?'

'There's been nothing in the paper about it,' said Grandpa, looking at Father.

'I've not seen Hazeldean for weeks. The last I heard was that Sir Thomas wouldn't make a decision. They intend to keep Lawton locked up, at least until after the Bills become law.'

'And they're not even admitting that they have him in custody?' asked Grandpa.

'No, and I've been sworn to secrecy. I suppose that applies to you all as well.'

'But how is his absence from Parliament being explained?' asked Rafe.

'The rumour is that he's in Antwerp on banking business. I suspect that came from Edward, but the constables still haven't found *him* either.'

Grandpa returned to his paper, then put it down again. 'Oh, Augustus, I have a large order for our vermin-killing preparation. I can't make it up, though, as we're running low on some supplies. Can Cully go to the suppliers for me?'

'Perhaps Rafe can go to Higham and Carter,' he said. 'Cully can accompany *him*.'

'I've some samples to process this morning, Rafe,' I said. 'We'll go after I've finished.'

'*Urine* trouble then, Cully,' Grandpa said as he disappeared behind his newspaper once more with a wheezy chuckle.

'Oh, Grandpa!' I said, laughing as well.

'A good pun, Cully, is its own *reword*.' He chuckled again.

Higham and Carter had their premises on Holborn Hill, just a ten-minute walk from Temple Bar. We set off just after one o'clock. Rafe had insisted on putting on a clean stock at the collar and also took off his apron to wear his frockcoat. He didn't say so, but I knew he wanted to make a good impression the first time he represented our family. In his top pocket was a letter of introduction from Father, authorising him to charge purchases to our account, together with Grandpa's list of supplies, many of which were poisons. He slung a satchel over his shoulder.

We walked up Holborn Hill, the street busy with horses and carts. The pavement was also busy, and we were forced to sidestep people coming towards us.

Inside Higham and Carter, I introduced Rafe to the chief clerk, Mr Terry, and Rafe handed him his letter of introduction and list of supplies. The clerk manoeuvred his ladder up and down the shelves behind the counter, climbing to retrieve jars, canisters and labelled glass bottles for the emollients, herbs, compounds, minerals and animal fats that we used in our apothecary shop. He carefully weighed them out, fulfilling Grandpa's list meticulously. It took him about twenty minutes; then he looked up at Rafe, the list in his hand. 'Poisons,' he said, 'I need to go into the back for these.' When he disappeared, Rafe started to fill the shoulder bag.

Rather than just wait, I took the opportunity to saunter outside onto the street. I shivered slightly in the chilly air and pulled my cape tighter around my shoulders. The spicy smell of cinnamon was on the air from a bakery two shops down; it made me feel hungry. Suddenly, I became aware of a carriage pulling up beside me, and the door swung open.

I turned to go back into the suppliers when I heard somebody call my name. 'Please get into the carriage, Augusta. I need to talk to you.'

It was Edward Lawton. I walked to the open door and peered inside the carriage.

'What do you want, Edward?' I asked. There was no politeness now that I knew who he really was.

'We can't talk like this, Augusta. Please get in.'

I sensed danger but got in anyway. I sat facing Edward. 'What is it you want, Edward?' I raised a curious eyebrow.

He reached across for the handle to the carriage door and slammed it shut. With the head of his cane, he tapped the carriage roof, and the driver set the horses to trot. I looked up in alarm.

'Are you kidnapping me then?' I demanded, shooting Edward an angry look.

'I hope it doesn't come to that,' he replied softly, 'and may I say you're looking particularly fetching today, Augusta.'

I knew this was pure flattery. I was in my work clothes, an apron over my cream housedress, my hair tucked into a cap. How could I ever have trusted this man? His insincerity was palpable. I wondered what else I had failed to see.

'Don't take me for a fool, Edward,' I said. 'Let's dispense with the blandishments, shall we? Just tell me what you want.'

He sat back and I looked out of the window. We had left Holborn Hill and were now on Newgate Street.

'Where are you taking me?' I asked.

'Oh, nowhere in particular, Augusta,' he said. 'The coachman has orders just to drive around while we talk.'

'So talk,' I said as assertively as I could.

'I believe the Home Department is holding my father, but they haven't charged him or even released any information about him. I have used some of his contacts in government, but they've not been able to tell me what's going on.'

'Or they have found out that you are wanted as well and *won't* tell you,' I countered.

He sighed. 'That's a possibility I have also considered. You are very astute, Augusta.'

'Well, *I'll* tell you what they won't tell you. Your father is being held in the cells at Bow Street, along with four of your *premières*. A fifth one was killed.'

'That much I know,' he said.

'So what do you want from me?'

'I want a go-between.'

'Me? What makes you think they'll talk to me?'

'They probably won't, but Hazeldean will listen to your father. I need him to take a message for me.'

'Why don't you just write to Hazeldean, or preferably the Home Secretary?'

'It's not the way of the Brotherhood.'

'And if my father refuses?'

'Oh, he won't, not if he wants his daughter back.'

His words were delivered without any malice, with all the cordiality of a gentleman. *So it is a kidnapping*, I thought to myself. I looked out of the window again; we had now moved onto Cheapside, getting further away all the time. The danger I was in became apparent.

Suddenly, a blur flashed past the window. A figure leapt up onto the cab alongside the coachman. The figure was now out of sight, but I knew who it was — Rafe; he must have seen me get into the carriage and then run after it, all the way up Holborn Hill, onto Newgate Street and then Cheapside. I heard a commotion above us, and the carriage jerked.

'What's going on, Ambrose?' Edward shouted up, tapping his cane against the roof, but there was no response. He released the leather strap so that the window glass fell, then leaned out and saw his coachman engaged in a struggle. When he brought his head back inside, I saw fear on his face.

'We may have to run,' he said to me.

'You may have to, but I won't be coming with you,' I replied, fixing him with a fiery stare. I knew I had to stay with Rafe at all costs.

I heard a cry of 'Whoa!' and the carriage came to a halt. Rafe must have gained control of the reins. Then a body fell from the cab to the floor and thudded against the ground. I heard a wail of pain. For a heartbeat, there was silence. The man stirred, regained his feet, and a bloodied face appeared at Edward's window. It was the coachman.

Edward gestured for him to go back up to the cab and tackle Rafe, but there was no more fight in the man. He shook his head and ran off.

Edward grabbed my wrist and opened the carriage door. 'You're coming with me!' he shouted and tried to leave the carriage, pulling me with him. I resisted with all my might, pulling myself back inside. Edward looked back at me, his face contorted with anger. He opened his mouth to speak again, but before he could say anything, he was shoved back inside the carriage.

He let me go as he fell onto his hands and knees in the well of the carriage. Rafe followed him inside and shut the door. I noticed he was breathing heavily, having run so far and tussled with the driver. Edward righted himself and raised his cane to strike Rafe. But it was a long cane, and as he pulled it back, it hit the ceiling and lost all momentum.

Before he could try again, Rafe thrust the heel of his hand forcefully forward onto the bridge of Edward's nose. As he recoiled from the blow, Rafe curled his hands into fists and then thrust them simultaneously against Edward's ears. In those two actions, he had immediately disabled him — something he must have learned at Samuel Medina's academy. He snatched the cane from Edward's hand.

Rafe sat back and looked at Edward. 'This cane is much too big to use in a confined space, sir. You should remember that for next time. A cudgel would be better. If that is too ungentlemanly for you, bring a pistol.' I wasn't sure if he was taunting Edward or not, but I could see that Edward's condescending glare had been replaced by an expression of bewilderment.

Rafe continued, 'Your nose will smart for some days, but your eyes will stop streaming shortly, and the ringing in your ears will cease.'

'You won't get away with this; I'll have you flogged! I'll —'

'You'll do what, Edward? Call a constable?' I said. 'Shall I do it for you?'

I put my hand on the door handle theatrically. That shut him up. I turned to Rafe. 'Well done,' I said. 'He was going to kidnap me to get Father to do his bidding.'

'What shall we do with him?' Rafe asked. 'Take him to the magistrate at Bow Street?'

I knew this was the right thing to do, but I also knew that Edward and his father would be hanged if we did so. Their lives were in our hands. 'I don't know,' I mumbled.

'Shall we let Dr Swift decide?' Rafe asked.

'Yes,' I agreed, 'we'll let Father decide.'

When we arrived home, Father was in his clinic. I called for him to come. He looked alarmed when he saw Edward standing beside Rafe, his head bowed. Mother appeared a moment later and put her hand to her mouth. All of Edward's charisma and bravado was gone; his hair was ruffled, and there was dried blood under his nose and on his stock. The charming man she had so admired had now been diminished. It was Father who spoke first.

'What's going on?' he asked.

I told him the whole story, and when I had finished he walked over to Rafe. 'Thank you, my boy,' he said, shaking his hand vigorously. 'Those lessons at Samuel Medina's academy have served you well.'

'What shall we do with Edward, Father?' I asked.

Father let out a deep sigh. I knew he had been troubled by helping to catch Edward's father, Henry Lawton, although he was a contemptible man. Father was aware that his actions had helped Pitt. I saw him wrestle with his dilemma. He opened his mouth to speak, but I cut across him.

'What's that proverb you like to quote?' I asked.

He frowned. 'Which one?'

'The one about anger,' I said.

'Ah, yes: *The best answer will come from the person who is not angry.* Thank you, Cully, for reminding me of that. Yes, I will allow my anger to subside before deciding.'

Father struggled with his conundrum late into the night. To hand Edward over to the magistrate would lead to the deaths of all those held in custody, perhaps many more. But if he acted as their go-between, those same men might evade the justice they deserved. And what of the country? It desperately needed reform, but his own actions may have already put that back many years.

Before I went to bed, I threw some logs on the fire and sparks flew, but he didn't notice. I wished him goodnight, but I knew my words went unheard.

The following morning I rose early. Father's seat was empty; he had gone to bed, but the room smelled of whisky and tobacco. *He must have been up late,* I thought. I made myself a cup of chocolate and was sipping it when Father came down. He smiled at me lovingly; I was encouraged.

'Have you decided what to do?' I asked.

He sat down next to me, his smile broadening. 'Yes, I think so,' he said.

I looked at him, eager for him to explain.

'Consider this,' he said tentatively. 'If I watch a dog chasing its tail, who is engaged in the more pointless task? Me or the dog?'

'I don't understand, Father,' I said, perplexed.

'Use the method I have taught you, Cully.'

I put down my cup. 'Well, the dog can't catch his tail,' I began hesitantly, 'so his actions are pointless.' I thought I was pretty safe with that observation.

'More pointless than me watching, do you think?'

I considered this. 'I suppose the dog doesn't know that his tail will always be out of reach, so to him it is not pointless.'

'Good, Cully,' Father enthused. 'So what is your conclusion?'

'Because *you* know it is pointless, *you* are engaged in the most futile act.'

'That's right.'

I still didn't see the relevance, though, and Father explained.

'Substitute the word *useful* for the word *pointless*, and consider what Pitt and Lawton are doing.'

I began to see his reasoning. Useful and pointless were opposite sides of the same coin. 'You mean that both the Prime Minister and Mr Lawton are engaged in self-interest, Pitt with his gagging legislation and Lawton trying to stop him, but they have closed their minds to what is best for the country.'

'Nearly, Cully. Both believe they are acting in the country's best interests, but when considering this, they only see their own interests; they are blind to what the country as a whole needs.'

'So they are the dogs; they don't even know they are acting out of self-interest.'

'Precisely, Cully.'

'So it is down to *you* to act in the best interests of the country.'

'And what might those be?'

'Well, the Brotherhood of the Parole is an evil organisation, even if it has been working for good in trying to stop the gagging legislation. So you want it stopped.'

'I do, Cully, but I also want the government to embrace reform.'

'But that battle has already been lost, Father. Pitt has his gagging legislation in place.'

'For the time being, yes, but the fight has to go on. We need a strong opposition.'

Father agreed to act as a go-between for Edward Lawton and the Home Department. Edward was kept secretly in our house during this period. Initially, both parties wouldn't concede any of their demands, but Father put together a set of proposals. Eventually, an understanding was reached. Henry Lawton, Mary Gayle and his *premières* were released in exchange for the names of all the members of the Brotherhood. So effectively, the organisation was closed down, though they all now escaped punishment for their crimes.

Pitt and his government had protected the reputation of many influential people. The government would probably have fallen by any resulting scandal. Henry Lawton feared that government agents would eliminate both him and his son after their release, and rearrest his men. He asked Father to hold a list of the people that had hired the Brotherhood, to be disclosed in the event of his death, but Father declined. He had not spent several months in fear of his life from the Brotherhood, just to replace that with fear of government agents.

Father proposed that sealed letters be given to three unidentified men who would be above reproach, to be opened on the suspicious death of any of these men, or Henry and Edward. There was a bishop, a university academic, and a continental banker.

As part of the deal, Henry Lawton was forced to give up his seat in the House of Commons, but he simply bequeathed it to his son, Edward. Father, not a man usually given to profanities, had some choice words to say about this.

Our lives returned to normal. Father continued to run his free clinic but remained a consultant for the Home Department. Rafe turned twenty-one and would complete his apprenticeship within a year, but wanted to continue working with the family, keen to learn as much as he could from my remarkable father. I still had dreams of running the apothecary shop, despite knowing that the Guild would not accept me, and Mother wanted to see me married. But I was formulating my own plans about that.

Knowing that we were all safe was comforting. But sometimes the days seemed so dull. Strangely, I missed the adventure of the last few months.

HISTORICAL NOTES

I have given Augustus Swift an extremely analytical mind. He has developed his 'method' from his work as a diagnostician, supplemented by his study of the logic of the Greek philosophers and their Muslim successors.

The Prime Minister, William Pitt the Younger, and the magistrate, Samson Wright, are historical figures. All the other characters in the novel are fictional. There seems little doubt that professional historians assess Pitt the Younger as a brilliant man with a brilliant mind. He was Prime Minister for nineteen years, a very long period indeed, and at a time of several national crises. But he is also remembered for his 'reign of terror', during which he orchestrated an attack on the civil liberties of the British people at the time of the emergence of enlightened thought. This aspect of his career brings him into conflict with my fictional character, Swift, a man firmly entrenched in the principles of that Enlightenment.

Mary Gayle and her prophesying hen are based on Mary Bateman, an early con-artist known as the Yorkshire Witch. In 1806 she created the hoax known as the 'Prophet Hen of Leeds', in which eggs laid by a hen were purported to predict the end of the world. She was hanged in 1809 after being found guilty of fraud and the poisoning of one Rebecca Perigo.

St Olave's Church is real and is situated in the City of London. It is one of the few medieval churches to survive the Great Fire of London. The description I have used and its history should be accurate. There is no triquetra symbol there, however, which is a fiction of my making.

The Treasonable and Seditious Practices Act and the Seditious Meetings Act were enacted in 1795. A further six Acts were passed in 1819 and were adopted to suppress sedition further. These six Acts led to further unrest, culminating in an attempt to kill all the British Cabinet ministers and the Prime Minister, Lord Liverpool, in 1820. It was known as the Cato Street Conspiracy. It was foiled by the police and the Home Department. They had an informer amongst the conspirators but, had it succeeded, they intended to overthrow the government and replace it with a revolutionary committee.

In 1808 Friedrich Niethammer coined the word 'humanism' and by 1836 the term had been absorbed into the English language. However, historians agree that the concept predates the label invented to describe it. 'Industrial Revolution', 'Enlightenment' and 'Radical' are all names allocated by history in retrospect. They weren't recognised at the time.

A NOTE TO THE READER

Dear Reader,

I hope you enjoyed *Brotherhood of Death* and the adventures of Augustus Swift and his daughter, Cully.

This is the first book in the Augustus Swift Investigations series. Set mainly in London in the 1790s, it is set thirty years or so before the first Metropolitan Police force was set up and half a century before the first criminal investigation department was established. Swift is an unlikely and reluctant detective, but his profession as a physician has taught him the skills of diagnosis and, through his study of the Islamic philosophers, the power of logical thought. These are skills that the magistrate at Bow Street and the Bow Street Runners do not have.

This is a decadent period. In 1795, political power rested firmly in the hands of the aristocratic landowners, as it had done for centuries. They retained power by way of a corrupt voting system, seeing no dishonour in denying reform at the time of the Enlightenment — and Swift is passionately a man of the Enlightenment.

Nowadays, reviews by knowledgeable readers are essential for a writer's success. If you found this book entertaining, I would be grateful if you would consider leaving a review on **Amazon** and **Goodreads**. I love hearing from readers, and you can contact me via my website: **www.stephentaylorauthor.com**.

Thank you!

Stephen Taylor

Sapere Books is an exciting new publisher of brilliant fiction and popular history.

To find out more about our latest releases and our monthly bargain books visit our website: **saperebooks.com**

RELATIONAL PERSPECTIVES IN ORGANIZATIONAL STUDIES

Relational Perspectives in Organizational Studies

A Research Companion

Edited by

Olivia Kyriakidou

Department of Business Administration, University of the Aegean, Greece

Mustafa F. Özbilgin

School of Business and Management, Queen Mary, University of London, UK

Edward Elgar
Cheltenham, UK • Northampton, MA, USA

Published by
Edward Elgar Publishing Limited
Glensanda House
Montpellier Parade
Cheltenham
Glos GL50 1UA
UK

Edward Elgar Publishing, Inc.
136 West Street
Suite 202
Northampton
Massachusetts 01060
USA

A catalogue record for this book
is available from the British Library

Library of Congress Cataloguing in Publication Data
Relational perspectives in organizational studies : a research companion /
   [edited by] Olivia Kyriakidou, Mustafa Özbilgin.
      p. cm.
      1. Organizational behavior—Research. 2. Organizational learning—Research.
   3. Interorganizational relations—Research. 4. Communication in organizations—
   Research. 5. Business networks—Research. 6. Complex organizations—Research
   7. Organizational sociology—Research. I. Kyriakidou, Olivia, 1972–
   II. Özbilgin, Mustafa.

   HD58.7.R45   2006
   302.3'5–dc22   2005052086

ISBN-13 978 1 84542 125 0
ISBN-10 1 84542 125 6

Printed and bound in Great Britain by MPG Books Ltd, Bodmin, Cornwall